PRAISE FC

'Read once foi

pleasure of seeing how it was done.'
The Bookbag on *The One I Was*

'A beautifully crafted piece of literary fiction. . . . Adding to the sympathetic characters, page-turning secrets, and bits of little-known history is a gorgeous style of writing.'
The Happy Book Reviewer on *The One I Was*

'Grips like a vice with the disturbing mystery at its heart.'
Lancashire Evening Post on *The History Room*

'A fantastic summer read which will please readers of all types of fiction.'
The Bookbag on *The History Room*

'Eliza Graham's subtlety, intelligence and historical sense make her storytelling rich in suspense, atmosphere and characterisation. Fans of Sadie Jones, Kate Morton or Susan Lewis will love this cleverly crafted tale of family secrets.'
Waterstones Books Quarterly on *Jubilee*

'An evocative, riveting tale of survival and the triumph of the human spirit in the aftermath of war.'
Pam Jenoff, author of *The Kommandant's Girl*, on *Restitution*

'The novel is probing, sensitive and moving.'
Irish Book Review on *Playing with the Moon*

'. . . Engaging and . . . an emotional read.'
Brighton Argus on *Playing with the Moon*

THE ONE I WAS

ALSO BY ELIZA GRAHAM

Playing with the Moon

Restitution

Jubilee

The History Room

Blitz Kid

THE ONE I WAS

Eliza Graham

This is a work of fiction. Names, characters, organizations, places, events, and incidents are either products of the author's imagination or are used fictitiously.

Published by Lake Union Publishing, Seattle

www.apub.com

ISBN-13: 978-1477829318
ISBN-10: 1477829318

Cover design by bürosüd° München, www.buerosued.de

Library of Congress Control Number: 2014920272

Printed in the United States of America

THE ONE I WAS

1.
ROSAMOND

Every atom of my body screamed at me to run away from the elegant and classical white house at whose door I stood.

I was a forty-something woman, a professional, a nurse, but I felt like a twelve-year-old again. I forced myself to push the doorbell. Sarah, the housekeeper, opened the front door and let me in. I heard myself exchanging pleasantries with her while my heart beat out a tattoo. I took stock of my surroundings. Duck-egg walls. A chandelier of twisted metal and crystal, hanging from the ceiling like an icicle. I looked up the staircase, trying to accustom myself to being back at Fairfleet again. My fingers clenched the handles of my suitcase as I drew in a long breath. The house smelled of new paint and the large white lilies on the console table. An older, deeper smell undercut the scent: polished wood and old stone, but it should have been bitter like burning almonds, to remind me of my guilt.

The telephone rang. Sarah frowned. 'That'll be the district nurse. Excuse me one moment, Rosamond.'

Some of the balustrading on the staircase had been replaced, but the work had been done with sensitivity; only someone who knew where to look would have spotted the new spindles. The flagstones replacing the old parquet floor might have been there for centuries. What had I expected – that the house would somehow remember what had happened on a clear, winter's morning just like this, thirty years ago?

I tried to clear my mind, to remember why I was here. I thought about my patient, Benny Gault, and his arrival at this house. Just before the war Fairfleet had taken in a group of Jewish refugee boys from Germany, made them a home while they grew up, and sent them back out into the world to make good lives for themselves. And then the adult Benny Gault had returned years later to buy Fairfleet and make it his own. Now he lay dying upstairs.

Sarah came back in. 'Sorry about that. Come through to the kitchen, Rosamond.'

I moved onwards into the house. I felt more relaxed now I wasn't dwelling on myself and my past. I was thinking about how Benny must have felt when he'd first arrived in England. Homesick? Relieved? Excited? Possibly all of these.

2.
BENJAMIN, 1939

The boy clutched his football. The label round his neck flapped in the breeze, cutting into his skin. Now that they'd docked at Harwich, his stomach had stopped heaving. He stood at the top of the gangplank, took in deep breaths of the salt-and-oil air that rasped his throat. Where were the little kids he'd looked after on the voyage? A woman in nurse's uniform was already steering them away. Someone pushed him gently down the gangplank.

It looked different, England: the cars, dockers, buildings. People were smiling at them, even the policemen in their tall helmets and capes. One of them was holding a small girl's hand, picking up her suitcase, snow falling on them.

All very foreign. All very safe. He had to get the hell out.

He turned around. He'd hide on the boat. But there was no fighting the tide of children streaming down the gangplank. Boys cursed him and girls tutted as he shoved into them. He gave up and let them push him down to dry land. Not that it was very dry. It had obviously rained here. And now it was snowing, white flakes dissolving into the black ground. Everything swayed as Benny walked along the quay. Perhaps it took a while to get used to being on land again. The English dockers were shouting in that up-and-down, up-and-down language he couldn't understand. HARWICH, he read on a sign.

Then they were on a bus, the air thick with the reek of long journeys and farewells and not being sure where the toilets had been and hoping the big boys wouldn't give you trouble. Act your age, he told himself. You're eleven, not six. A plump woman in a hat that looked like a squashed cake wiped noses and handed round wrapped sweets. Someone was sick, very quietly, into a paper bag. A child of about four wept, face buried in his lap, tears running down his knees. The seven-year-old girl twins stared at their hands, their golden curls now less smoothly brushed, stains on the fronts of their coats.

Then the camp: a huge, metal-clad structure. Not like the camps he'd heard about at home. The woman in the squashed-cake hat ushered them inside to trestle tables, where they were served a hot stew he was too tired to identify. Young men and women led them to little houses like miniature Alpine chalets, where they were to sleep, even though it wasn't yet night. Groups of three or four. The other boys in his hut complete strangers. Good. He laid his football at the end of the bunk. Certain he wouldn't sleep. Closed his eyes to block out everything. Thought of his bedroom back at home. Quiet. Shuttered. Football posters on the wall. Boxes of construction kits. A bookcase of books. *Emil and the Detectives* was his favourite; be good to have it here now and flick through its pages. A dull ache of homesickness inside him now. Try to ignore it, feel the safe roundness of the football at your feet and . . .

When he woke it was morning. He was still wearing his outer clothes. If he'd been at home there'd have been trouble.

They spoke German here – he heard them calling out as they walked along outside the chalets, knocking on doors, encouraging kids to wash before breakfast was served.

He'd tell them he'd changed his mind and wanted to go home. But he'd seen them on the boat, hushing kids who cried for lost homes and families. Telling them how fortunate they were, how their parents and friends were so relieved they were safe and would be sad if the children returned to the danger.

Well he was no little kid. He wasn't going to blub. He'd force down the memories of the people at home so they wouldn't trouble him any more.

Perhaps he'd only be in England for a few months anyway, if the war didn't happen. They might be pleased to see him back in Germany after an absence.

~

A couple of days passed. They were kind enough here. He was even growing used to English cooking: strong-smelling kippers for breakfast with a thick oat soup called porridge, which coated your insides like a warm glue.

At home breakfast meant warm bread rolls from the baker's. Eggs boiled so that their yellows were still soft. Slices of nutty cheese.

Thinking about these past meals sharpened the persistent ache inside him into a more painful stab of homesickness. He looked around for distraction. The children were wearing coats and scarves to breakfast in this huge glass-and-iron edifice where once, they'd been told, holidaymakers had enjoyed cabarets, and fish with the fried potatoes the British called chips. Were all English homes cold like this? A vase of chrysanthemums sat on the table. At home these were flowers you took to the cemetery for your mother's grave. The floor was wet from snowy footsteps.

Today was Sunday: market day for English families seeking foreign children. He'd already heard rumours that nobody really wanted kids like him: male, over eight.

'Try smiling,' he overheard a youth worker telling a boy of about his age. 'It helps.'

Benny practised smiling. His facial muscles ached. He'd laughed once since he'd been here at Dovercourt: at a clown performing in one of the evening shows. But you could laugh and not really be happy.

'Why don't you join in prayers?' one of his room-mates in the wooden chalet had asked him this morning, frowning.

Benny tried to make a relaxed but dismissive gesture with his hand.

'Weren't you observant at home?' The boy folded a towel into neat squares while he addressed Benny, eyes narrowed.

Silence seemed the safest response.

'Perhaps . . .' the boy's nose wrinkled, 'you're a secular Jew?'

Benny had thrown his football at the boy, hitting him in the midriff and preventing further questions.

Now the would-be buyers shuffled into the hall to examine the wares. The blonde Berlin twins drew a flock of clucking matrons. Those girls would be sitting in front of the fire with doting foster parents before supper time.

Benny arranged his face into what he hoped was a nonchalant confidence. Nobody came near him. He fiddled with the petals on the chrysanthemums.

A middle-aged man wearing a smart black coat and clasping a bowler hat walked over to the table and stared at him.

'Good afternoon.' Benny stood up and spoke in his best English, deciding against a heel click.

'Benjamin Goldman, sir,' said a nearby youth worker in German. 'Eleven, as you may know, from a small town near Berlin. Excellent school reports. His father was a successful businessman until, well, things took a turn.'

The middle-aged man observed him kindly for a moment, slipped a bar of chocolate across the table, murmured a farewell and walked away. Probably not impressed with Benny. None of the other English visitors came near him. He wasn't sent to collect his possessions from the chalet so that he could go home with an English family. He ate his chocolate.

This indifference was a sign. He'd talk to one of the friendly volunteers, beg to be sent back to Germany. Plenty at home who'd jump at the opportunity to replace him.

The visitors left and supper was laid. While they were eating, someone read out a list of kids' names over the megaphone. He paid little attention, knowing he had failed to impress this afternoon.

'. . . and Benjamin Goldman,' the man read out. 'Please come to the table at the side of the hall.'

It took a second to realize that meant him. He forced himself to amble over to the table as though he wasn't surprised or excited. Five other boys waited there. A youth worker sat behind the table with a clipboard.

'Ah, Benjamin. Good news. They're ready for you now at Fairfleet.'

Fairfleet? He tried not to let his confusion show. *Don't draw attention to yourself.*

'The snow blocked the road and the bus couldn't get through.'

The youth worker was speaking in German, but it might as well have been English for all his words meant.

'You must be impatient to start your new life.' The young man grinned. 'Fairfleet will certainly be more luxurious than here.'

'Don't know much about it,' he mumbled.

'Your parents –' The youth worker flushed. 'The orphanage . . . were sent a letter with all the information. Perhaps it went astray?'

Best just to nod.

'Fairfleet's a large house in the countryside near Oxford. Lord and Lady Dorner are taking you in.'

Benny blinked.

'There'll be lots of fresh air and exercise.'

Hopefully not like a Hitler Youth camp back in Germany. Plenty of fresh air and exercise there. And songs. And kicks and blows behind the shower blocks if you weren't enthusiastic enough.

'Cheer up.' The youth worker made a final tick on his sheet and stood up. 'We're running English lessons from tomorrow. You've got two days to learn a bit of the language.'

Two days. He took himself back to the chalet, lay on his bunk, thinking. Whatever Fairfleet was, it had to be better than here. But if he went along with events, he'd be even more caught up in the mess he'd made for himself. What was the alternative?

He needed to forget about all of it. Forget Rudi and what Rudi had done and the last time they'd been together.

Rudi and Benny: two friends who'd tried to sort things out, tried to beat the system, even though they were only eleven and most grown-ups were too scared to try.

They'd done their best, but it hadn't worked.

3.

By the following morning Benny felt calmer. He strolled around the camp, watching some of the younger kids playing on swings and slides between the fir trees. Someone had told him about an indoor amusement area and he'd found it. Table tennis and a badminton net. He'd thought he might be tempted to play some kind of game but found himself feeling in continued need of solitude. He slipped into the communal dining room, uncertain whether he was supposed to be here outside meal times. Someone had left a pile of old English comics on a chair. *Crackers,* the title said. Benny settled himself on the ground in a quiet corner and flicked through them. He could follow the stories all right: parents on your back about untidy bedrooms, daft teachers, naughty dogs: some of the words were easy to decipher. But most of it was baffling.

A bell rang. Lessons. He stood up, uncertain where to go. But the doors opened and children streamed in, chatting. Nobody seemed to notice Benny. A blackboard was pulled out. A woman in a suit came in and pointed to the chairs.

He sat down with the others. Someone handed him an exercise book.

The teacher wrote the words on the blackboard, pronouncing them as she did. Benny copied them onto the sheet of paper he'd been given, lips silently pronouncing the words, trying to make the 'th' sound the way the English spoke it.

After lunch lessons became more relaxed. The same teacher took them on a walk through the slushy grass to the seafront, the wind fierce against their cheeks, the sea a leaden grey. Afterwards they returned to the amusement centre to learn the words of 'Ten Green Bottles'. A young woman taught them how to do the Lambeth Walk. They danced again after supper in the dining hall. A group of girls and boys performed the dance called the Hora. Benny watched for a while and then joined in.

They had to have showers later that night. He grabbed his towel and dashed off to the cubicle, standing under the warm water before the rest of his room-mates had even removed their socks. 'Someone's keen to get clean,' a youth worker commented as Benny wrapped his towel around him. 'Good for you, young Goldman.'

Another middle-aged man came for them on the Thursday. Not as smartly dressed as the bowler-hat man. He wore round spectacles and a tweed jacket. Dr Dawes, his name was. A university man from the town of Oxford, which wasn't that far away from Fairfleet. He told them he was going to be their tutor at Fairfleet.

'Go and fetch your luggage, boys.'

Of course the refugee Benjamin Goldman had nothing except a football and a satchel containing a single withered apple, two German exercise books with his name on them and a pencil box.

'I need the lavatory,' he called, running back into the chalet. He stuffed the exercise books under the mattress of his bed.

'No suitcase, Benjamin?' Dr Dawes was ticking names off a list in front of a shiny green charabanc. He lifted his head, showing mild irritation behind the glasses. 'You're supposed to have a change of clothes and underwear.'

'There wasn't time.' He blushed. Some of the kids here had even brought toys with them. Benny tried hard not to think of the boxes of building blocks and construction kits he'd left behind. And his train set.

Dr Dawes pushed his spectacles back up his nose. 'I remember your circumstances now. Forgive me.' He leant towards Benny so that the others couldn't hear. 'Lord Dorner is well off and will ensure you have everything you need. He's sponsoring twenty Jewish boys and girls, but you six are the only ones he's taking into his own home.'

'Why us?' Benny wasn't used to asking adults questions. At home it was generally safer to let them do any questioning. Safer still not to get yourself into situations where questions were asked. But Dr Dawes didn't seem to mind.

'He asked for bright boys.' The tutor gestured that Benny should climb into the charabanc. 'Lord Dorner wants to educate you privately so that you can do well over here, perhaps even go to university. We had reports on you from the Jewish refugee council in your town.'

Benjamin Goldman had certainly been regarded as bright, working out the answers to sums before others had even copied down the questions from the blackboard. Sometimes other children had resented this. They'd muttered about sharp Yids. Like most of the Jewish kids, Benjamin had left that school and taken lessons in a Jewish school set up in someone's basement.

The charabanc journey to Fairfleet lasted most of the day because of the snow. Dr Dawes said this was because the roads weren't good in winter, not like the new autobahns in Germany, he added.

At least this time nobody threw up.

In the afternoon the charabanc pulled off a small country lane into a driveway. FAIRFLEET, the sign said. The house itself was a white rectangular structure, one side of which was bathed in the last of the pink winter sunset.

'Eighteenth century,' Dr Dawes said proudly, as though it were his own home. 'In the Palladian style. Small for its type,' he admitted ruefully. 'The owner captured a French ship in one of many wars against France. He won prize money for depriving the enemy of an important vessel. Hence the name Fairfleet, the English word "fleet" meaning a group of ships.'

Hitler himself would like the sound of plunder like this from defeated enemies, Benny reflected.

The charabanc drove round to the back of the house.

'Servants' entrance,' muttered David, the boy sitting next to him. A thin-faced, aproned girl of about eighteen stood at the door, arms crossed, frowning.

'Thrilled to see us, isn't she?' David whispered.

Dr Dawes got out first and said something to her. The English he spoke sounded flowing yet precise and rhythmic. She answered in a sharp-pitched, jerky voice. Funny how the same language could sound so different.

They walked inside to a parquet-floored hall and up two flights of stairs.

'Put your bags down here for now and wash yourselves in the bathroom on the right,' Dr Dawes told them. 'Supper in ten minutes. The kitchen's in the basement, three floors down.'

The girl said something else, sounding like a crow.

'Wash your hands properly before you come down,' Dr Dawes translated. 'Including your fingernails.'

As she went downstairs the tutor coughed and rubbed his nose. 'Alice has worked hard to prepare for your arrival. She's very efficient.'

'Efficient is good,' David said.

Dr Dawes gave a little smile.

The food at Fairfleet was more like what they were used to at home – better, actually, because there was plenty of beef in the stew.

A cheerful woman in her forties served them, chatting kindly in the language they couldn't understand.

'You won't be eating in the kitchen all the time,' Dr Dawes translated. 'Lord and Lady Dorner are away at present. And it's warmer in here.' Benny wasn't sorry to be down in the kitchen. The saucepans hanging from the ceiling rack and the dresser with its crockery reminded him of home. Something hit him below the ribs, a pang so strong it felt like a physical blow. He concentrated on his stew.

Later he lay in the bedroom he shared with David and Rainer. Proper beds, not bunks. They looked new. Moss-soft rugs on the floor. Heating that seemed to permeate the parts of his body that had been frozen since the boat had docked at Harwich.

Sniff, sniff. David might be weeping under his blankets, Benny couldn't be sure. Perhaps he just had a stuffy nose. Benny himself could weep too, but wasn't going to. Not yet.

~

A scream filled Benny's dreams. Someone was punishing a child and it was crying out. He sat up. Next to him David was also awake, rubbing his eyes. The two boys glanced at one another and tried to look as though the dreadful sound wasn't freezing their blood.

'It's a bird,' David said at last. 'Not a human.' As though to confirm what he had said, the bird screamed again. David smiled. 'Reminds me of the noises you hear in a zoo.'

Someone pounded on the door and called out.

'Time to get up,' David said. 'Come on, Rainer, lazybones.'

As he came downstairs, Benny noticed the view of the gardens from the window. To one side swept a line of hills like the white back of a sleeping beast. A window on the opposite side of the first floor showed him the gardens.

'They planned the house so there was always something to look at. You'll have to look at the animal hedges later on.'

He stared at the tutor, who gave him his gentle smile.

'Box trees clipped into the shape of a pig, fox, elephant and chicken. They call it topiary in English.'

After a breakfast of toast and boiled eggs, which everyone agreed was a great improvement on the porridge they'd suffered before, they went up to the specially furnished classroom on the ground floor. Six new wooden desks in two rows of three faced a blackboard. No photograph of Hitler on the wall, just a map of the world and a family tree of all the kings and queens of England.

'That's right, Benny.' Dr Dawes nodded approvingly. 'Familiarize yourself with all the history.'

The room smelled of new paper and fresh wood and overlooked the snowy lawn, which stretched out towards a small lake. Benny looked for the animal-shaped trees but couldn't see them from this side of the house.

Dr Dawes coughed to get their attention. 'This is all new and strange for you, boys,' he said in German. 'Let me explain what's in store for you. Britain expects that you refugees – aliens, you're unfortunately known as – will go into low-skilled work when you grow up.'

Benny had an image of himself ploughing fields or working down a mine.

'But that's not what Lord Dorner intends for you. He wants you to have the finest education the country can give you, if you're up to it. You'll have to work hard and make very good progress in English.' The classroom door swung open. The girl Alice came in with a bucket of coke.

'Soon you will be not only aliens but *enemy* aliens,' Dr Dawes went on.

Alice looked at them through her sandy eyelashes, clearly regarding them as exactly this. Dr Dawes said something to her in English. She went to the stove, its door squeaking as she opened it. The acrid smell of the coke as she shovelled it in caught the back of Benny's nose. For a second he was in the kitchen at home. He jabbed the sharpened point of his pencil against his palm until pain drove out the memory.

'It will be difficult,' Dr Dawes continued, looking from face to face, 'unless you adapt. These are some of the last German words you will hear in this classroom. All our lessons will be conducted in English.'

The boys sat up in shock, glancing at one another.

'You need to think in English, speak in English, sound English. Then you'll be accepted.'

Alice slammed the stove door as though in contradiction of the last claim. Dr Dawes didn't seem to notice. 'Eventually some of you may be called to fight Nazism as soldiers.' He switched to English. 'But for all of you, the fight starts now. In this classroom.'

4.

As promised, the morning's lessons continued in English. Benny felt the wires in his brain fizzing with new meanings. Maths involved problems using pounds, shillings and pence.

'One shilling and sixpence,' he said in halting English, responding to a question about the total paid for a basket of groceries.

'One and six.' Dr Dawes gave him an approving nod. Benjamin Goldman, known for being lightning quick at sums back home, was finding this all very hard but knew he had a position to maintain. He thought briefly of Rudi, how Rudi would daydream during maths, only paying attention when the teacher stood, ruler in hand, over his desk.

The same shriek that had woken them sounded through the window. The boys looked at one another, unsettled. Dr Dawes smiled. 'A peacock. *Ein Pfau.*' He wrote *peacock* on the blackboard, with a little picture of a bird with feathers fanned out behind it.

At break Benny took his football outside to the large lawn on the south side of the house and kicked it around with the other boys. He managed a good goal, one that would have been hard for Rudi to manage. It was fun playing here at Fairfleet with these boys. But there was still a numb ache under his ribs when he thought of how he'd played football with his friend back in Germany. The peacock stood on the terrace, observing them. At least it had stopped that frightful screaming. Its tail lacked the bright blue feathers of those he'd seen in pictures. Perhaps they moulted.

'Let's play again after lunch,' David said.

'Only if we speak in English,' Benny answered.

'Ha ha.'

'Seriously.' He picked up his ball. 'You want to play with my football, we use English. Only English.' He said the last two words in the language itself.

The others exchanged glances. 'Aren't you taking this a bit too seriously?' Rainer asked. Benny felt a little prickle of unease. He'd be marked out now as a teacher's pet. He didn't care. Back home it had always mattered to him what other boys thought. Not now. Becoming English mattered most. If the others felt differently, well, that was their choice.

'Do you think the lake's frozen?' Rainer broke the tension by pointing at the stretch of water. 'We could go skating.'

~

Every other night they had baths. The first few times it was easy to make excuses and dawdle so he was last and the others had left the steamy bathroom. But one night Rainer forgot his pyjama jacket and barged in as Benny was drying himself on one of the fluffy new white towels they'd all been given.

Benny felt Rainer's gaze.

'You're slow tonight,' the other boy said, plucking his pyjama jacket from the tiled floor and walking out. Benny took in a deep breath and let it out very slowly, watching the air condense on the mirror above the sink and turn into little drops of water.

'I am becoming an English boy,' he told his misted-over reflection. The real Benjamin Goldman was already a vague approximation of his former self.

~

As days passed it was easier and easier to become English. Benny started to think like the new person he'd become: the refugee who was blood-keen to suck up the new language and way of doing things. If the English held their cutlery a certain way, well, Benny would watch carefully and hold his knife and fork their way. If they drank tea with their breakfast, so would he.

When he met Alice Smith on the staircase he'd nod at her, ignoring the watchful expression in her pale green eyes. How easy it was if you acted like this, shrugged off any disapproval. At first the other boys had muttered about Benny's insistence on speaking English at all times, regarding him as a teacher's pet, as he'd anticipated. He'd relaxed a little now, allowing himself to talk to his room-mates last thing at night in their old language for a few minutes.

Lord Dorner, whom they still hadn't seen since arriving at Fairfleet two weeks earlier, had ordered crates of toys from Hamley's, which was apparently a large toyshop in London. The boys pulled English board games out of a crate.

'We had this at home,' Rainer said, pointing at a box set of Monopoly. 'But with Berlin streets.' There were Ludo and Scrabble as well. The largest crate contained a table-tennis set and bats. And a train set. Miles of track, a dozen engines, sleek liveried carriages, station buildings, bridges, points. Looking at them made something churn in Benny's stomach.

'You can take all that down the basement,' Alice told them. 'I don't want to be tripping over it when I'm vacuuming.'

The older boys muttered about kids' things, but Rainer and David carried the boxes down to one of the disused basement rooms and spent days arranging the train set on a large sheet of plywood the gardener found for them.

Benny tried to ignore their enthusiasm for the engines and points. He could still close his eyes and see the set he'd owned himself in Germany, still hear his father's voice.

'*You must take platform length into consideration when you're allocating wagons. And don't neglect the issue with the points. Or the signalling problem at that first junction.*'

Leave me alone, he told the voice. *You don't belong at Fairfleet.*

'Come on, Benny,' Rainer urged. 'Help us get this track sorted out.'

He mumbled an excuse and walked out of the room, carrying his football. On the left of the passage a bright rectangle of light had appeared. A side door to the garden. He hadn't noticed it before. He slipped through. The door took him out beside the tennis court. Alice Smith was shaking out rugs with a maid.

She scowled at Benny. 'That door's not to be used.'

'I am sorry,' he said.

She gave the rug a particularly vicious shake. 'I just open it once or twice a year to air the basement. You boys don't half try it on.'

The peacock strode towards them. Benny heard the rug flicking, Alice shooing it away. It cried at the bad treatment and Benny drove his fingernails into his palms, thinking again of tormented children.

A large oak stood at the edge of the back lawn. Benny kicked the ball again and again against its rough bark. Every slap of the leather was a slap against his own memory. When he came inside again he felt better. As long as he didn't have to play with the trains.

~

He could be this reborn Benny during the day. But sometimes at night he remembered that he didn't deserve this fresh chance at Fairfleet, with its soft-carpeted rooms and well-stocked library, its lawns where football could be played. His mind flitted to his old home, its tiled kitchen with pots and pans hanging from a ceiling rack and the stove emitting its constant warmth. He thought of his father, as he had once been, years ago, tumbling him onto the ground and pretending to be a bear, chasing him round the garden. He thought of his mother as she'd been before she fell ill, reading him a story before he fell asleep, buying him a bunch of red balloons once when she'd seen him gazing at the man selling them at the park gates.

Somewhere in his home town, another boy would be lying in bed. Probably not a comfortable bed like this one. That boy would be reviewing the past day: stones whizzing through the air to strike his neck as he walked through the streets, youths in uniform jeering at him.

'*Es tut mir leid*,' he muttered in the language he'd forbidden himself to use. 'I'm sorry.'

He buried his face in the soft, downy pillow and begged sleep to come.

5.

Weeks passed. Benny felt some of the ache inside him fade. Dr Dawes praised his rapid progress in English. And he was the best footballer – that was also clear. This status brought him grudging approval from the older boys. He still kept a slight distance between himself and the others, never hurrying to join them when they gathered for cocoa at break time or trooped downstairs to play table tennis in the basement after supper. Back home, he'd been eager for approval, to be part of the gang. He'd only ever been tolerated, not admired.

But in England even the older boys seemed to like Benny. And once there was even a near scuffle between Rainer and David about who was going to sit next to him at lunchtime.

Sometimes, at night, in the room they shared, he'd hear a repressed sob. One of the others was still missing home. Benny still hadn't wept, too wary to relax enough. Those last days in Germany had numbed his cells. Perhaps gentler memories would eventually ooze through him until he wept like Rainer and David.

The boys had yet to meet their benefactor. Meet him properly, that was. Dr Dawes assured them that Lord Dorner had indeed travelled to Dovercourt and seen each of them. Benny tried to remember when. Of course: that middle-aged man clutching the bowler hat who'd silently approached him at the breakfast table.

Someone knocked on the door while they were studying English adjectives. Lord Dorner was dressed more casually this morning, in sleeveless knitted pullover and corduroy trousers. He entered the room as though worried he'd be told off for interrupting, as though this school room weren't part of his own house and he weren't their host.

'You wouldn't think he was an important man, would you?' Rainer muttered to Benny.

Lord Dorner said little but stood with his arms behind his back, rocking slightly on the balls of his feet, as Dr Dawes listed the subjects they were studying.

'I'm glad you are working hard. I will buy some bicycles for you so you can see the countryside when the weather brightens up,' he said, in slow but accurate German.

Dr Dawes nodded at Ernst.

'Sir, we like to zank you for zer games you have bought for us.' It had probably taken Ernst all morning to master the phrase. Benny knew he could have done much, much better. English was going to be his language. Nobody would ever guess where he'd come from originally.

The door opened again. A woman came inside just as the halting winter sun came out from behind a cloud to shine directly on her. She was all shades of gold. Pale blonde hair. Apricot-tanned skin. A very soft jacket made from some kind of leather or suede, the colour of honey, lined with sheepskin. Riding breeches over long, shapely legs. Boots the colour of horse chestnuts.

'His wife, Lady Dorner?' whispered Rainer. 'Must be.'

'Harriet.' Lord Dorner laid a hand on her arm. 'How was the flying?' he asked in German.

'Bitingly cold but quite, quite exhilarating,' she replied in the same language, smiling at her husband and the boys. The smile warmed something deep inside Benny and made him sit up straighter. He knew little about women, but surely Lady Dorner was far younger than her husband?

'Let me know if there's anything the boys need, Dr Dawes,' she continued in German, very clear and well pronounced. 'Books. Comics. Sweets.' The last word was said with a twinkle.

'You've already been most kind, Lady Dorner. We have all we need.' Dr Dawes flushed as he replied in his careful German. 'But I am afraid we must only ever talk in English in front of the boys.'

She laughed. 'We're undoing all your hard work, aren't we?'

'Not at all.' His blush was now deep purple.

Rainer nudged Benny. 'He fancies her.'

With a nod to the boys Lady Dorner left. Her husband spoke quietly to the tutor for a moment. Dr Dawes removed his spectacles and wiped them on a handkerchief, looking anxious. Lord Dorner gave another shy smile, closing the door quietly behind him.

The boys went back to their adjectives: words describing nouns. Hot, warm, cool, cold. Benny wrote them out, but not in a list, using proper sentences. Dr Dawes stood beside his desk, looking at what he'd written.

'Benny?' He shook his head. 'How can the sun be both hot and cool? Try again.'

'*Dummkopf*,' whispered Ernst, who was hardly in a position to comment.

But Benny knew he was right. Hadn't she been like the sun? She made you warm to look at, but there was a cool poise to Lady Dorner, too: as though she'd been carved out of marble.

'Put down your pens now, boys.' Dr Dawes moved in front of the blackboard, rubbing an ear. 'Now then, boys.' The smile he attempted didn't quite have the effect of relaxing them. 'I have to tell you that war seems even more likely than ever. I know you'll be worried about your families at home. Lord Dorner tells me he'll do all he can to bring out close family members, for those of you who have them. But it's going to be hard.'

War. An image of the people at home threatened Benny's composure. But only for a moment.

He lowered his head back to his English exercise book, concentrating hard on the sentences. The words that others found so hard to master felt warm and pliant under his pen's nib.

6.
ROSAMOND

Seventy years later

And Benny himself is such an interesting man. This job seems just perfect for you.' Jo, the nursing agency manager, was upbeat as she told me about the new client at Fairfleet. It meant a lot to her to match the right nurse with the right patient. That's why she'd started her own agency, specializing in end-of-life cases.

And Benny himself certainly was intriguing. If you read broadsheet newspapers and watched documentaries you'd have heard of Benny Gault.

'He's reaching end stage, but is still very alert and reasonably comfortable. He needs someone who can talk to him about books, travel and politics as well as nurse him as things progress. There's just Benny and his housekeeper. Fairfleet is a big house and she's finding it hard to manage. I thought of you immediately.'

I said nothing; my head was a kaleidoscope of memories and fears.

'Rosamond?

I swallowed. 'I'll have to think about it. There's James, you see, and . . .'

And so much more.

'I know.' A tactful pause. 'I know you're still getting over . . . But this patient really needs someone like you, Rosamond. And it's an interesting house to live in, Fairfleet.'

I knew that.

'I just don't think I can.'

'Of course you have the final say.' But she sounded disappointed in me. 'Why don't you have a think about it? Talk to James?'

I mumbled something about calling her back in a day's time. James was listening to the conversation. It was early evening and he was home on time, compensating for long nights leading up to a school drama production last week. In front of him on the kitchen table lay a pile of school books for marking.

'What was all that?' His face was furrowed with concern. Impatience at his still worrying about me swept through me.

'Just a job.'

'One you don't want?'

I said nothing.

'Why not?'

I shrugged. He looked surprised. 'Jo knows you quite well, doesn't she? You always say she has an instinct for matching you to people you can best help.'

It was true. I'd been to homes both prosperous and humble. Nursed men and women, old and young, dying of all kinds of illness. And Jo had always found a connection between these people and me that went beyond simply that of nurse and patient. She had a talent for recreating families. Sometimes I found I was nursing someone who'd had a daughter my age, who'd died or emigrated or become estranged. Or an elderly woman who reminded me of my grandmother. In so far as anyone could ever resemble her.

'It's at Fairfleet,' I muttered.

'Fairfleet?'

'My grandmother's house.'

'Your grandmother who flew the Spitfires?'

I smiled and the tension lifted briefly. Granny and her beloved planes.

'Rather nice to go back to a place with happy memories.'

I felt my body freeze. I was silent, but it must have been painted there on my face for him to see. 'Rosamond?'

I fiddled with the corner of one of the exercise books.

'Hang on. Fairfleet . . .' The name was resonating with him. 'That was where your . . . ?'

'Yes.' I didn't want him to say aloud what had happened at Fairfleet, couldn't face hearing it all mentioned here in the futuristically modern kitchen of my safe London apartment. My fingers were still fiddling with the cover of the exercise book. He took it gently from me.

'Don't despoil school property. But, my God, no wonder you don't want to go back to Fairfleet. Call Jo back, tell her on no account are you taking the job.'

Unlike James to dictate to me. But that wasn't why I remained silent, fingers drumming the sleek kitchen counter.

'She'll understand that Fairfleet is one place you really can't go to. Especially now.'

I walked over to the window and stared out at the Thames below. Lights twinkled along the side of the river. A police launch shot past. From this height you couldn't hear much, but down there, people were going about their lives heedless of me and what had happened to me. Many people dealt with worse. I could ring Jo back. Explain in a rational adult way that matched my rational professional persona what had happened at Fairfleet thirty years ago. She'd understand, of course she would. Nobody could blame me for turning down this job. Especially now.

Or I could do it. Return to Fairfleet under my married name of Rosamond Hunter. I'd ditched the husband but retained the surname.

My hair had darkened as I'd grown older instead of staying the blonde that my mother and grandmother had kept. I encouraged this change, having it regularly tinted so that it was now chestnut. I hadn't inherited the striking facial features of my grandmother and mother. And who in the area would even remember Rose Madison? We hadn't played with children in the village, or attended local schools.

Rosamond Hunter. Rose Madison. The same person, only different.

'Rosamond?' James had been watching me, face full of concern.

'I could go back,' I said. 'I know the house. I know a bit about Benny Gault. He lived in the house during the war, you know. My grandmother took him in.'

'And all those things would be wonderful if that's as far as it went, if you just paid a visit,' James said. 'You could reminisce about your grandmother. Did she ever talk about Benny?'

I tried to remember. 'I don't think she did,' I said. 'No more than the other boys from Germany they took in. He wouldn't know who I was.' My mind went back to my change of name. 'It was all such a long time ago.'

'You're seriously thinking of taking this job?' James put down his wine glass. 'Rosamond?' The way he pronounced my name made it clear just how much he disapproved.

'I don't know.' I turned my back on him and returned to the view over the Thames, watching the wide, dark expanse of water pulling everything down towards the sea, where all memories and events finally met and mingled. 'I just don't know.'

But later that same evening, when James was taking a shower, I rang Jo on her mobile and told her I'd like to accept the job at Fairfleet. I didn't tell her any of the reasons why doing so might not be a good idea.

~

'Don't go back. There's nothing for you at Fairfleet now.'

Half of me was touched by the obvious concern in my brother's voice. Half was annoyed by Andrew's insistence that he knew what was good for me. And if it were possible to have a third half, that half would have been exasperated that James, the man I lived with, who was watching me while I had this telephone conversation with a similar kind of anxiety on his face. These two males were trying to force me to do what they wanted and I wasn't going to have it. I reminded myself that it was only concern that motivated them.

'We all die,' I explained to James, when I finished the call to my brother. 'It's one of the most important things, perhaps the most important thing, that happens to us. It matters that it's done well. And I think I can help Benny, I really do.'

James took my hand. 'I understand that. But I just wonder whether going back to Fairfleet is not really about Benny but more to do with what happened when you were a child.'

'Everyone always wants to psychoanalyze me.' I pulled back my hand. 'You. My brother. My ex, Charles. I'm fine.'

'There's nothing wrong with using a traumatic experience to do something good for other people. I understand that.' His voice was gentle. 'But is now the best time for you to go to Fairfleet?'

'I'm feeling much better.' Instinctively, though, I felt myself hunch in the chair. I hadn't been able to think of any better way of reconciling myself to what had happened.

Benny and I certainly seemed to hit it off at our preliminary meeting, at a coffee shop in a nearby town, probably one of Benny's last outings. He was in early old age and had probably looked young and fit for his years until a few months ago. Face starting to fold in on itself, slightly yellow-skinned. Eyes still bright and sharp, inquisitive as they took me in. Still a handsome man. Benny Gault, journalist and writer.

We talked mainly about books and my travels abroad. Nothing was mentioned about his illness and I didn't ask for details. There'd be time enough for all that. What mattered now was seeing whether he liked me, would trust me to care for him.

'We'll ring the agency,' Sarah, the housekeeper, said. 'Thank you for coming to meet us, Rosamond.' She passed Benny his stick.

'Yes, it was interesting.' Benny gave me a probing look. Perhaps he could see into the very heart of me. Or perhaps that was how he was with all newcomers.

He seemed weak, halting at the door on his way out and leaning on his stick and staring out towards a statue of King Alfred in the marketplace. Probably noting the scene in his memory because he wouldn't see it again. He looked at it all for a full minute, then turned to me.

'No need to keep you waiting to find out from the agency, Rosamond. If you can put up with a cranky old invalid, I'd like you to come and stay at Fairfleet.' There was a softness to his voice as he said the name of the house. 'Do you know the area?'

'Not as much as I'd like.'

'The house is beautiful,' he said. 'Perhaps I shouldn't say so as it's mine, but it's true. I think you'll like living there. Even if you do have to put up with me.'

Sarah tutted and tapped him on the arm. 'You're not that bad, Benny.'

~

So I made preparations for starting the job, leaving James reminders of how all the kitchen gadgets operated (although I barely ever cooked anything for myself).

'I wish you were spending Christmas with Catherine and me,' he said as I packed.

So did I, really. It was true that seeing James's undergraduate daughter would be a reminder of what had been lost. But I liked Catherine and she seemed to like me.

'What do you think you'll find at Fairfleet? How can it possibly help you to go back now?'

'It's not just me.'

'What do you mean?'

'It would show Andrew.'

'Show him what?'

'I think he felt, deep down, that Mum had somehow stopped loving us as much, had switched allegiance. If I could just show him something tangible, he might feel differently.'

'What do you mean by tangible?'

'There was a letter Mum wrote to her solicitor. Telling him what had happened. I think that letter shows how much she cared about us, how she wanted to put things right.'

'Does Andrew know about the letter?

'Yes. He gave it to me to hide. But neither of us read it.' There hadn't been time; that last afternoon had been a blur of panic and trying to outwit the enemy.

'Be very clear about your motives, Rosamond.' James might have been commenting on a badly written school essay.

'I'm not one of your sixth-formers,' I retorted.

'No, you're a professional nurse with a patient who needs you to have your mind completely on the job.'

'Yes, I'm a professional.' I shut my small case and snapped the catch shut. 'And of course I'll have my mind on the job. Frankly I'll be so busy looking after Benny there won't be time for much else.'

I still felt a little like a refugee myself as Sarah led me through to the kitchen a week later: uncertain what I would find at Fairfleet, how I would feel about things. I told myself that I was a woman in my early forties, rather than a girl not yet thirteen years old. I blinked hard to clear my vision of figures who weren't here, not now, not any more.

The patter of small feet raised me from my trance. A small terrier observed me, ears pricked. He sniffed my shoes, wagging his tail.

'Come on, Max,' Sarah said. He ran happily across the hallway. If a dog wasn't worried, it must be fine, I told myself.

As we reached the kitchen door I ducked instinctively.

'Well done – you spotted that low beam before I could warn you.' Sarah had turned just as I had entered the kitchen. 'I don't know why they didn't take it out when they moved the kitchen up from the basement after the war.'

The Little Miss Know-it-all inside me wanted to tell her it was because the lintel held up most of the supporting wall. I pushed Little Miss down and looked around the kitchen. A long oak table, dark and well waxed, covered in baking trays, a set of scales and ingredients, occupied the middle. Underneath the worktop lay the dog's bed: small and cosy. Max jumped into it and curled up. Outside on the lawn I caught a glimpse of the topiary walk: hedges cut into perfect cones and spirals, each sprinkled with frost, like giant Christmas decorations. I felt my heart beat more slowly.

Sarah cleared a space for my coffee mug. 'Cooking's a bit of a passion of mine. Benny doesn't eat much. He has friends down fairly regularly for short visits, but it'll be a treat to have someone else to cook for.' She looked wistful.

She must be lonely living here. At our first meeting she'd told me how the gardener only came in once a fortnight during the winter, and that the cleaner had been reduced to three mornings a week. Sarah herself was a slim woman, with only a few lines around her eyes. I wondered how long she'd been working as Benny's housekeeper.

She looked at my empty cup. 'Shall we go upstairs? Benny's been looking forward to seeing you.'

I followed Sarah across the stone-floored entrance hall, the dog pattering behind us. Once again I braced myself, but there was nothing. Stop, I told myself. Stop remembering.

'Benny still sleeps fairly well at night, he claims,' Sarah said, walking up the stairs ahead of me. 'He says he doesn't need you to sit up with him at the moment.' I murmured a response. My toes were like feelers, testing every inch, expecting to feel a shock at each step, relaxing a little as we approached the top and still nothing had happened. I was just walking up a staircase, that's all. I forced myself to think of my patient. At the coffee shop meeting Benny and Sarah had told me how the cancer had paced around like a tiger contained in a cage for the last five years, breaking out with renewed ferocity six months ago. Chemotherapy had not won this round. Further surgery or radiography were impossible, Jo had told me, filling me in on the medical information I'd need to nurse Benny.

'You've seen his notes, anyway,' Sarah said as we reached the landing. 'He's been growing sleepier over the last few days.'

That would be the effect of the opioid patch he now wore. 'Possibly he'll get used to the patch,' I said. 'Sometimes the drowsiness does wear off a bit.'

Though the doctor would probably need to increase the dosage soon.

'And sometimes he likes to talk. There's no family, you see. His wife died some years ago. Friends come down and help when they can. Benny's not demanding, far from it, but . . .'

'It's hard work.'

She gave me a grateful nod as we reached a bedroom door. 'But don't worry. We're not expecting you to do it all. We'll call in more help as we need it.'

I relaxed when I saw which room she was entering.

She opened the door. 'I'll just tell him you're here.' Max squeezed past her and ran ahead, obviously knowing he would be welcome. My stomach flipped. There's often this moment of nervousness at the very beginning of a job, I reminded myself.

Murmurs came from within the room.

'Come on in, Rosamond,' Sarah called. I was glad she was speaking in a normal tone. The dying usually prefer people to behave normally around them.

I let out the breath I'd been holding and walked in. A double-aspected room, windows overlooking both the gardens to the front of the house and the Downs to the south. My patient was lying in a four-poster bed, a smart aluminium laptop beside him. He smiled in a quizzical, amused way, as though he found this a strange way to be meeting me again. His proffered hand was paper-thin, the white skin stretched like a tent on its poles.

'I feel rude not getting up. What must you think?' The eyes rolled with the irony of it.

'I've seen worse. You haven't thrown a bedpan at me to welcome me.'

'Someone did that?'

'At least it was empty.'

'Could have been worse.' He grinned, the years slipping from him. 'Good to see you again, Rosamond. Make yourself at home before you do anything else. I've got some writing to do for a couple of hours, anyway. If I don't drop off, that is.' He touched his arm. 'Damn patch.'

He was more like a newspaper editor with a new reporter than a patient with a nurse. But his manner was easy and gentle. 'Leave Max up here, Sarah.'

'Until later, then.' I picked up the bag I'd left at the bedroom door. He raised a hand, already engrossed in whatever was on the laptop.

'That new computer only arrived a few days ago. He's been fiddling around with wi-fi connections,' Sarah said. 'It's really perked him up. She glanced at my bag. 'You travel light.'

Most of the time I simply wore black or grey jersey trousers with either a beige or grey cashmere v-neck over a t-shirt. Smart enough to look professional yet comfortable.

Other than these clothes and my underwear and toiletries, my bag contained my mobile and a tablet computer. I didn't own many other possessions.

'You live like a gypsy,' James had complained when he'd first got to know me. 'Even this apartment of yours is like a temporary refuelling point or something.'

I'd laughed, but taken his point. There'd been a period of time, lasting no more than a month or so, when I'd thought of moving, of finding a house with a garden. But that had all come to nothing.

'I suppose you're used to . . . this.' Sarah nodded over her shoulder at the door we'd just closed and blinked hard, a chink of emotion showing in her neatly made-up features.

'I've had plenty of experience, but you never get used to all of it. You shouldn't, really.' I suppose I'm like a kind of midwife for the dying. I hope so. Rather than help them arrive, I help them leave. I never hurry the pace of the departure, though. And my loyalty is always to the patient rather than anyone else. I hoped I understood this properly myself.

She paused, frowning, outside the door next to Benny's. For a moment I thought I was to sleep in there and clenched my suitcase handle. Sarah opened the door and looked inside. 'I heard something in there. Probably a bird hitting the window.'

Or a ghost, letting me know it was aware of my presence at Fairfleet.

Sarah closed the door, allowing me a glimpse of neatly arranged shoes under the dressing table and a well-ordered arrangement of make-up and perfume on the dressing table. Her own bedroom.

We followed the landing round to the right. Sarah opened a door. A west-facing room. In the evening pink light would flood in, warming the ivory walls.

'It's lovely, thank you.' I placed my suitcase on the bed, beside two thick and obviously new ecru towels. Sarah obviously had a gift for making rooms look welcoming. The wooden panelling had been left to speak for itself; the rest of the room was muted and neutral, except for the bluebell-coloured quilt on the bed, which matched the blue trim on the curtains. Sarah had piled new magazines on the small desk and arranged freesias in a square Perspex vase on the dressing table.

Four small candles in stainless-steel holders sat on a mirrored tile on the dressing table. I couldn't bear to have candles in my bedroom. I'd hide them away.

'If you've got everything you need, I'll let you unpack.' She reached the door and turned back. 'Oh . . .'

I stopped, hand still opening the wooden doors on the wall beside the dressing table.

'I was just going to tell you about the hidden wardrobe, but you're too quick for me!'

'Pure fluke.' I hoped I sounded casual. She left me to my unpacking.

'You won't be able to get away with it, you know,' James had said as I was leaving. 'You'll give yourself away. It'll be something small you let slip.' His face was creased with concern. 'Why not just tell them who you are?'

'Because they won't think I'm a suitable nurse.'

'You can't know that.'

'Oh, I do. Anyway, it's too late now. They're expecting me.' And I'd picked up my suitcase and kissed him goodbye. His face had worn the same resigned expression I remembered seeing on my ex-husband just before we'd broken up.

I washed my hands in the en-suite bathroom. The skin on my left arm was itching, as it often did at this time of year, when rooms were dry from central heating. I rolled up a sleeve and massaged the scar. I felt as I had when I was a child starting at a new school. To settle myself I switched on my phone and looked at the photos I'd stored on it. Mum. Dad. Granny. Andrew and me as children. It only took a minute for me to remember why I was here.

My unpacking didn't take long. Sarah had promised me a lunch of soup and sandwiches at half twelve. I put my sheepskin coat back on and went downstairs. 'Thought I'd stroll round the gardens,' I told Sarah, who was chopping vegetables. 'Benny sounds as though he wants to be left in peace for now.'

She rolled her eyes. 'He makes it very clear when he needs his privacy. But I like that. I know where I am with him.'

'I like things being clear, too.' I blushed.

'Make sure you take a look at the topiary,' she said. 'Beside the tennis court. We can't find anyone who can cut the wonderful animals they once had here, but our spirals and cones look rather elegant, I think.'

The topiary walk wasn't as I remembered, but I admired the frosted spires and cones – elegant, just like the house itself. I walked round the frosty lawns and flowerbeds towards the lake. If the weather stayed as cold as this the water might freeze. I couldn't resist a childlike rush of excitement.

Money had been spent on the house and grounds. Probably raised by selling parcels of land. A second wave of housing had sprung up at right angles to the original new-builds behind the lake.

The walled garden and tennis court were both in good repair, too, I noted. Benny and his wife had cherished Fairfleet. I walked on, eventually coming out at the front of the house. The drive led to the lane, itself leading to the village.

I headed back to the lake. The wind blew into my face, seeming to come across the water from the North Pole. Like a little girl I shivered and shoved my hands into my coat pockets. I needed gloves. The wind's rasping cold mocked my belief that I could handle being back at Fairfleet. The sun went behind a cloud. Fairfleet's gardens looked lonely and abandoned.

My car keys were still in my coat pocket. With a turn of the key in the ignition I could be away, never to see this place again. I could abandon my few possessions; they were all replaceable.

'Don't go back,' I heard Andrew tell me.

I stood there shivering, watching a flock of geese fly very low over the lake.

Then I forced myself to turn towards the back door of the house.

7.

The warmth of the kitchen relaxed me. My mind turned to practical matters. I'd packed for this job in a hurry, knowing that if I took time to consider what I needed for Fairfleet doubts might shake me. I needed more warm clothes. If I gave lunch a miss I could drive into Oxford, give myself a temporary escape from the house.

'I'm just going to do a quick bit of shopping before Benny needs me,' I told Sarah.

'What about your lunch?' Something smelled delicious. 'Here, let me serve you some quickly.' The red-pepper soup defrosted me completely.

She explained how to use the park-and-ride system and told me where the bus would drop me off in the city centre. As I went to pick up my handbag from my room I worried she'd consider me restless, dashing out on an errand no sooner than I'd arrived.

Oxford felt busier than I remembered it as a child. I stood blinking in the Cornmarket as crowds milled round me. Shoppers shivered, faces pinched and grey as they hurried between shops. Christmas might only be weeks away, but nobody seemed to be enjoying the shop displays or the groups of cold-looking school children singing carols. Ahead of me pedestrians veered suddenly to the right. An off-key busker? Probably a hole in the pavement, cordoned off. I heard shouts, a man's voice, deep and loud, screaming at passers-by. An arm waved above people's heads.

'Not him again,' a girl ahead of me muttered to her friend. 'Total nutcase. He was hassling some poor woman yesterday. The police should move him on.'

The drunk, if that's what he was, stood still, focusing into mid-distance, while he ranted at the crowd. He wore a long black coat, belted with a length of string and a woolly hat. He didn't appear any more threatening than the other drunks you saw everywhere in British towns. I scanned the street ahead for the department store I needed. Half two now. The short December day was almost at its ebb. I wasn't sure I'd remember how to navigate the maze of country lanes around Fairfleet in the dark.

The drunk drew breath as I passed him. For a second I could make out the screech of bus brakes and the laughter of a group of students on the other side of the road. Something clenched my arm. I looked down and saw the drunk's hand on my sheepskin sleeve. His nails were bitten and cracked, the skin red and chapped, mottled with some skin complaint. I tried to shake the hand off.

'I know all about you.' His blue eyes bored into mine. A small dent pitted the side of his head, as though someone had once bashed his skull. A grubby beard covered his jaw. I wanted to scream.

'Think I'm stupid?' he went on. 'I know what you are.' He nodded slowly to himself.

Shoppers turned to gawp at us.

'Get off.' I shook his hand harder, heart thumping. 'Let me go.'

'You don't fool me!' he roared.

'Bloody leave her alone.' The girls who'd been muttering about the drunk came towards us. One of them waved a mobile phone. 'I've got a photo. I'll text it to the police.'

He stared at them and then at the hand he'd placed on my arm. He let me go, stepping back into a doorway, still nodding towards me.

'Should be her on the streets. Not me.' He spat the last words at me, hunched his shoulders and shuffled off towards a coffee shop, presumably to harass people going inside in search of warmth.

'You want us to call the police?' The first girl waved her mobile.

'No.' The word sounded harsh. I softened it with a smile. 'He's just a drunk. I'll leave it. Thanks anyway.'

They walked on. 'Nutter,' one of them muttered. I wondered whether she meant him or me.

I reached the warm department store and forced myself to concentrate on the counters of make-up and the Christmas decorations around the moving staircase, the hubbub of the shoppers.

8.

By the time I reached women's fashions on the first floor my heartbeat was back to normal. I concentrated on the racks of cashmere, managing to ask an assistant to bring me the sizes I needed without my voice shaking.

'This one is more expensive.' The assistant looked me over. 'But the quality of the cashmere is excellent.'

The taupe jumper felt like a warm waterfall running through my fingers. 'I'll take it,' I said. 'And the charcoal version, too.'

I saw her raise her eyebrows slightly and give me an approving nod. I hadn't even looked at the price tags, just picking out whatever appealed. Lady Muck, James sometimes called me, affectionately. At least I hoped it was affectionately.

'Quality lasts,' had always been my rejoinder. That was what my grandmother and mother had believed. One perfect coat rather than two or three mediocre ones. Good-quality woollens because they could be washed again and again.

So two or three times a year I bought whatever I needed, without looking at price tags. I had accustomed myself to my wealth by now; we were old partners, making the best of one another. But as I replaced my credit card in my purse I couldn't help thinking of the lack of money affecting so many people these days. The drunk's face flashed into my mind. I shivered, even though the store was heated to tropical temperatures. Downstairs I picked up a pair of warm leather gloves, lined with sheepskin.

I was careful to make a detour back to the bus stop to avoid the Cornmarket, in case the drunk was still looking out for me. Perhaps he'd guessed I'd come in on a park-and-ride bus and was hanging around by the bus stop. Stop it, I told myself. You're being paranoid, seeing things in his raddled expression that weren't there.

As I stood at the stop I opened the store bag and unfolded the tissue paper to let my fingers touch the soft cashmere jumpers. The smooth, warm fibres soothed me. I could manage this. My mobile trilled, alerting me to a text message. *Pls. let me know how it's going. J.x.*

It must be break time. James would be in the staff room, grabbing a coffee. Worrying about me.

All fine. xxx. My fingers tingled as I typed the lie.

Evening was already falling as I drove the last miles back to Fairfleet, the pale sun dropping below the hills. There were more streetlights lining the roads than I remembered, but when I turned off the lane into Fairfleet's drive the darkness curled itself around the car. I felt the now familiar mixture of excitement and anxiety. Proper inky winter night-time: a period for reflection.

I let myself into the house and went up to my room to unpack my purchases. As I passed Benny's door I heard a low murmur of voices. Sarah and Benny, perhaps talking about the new arrival who'd dashed off so precipitously to buy something or other.

Time to push my personal considerations to one side. I put on my new taupe jumper over my long-sleeved silk t-shirt and prepared myself for Benny, trying to erase thoughts of the drunk's grimy hand on my arm. I was safe here at Fairfleet. And my patient needed my energy and concentration now. As I applied a thin layer of eye-liner I felt myself slipping into my professional persona.

Benny was sitting up in bed when I went in, finishing a sorbet of some kind. Good choice for a patient with a dry mouth and possible nausea. Max still lay on the rug beside the bed, greeting me with a gentle wag of his tail. The smart laptop sat on the bed-side table.

'Nice jumper.' Benny's eyes glinted with something. Amuse-ment? Irony? I decided not to analyze it. This evening his voice still sounded as it had on the television and radio: very English-sounding, but with the slightest note that might, if you listened carefully, make you aware of the fact he hadn't been born in this country. Unlike other famous or successful people I'd nursed, he hadn't surrounded himself with photographs of himself with fellow famous people. No awards on his book shelves, no press cuttings framed and displayed on the walls.

'Thank you. I'll just clear this.' I took the sorbet bowl and car-ried it out on the tray, leaving it on the small table outside the door for Sarah to collect. She'd told me he hated having used plates and cutlery left in his room.

'I've been working on that laptop too long. My eyes feel tired. Or perhaps it's the patch.' He stopped. I sensed there was more to say.

'Is the patch keeping you comfortable?'

'Yes. The doctor explained . . . that it wouldn't be enough to take me . . . through. I'll probably need a syringe pump soon, he said.'

And once that arrived, Benny would spend more time sleeping.

'Would you read to me? It's *Great Expectations*.' The book was on the bedside table, underneath the open laptop. As I moved the laptop Benny made an anxious sound.

'Don't worry,' I said. 'I won't drop it.'

He didn't say anything. I wondered if he'd been concerned I'd read what was on the screen. I wouldn't have dreamed of looking at the words, but in any case the laptop had already gone into sleep mode.

I found a page in the book marked with a used envelope.

'Pip's just arrived in London.' There was a note of challenge in Benny's voice. 'He's the new boy, the kid from out of town, and he needs to learn the new way of doing things. And quickly.'

Like Benny himself had had to, I thought. When he'd come here just before the war. Or like I was having to, now.

'Is it a novel you know well?'

'I've read it a few times. I like it for its apparent simplicity. Fewer characters to keep in your mind than in most of Dickens' novels. But the simplicity is deceptive.'

'It usually is.' I'd spoken without thinking. He gave me a searching look. I began to read, moving my eyes from the page to his face from time to time, to check I wasn't reading too fast or slowly, or with too much or little expression. Benny's eyes stayed on the wall opposite his bed, as if the text were written on its cream surface. I read on.

'Magwitch,' he muttered. 'What a terrifying apparition for a young boy.'

I agreed, though we hadn't been reading about Magwitch in this chapter. And tonight I didn't want to let that frightening outcast, who'd returned after so many years' absence, into my mind.

'Your one worst nightmare, waiting to reappear,' Benny went on. 'But Pip doesn't know that yet.'

My mouth felt as dry as the pages in the book. Had Benny guessed what had happened in Oxford? Impossible. I was being fanciful, not the calm, professional nurse who ought to have cleared her mind of the incident before coming to her patient's bedside.

'Nor do we readers,' I said. 'If we do, it's only because we've read the book before and know how the story goes.'

'We know how the story goes,' he repeated softly.

After a while his breathing grew slower and his breaths longer. I replaced the envelope in the book, noticing in passing that it was addressed to Benny and had a modern-looking German stamp on it. Benny looked peaceful now.

I rose and busied myself tidying the very few things in the room that Sarah hadn't already tidied. When I looked at him again he was sleeping, breathing peacefully. I wondered whether he dreamed and if so, of what. He'd had a long and full life. Did his mind return to the triumphs? Or did he drift back to his early childhood, as so many people did at the end of their lives?

I went down to Sarah, leaving Benny alone with the dog.

'Sleeping, is he?' She lifted her head from a recipe book. 'He's had a better day. Perhaps you're doing him good already, Rosamond.'

'It's probably the patch, but I hope I can help make him feel at peace and cared for.' I sat down at the table and watched her as she gathered ingredients together. 'But you've certainly looked after him very well.'

'Sometimes he has such terrible dreams. Could it be the drugs?'

'Might be. We'll talk to the doctor. There may be antipsychotics or sedatives that will help with that.'

'Good luck getting him to agree to taking those. But he's scared of something.' She took an egg out of a carton and cracked it on the side of a Pyrex bowl. 'I think it's to do with all that happened just before he came to England. He left Germany a month or so after Kristallnacht. They smashed Jewish shop windows in his town. And some of the houses were targeted too, he told me.'

'It must have been a relief to be safe.' But I wondered what had happened to Benny's family, whether he'd felt homesick, alone, lost, in his new home. He must have done.

'The Dorners took good care of the boys they took in. That's probably why Benny bought this house, because of the happy memories. But it can't have been easy for him. He even changed his name eventually, to make himself seem more English and less German-Jewish.'

I didn't know this. 'What was he called originally?'

'Benjamin Goldman. He became Benny Gault as the years went by. Sounded more English, he told me.'

Names were important: I knew that, hypocrite that I was, coming back here with a name that, while legally mine, obscured so much.

'Benny always wanted to belong.' Sarah broke the shell and expertly held the yolk back, allowing the white to flop into the Pyrex bowl. 'There have been Kindertransport reunions over the years, but he never attends. Always sends large cheques for memorials. And to other refugee organizations, though I probably shouldn't tell you that.' She tipped the yolk into a tea cup. 'But apart from the boys he grew up with here, he keeps himself apart from his past. And three of the old Dorner boys are overseas. Of the two others still in Britain, one's a carer for his sick wife and the other lives in Edinburgh. They ring and email, but they can't easily visit. Shame, because they're the ones who really understand the early trouble.'

Benny and I had both known early trouble. And we'd both found ways of insulating ourselves from discomforting echoes: he in this old country house with its sweeping views and fine furniture, me in my minimalist flat with its few starkly fashionable pieces.

'I'll get my book,' I said, rising from the chair.

But my book wasn't on my mind. I was thinking of that missing letter my mother had written years ago.

~

Next morning, after I'd helped Benny wash and given him his medication, he said he wanted to sit up in his armchair and do his crossword. 'Please put the laptop on the dressing table. I'll want to write later.' He looked distracted this morning, mind already on the words he wanted to tap out. I didn't know whether he would welcome any interest in the writing. Half of me thought a journalist would like people talking about his work – relish the interest, in fact. But the other half detected a desire in Benny to be left to whatever he was writing, without questions.

He had clothes to be washed. Sarah had already told me that the utility room was down in the basement. A chance for me to descend the stone steps. My pulse beat fast and my mouth felt chalky-dry. But when I reached the ground floor, holding the laundry basket, Sarah herself was unlocking the basement door.

'I'm on my way down to see if the towels have finished in the dryer.' She held out her arms for the basket. 'I'll take those down for you, Rosamond.'

I made an attempt to protest, but she was having none of it. 'If Benny's doing his crossword he'll be quite happy for an hour.' She nodded at the window by the front door. 'The sun's come out. Go for a walk, Rosamond.'

I started to demur, even as relief flooded me.

'I need eggs,' she said. 'They sell them in the village shop. You'd be doing me a favour if you walked down there for me. Perhaps take Max with you?'

I'd forgotten about the shop when I'd decided to come back to Fairfleet. We hadn't visited it that often when I'd lived here before, so long ago. Just at the very end.

The shop had been given a make-over. The vivid tangerine-and-yellow Battenberg cakes and fondant fancies had gone, replaced with organic tea loaves, arranged in lined baskets. Instead of

Black Tower and Blue Nun, bottles of Pinot Grigio and Chilean Sauvignon stood on stripped wooden shelves.

A middle-aged woman was serving customers behind the till and an older woman sat on a chair in the corner reading an *Express*, a walking stick propped up against the shelves of washing powder beside her. Mother and daughter, I concluded.

I took the eggs to the counter. The woman lifted her head. I recognized her. My heart thumped as I bent my head over my purse, as though searching for the correct change. The *tap, step, tap, step* of the old woman coming towards the till made me look up. She watched me silently.

'I'll put the kettle on in a moment, Mum,' the shopkeeper said, taking my coins.

I felt both sets of eyes on me as I left the shop after a hastily muttered thank-you. I untied Max from the hook outside the door and we walked briskly back up the lane to Fairfleet. Had that woman recognized me? No way of telling.

I was looking forward to returning to Benny's room. As a young woman I would never have dreamed that my career would have been spent in sickrooms. But my job suited me and I suited my job.

As Sarah had predicted, Benny was still working on his crossword when I returned to him. 'With you in a moment. Just let me finish this clue.' He sounded brisk. Perhaps my reappearance had reminded him of his decline.

'I can still just about do these things,' he said with satisfaction, putting down his pen.

'Cryptic crosswords baffle me.'

'You need someone to teach you the tricks. I had a very good tutor during the war. So good I'm surprised he wasn't bundled off to Bletchley Park to break ciphers.'

I'd always wondered why the boys hadn't been sent to school. Seeming to read my thoughts, Benny went on, 'Lord Dorner, my benefactor, was worried about anti-Semitism in English schools.'

'Ironic.'

'There was a lot of anxiety about foreign Jews flooding the professions. We were supposed to go into manual work when we grew up.'

'No wonder he thought it was easier to educate you privately.' Hard to imagine a parallel existence for Benny Gault as a miner or farm labourer.

'And Lady Dorner?' I stooped to pick up a throw that had fallen onto the carpet and folded it carefully on the end of the bed. 'Was she welcoming?'

'She flew for the auxiliary air transport so she was away for a lot of the time.'

I tried to reflect both interest and surprise in my expression, thinking back to James's warnings. 'You'll find it a strain,' he had said. 'When they tell you things you already know and you have to pretend you're hearing them for the first time.'

'Just because you teach drama doesn't mean you have to treat this whole assignment as though I'm going on stage.'

'Oh but you will be on stage, Rosamond,' he'd told me.

Benny was staring out of the window, caught up in the past. 'Harriet Dorner was quite a woman,' he said softly. 'One of a kind.'

I know, I said silently.

'Tell me about her.' I sat back in my armchair.

'She was tall and athletic. Very pretty. Younger than her husband. He adored her. He indulged her in her flying lessons before the war. Probably never dreamed she'd end up doing the things she did. She flew planes from one airfield to another so that they were in the right position for the RAF. Dangerous work. Those women weren't armed. Often they lacked basic navigational tools, as well.'

I remembered hearing about a flight across the Highlands in thick cloud, the terror that a hidden mountain top would suddenly appear.

'She was away for long periods,' Benny went on. 'But she'd sometimes come home for weekends or an occasional week. She'd be walking around the gardens when I was playing football outside.' He grinned, his gaunt features losing decades. 'I remember her telling me off for hitting a peony with the ball. Must have been the first spring of the war, May 1940. The Germans had invaded the Low Countries. Everyone was on edge.'

9.

The space between the lilac tree and the peony was almost exactly the width of a goal, Benny estimated. Situated right at the far end of the lawn, there was a good run-up, too. The others were busy playing with the train set, but now the rain had stopped, Benny needed to be outside.

He took aim. The first kick was a good one, but the ball flew three feet to the left of the lilac. He ran after it, the damp grass squelching under his plimsolls. Really he needed proper boots, like the ones he'd left at home.

The second kick was still wide. Again he ran after the ball, plucked it out of the bushes. The third shot hit the tree, sending out the aroma of lilac. Fleetingly Benny's mother was there in the garden too. He remembered her cutting sprigs of lilac blossom to bring inside.

When he aimed the ball again it was a disaster. A spray of dark red petals dropped onto the lawn.

'Boy!' The voice was a commanding one. He turned round to see Lady Dorner in a mackintosh, eyes blazing. 'That's my peony you're destroying.'

'I'm sorry.' And he was. He'd never imagined she could look as furious as this. What could he do? She glared at him as she strode towards him.

'That is a very beautiful plant that flowers for about a fortnight once a year. You have destroyed at least three of the blossoms, Benny.'

He felt his cheeks warm.

'Can't you use one of the oaks? God knows, they're sturdy enough.'

'Yes. Sorry, Lady Dorner.' He gazed at his plimsolls.

'What were you trying to do? Blast it to death?'

'To make my football kick more . . . sharp.' He was speaking in English, almost without thinking about it – not perfectly, he knew, but well enough. Perhaps she appreciated this too. The glare softened.

'I was just taking a stroll or else I wouldn't have known what you were up to.'

'I was not knowing you were at home, Lady Dorner.' The wrong thing to say. Made it sound as though he was only sorry he'd been caught, not about damaging the shrub.

'They gave me a few days off. God knows why at a time like this.' She nodded at the ball, still lying beside the scattered red petals. 'You're very determined, Benny.'

He shuffled.

'Do the others play football?'

'Yes, but they like the train set and ping-pong, too.'

'You need a proper goal, really.' She frowned. 'Not sure where we'd get such a thing.'

'I could perhaps put a paint mark on one of the oaks, so.' He drew a cross in the air. 'If you say this is not a bad thing to do?' He'd had this idea before but had never been able to find any paint. There was probably some in the basement, but Alice Smith guarded the place like a warden. And she wouldn't approve of him defacing the Dorners' trees.

Harriet Dorner looked at her watch. 'I wonder if we have time to sort this out before your lunch is served. Let's have a look.'

Funny how she knew what time their meals were, even though she was away such a lot. He followed her across the lawn. 'I know what it's like,' she went on. 'When I was learning to fly I had to keep on doing things over and over again until they were perfect, until I could do them almost with my eyes closed. You have to be obsessive.'

He frowned at the unknown last word.

'You have to want to do it very badly,' she explained. 'You'll probably find it hard to get hold of paint, won't you? Oh.' Her eyes widened. 'I've just had an idea. Stay there.' She seemed to reach the house in a few long strides. He waited on the lawn. If one of the others happened to come upstairs and see him standing there they'd wonder what on earth was happening.

But she was back in mere minutes, holding something small in her hand. A little glass flask, he saw, with a black top.

'Nail polish.' She gave him a grin. 'Arctic Rose, it's called. I know your old Fuehrer doesn't approve of make-up for women, but it has its uses.'

She unscrewed the lid and painted a very pale pink cross on the bark of the old tree.

'Looks better on the tree than it ever did on my fingernails. That's your target.' She gave the bark a pat of approval. 'This old boy has seen it all. He'd have been a youngster when they fought the Battle of Trafalgar, Benny.' She looked concerned. 'Sorry, you probably don't know what I am talking about.'

'Oh yes,' he assured her. 'We have learned about Napoleon. And there was also Waterloo, where a German army helped you.'

Her gust of laughter made him blink. 'Quite right, Benny.'

'But please do not think I am admiring the Germans still.'

'Lots to admire once. Your English is really very good.' She reached inside a pocket and pulled out a cigarette case and lighter.

'I work very hard on it.' He must have looked serious because the lips holding the cigarette as she lit it were smiling at him.

'I hope you have fun, Benny, as well as working hard.'

'Yes, but other things are more important than fun.'

She turned her head to gaze back at the house. 'That's a hard lesson to learn so young.' Her words sounded heartfelt. Surely if you were a grown-up you could choose to lead the life you wanted, even in warfare? She was flying planes, wasn't she? Taking them from airfield to airfield to supply the RAF against Hitler as he moved across northwest Europe.

As though knowing what he was thinking she looked back at him. 'Not that I've had to learn it myself, yet,' she said with a smile that sent every atom in his body buzzing and brought a smile to his own face. 'I'm lucky: my passion is useful for the country. Otherwise I'd be knitting socks and growing vegetables.' She took a puff on the cigarette and raised a shaped eyebrow. Her eyebrows weren't like other people's: they were like punctuation marks expressing a view of life he wasn't sure he understood. He smiled.

'That's better,' she said.

'Where did you keep your plane?' he asked now, feeling bolder. 'Not here?' He looked towards the fields beyond the lake.

'I had a little two-seater Hawk. I kept her at an aerodrome about five miles from here. She and I flew all over the country. Further, sometimes. It was fun.' She looked wistful.

'Where is she now?'

'I sold her when the war started. It was time to start trying my hand at more serious flying. Luckily for me I managed to persuade them to let me deliver Tiger Moths to training stations and hangars. That's what I've been doing these last months. Freezing work, it's been, in this bitter winter and spring. And the RAF men don't always like us doing it.'

'Because you are women?'

'Yes.' They looked at one another with an understanding: outsiders both. Benny felt a sympathy between them he couldn't have described, especially not in English.

'But I am doing what I need to do,' she said, very softly. 'And when I return, tomorrow, this crisis will force them to use women pilots even more effectively.' She smiled at the confusion on his face. 'Effectively means better, Benny. They'll have to let us fly all kinds of planes.' Her chin jutted as she said it. 'We will have earned that right.'

'Yes.' He knew *that* feeling well enough. He picked up his ball, feeling very strange, suddenly. 'Perhaps I should practise now, before lunch is served.'

'Alice Smith gets cross, doesn't she, if you're late for meals?' All seriousness left her face and she looked as though she might almost wink at him. 'Don't mind Smithy. She's a good sort, really. I'll see you soon, Benny. In the meantime, keep working on that shot. And keep being obsessive about it.'

'Sometimes people think it is strange to try so hard,' he said.

'The world depends on some of us refusing to be the same as everyone else.'

He watched her stride back towards the house.

'She'd have liked seeing you work away at something, building real skill,' I told Benny, seeing my grandmother through his eyes as she strode across the lawn. 'She'd have liked you being yourself, even if it meant you stood out.'

He looked surprised. I wanted to kick myself: I sounded far too familiar with Harriet Dorner, a woman I wasn't supposed to have known.

'I mean, she must have worked very hard to become one of the first women pilots in the war,' I went on, hastily. 'It can't have been easy. People were very chauvinistic in the forties.'

'So it was just you boys and Dr Dawes in the house most of the time?' It must have been a very male, very intense kind of atmosphere.

'And Alice Smith. She became more of a housekeeper than a maid during the first years of the war, before she went to work in a factory.'

I bent my head and pretended to rub the top of my hand.

'But even Alice couldn't manage when disease broke out. That would have been the late spring of 1942? No, a year later. Two of the other boys fell ill. Diphtheria. Harriet came home to help nurse them.'

'A frightening disease.'

He nodded. 'Indeed.'

He started telling me about that long-ago early summer, how the diphtheria had hung around the village. And I listened, finding a curious release in hearing these stories as though I were a stranger.

10.
1943

At Fairfleet they'd thought themselves safe from disease, separated as they were by half a mile from the village. But, as Alice Smith pointed out, those boys were always taking themselves off to kick a ball around on the village green with the local boys, or hanging round the village shop, vainly hoping that sweets might reappear. All sorts of opportunities for germs to insinuate themselves inside the precious walls of Fairfleet. Alice looked concerned, probably on account of the extra work any sickness would cause her.

'Don't worry, Benny,' Dr Dawes, the tutor, said, noticing the anxiety on his face.

But how could Benny not worry? Dr Dawes didn't know what had happened in those last days in Germany.

The doctor came up to the house and Dr Dawes and Benny waited for him on the landing of the second floor.

'There's little doubt, I'm afraid.' He came out of the bedroom, rolling down his sleeves. 'At least the older boys are away at the moment.'

Ernst and Richard were at a Pioneer Corps training camp. Peter was spending a fortnight with a distant Jewish cousin in Oxford.

Which just left Benny.

He followed the two men downstairs. 'One of those lads is quite ill,' the doctor said when they reached the ground floor. 'The other one is through the worst of it now.' He seemed kind enough but never seemed to remember their names.

'Keep, erm, this young fellow out of the way.' The doctor nodded at Benny.

'There was diphtheria in our town in Germany.' The words fell out before Benny could stop them. An image of a boy coughing and gasping for breath flashed across his memory. He clutched the banister.

'Eh, what's that, boy?' The doctor, who'd been replacing his hat, looked at him sharply. 'Did you have someone in the family with diphtheria?'

'A school friend,' Benny said.

'Well, you look hale and hearty enough. They'll be signing you up if the war goes on long enough.'

'Benny's barely fifteen,' Dr Dawes said gently.

'Tall for his age, isn't he? I must say, I always think of you Jews as being bookish, indoor kind of chaps.' The doctor guffawed. 'But you look as though you'd do well in a rugger match. Do you like rugger, boy?'

'I prefer football,' Benny said.

'Do you, by Jove?' The doctor turned to Dr Dawes. 'And barely a trace of an accent. Could pass as one of us. Never understood this anti-Semitism business. I mean, some hook-nosed, straggly-bearded youth in a black cap might make you stare at him, but a lad like this?' He patted Benny on the shoulder.

'Prejudice is indeed a mysterious beast.' Dr Dawes opened the front door to let him out.

Alice Smith had been waiting on the staircase when they'd seen the doctor out, arms folded into their customary expression of interrogation.

'Am I to put Benny into a room on the first floor by himself then?'

'Probably a good idea.' The apology for the extra work was audible in Dr Dawes's voice.

'More trouble for me if he goes down with the diphtheria too,' she admitted grudgingly.

Dr Dawes went up to see the invalids.

For the first time since he'd left Germany four years ago Benny was alone, unsupervised. Unobserved. He felt curiously light. He could go and read in the library, but there was always a chance Alice Smith would come in to dust and tut at him for being in her way, or for reading while it was so sunny outside. Perhaps he'd go outside and kick his ball around. But then she'd probably come out to chide him for not getting on with something more useful.

Benny jangled the coppers in his pocket and thought of his sweet coupons upstairs. There was a chance that the village shop might have fresh deliveries. Not that he could remember seeing chocolate or bulls-eyes for months and months now, probably longer. He ambled down the drive towards the lane. It was a clear, sunny day and he didn't miss the classroom.

There was a new girl in the shop, Rainer'd told him before he fell sick. Not quite a stunner, but worth a look. Before today Benny had had no intention of going to peep at her. It felt as though he were Rainer's stand-in. And yet something in him stirred at the thought of the unseen girl.

And it was better than hanging around at Fairfleet and feeling the anxiety sweep downstairs from the sickroom.

11.

The shop met Benny's low expectations. He walked round the shelves slowly, just in case there was something more exciting than the usual drably labelled tins and jars. Unbidden, an image of a cake shop at home wound itself around his mind. He must have been tiny, out shopping with his mother. They'd stopped to buy a tart for lunch. While his mother was paying he ogled the rows of chocolate-and-marzipan beetles at his eye level at the glass counter. She noticed his round eyes and bought him one. His mother had been like that: kinder than most of the other mothers, a believer in enjoying life.

'Hello.' A girl came out of the shadows at the back of the shop, tins in her hands, apron around her slender waist. It had to be the kid Rainer'd mentioned. Not a stunner, no.

'Hello.' She was about his age. Was she going to order him out of the shop on the grounds of possible infection?

'I'm his niece,' she said, nodding towards the man behind the counter. 'Come to stay.'

'Bombed out?'

'No. My mum's got a job in a factory and they think I need looking after.' She rolled her eyes. She didn't look like someone who needed looking after. Perhaps that was what her mother had been worried about. The newspapers talked about young people behaving wildly in bombed-out London houses. Certainly sounded livelier than it was down here. The girl spoke in a slight accent, he noticed.

'Quiet here, isn't it?' She looked out towards the lane. When Benny'd first arrived at Fairfleet he'd missed the noises of a town, too: the clanking of trams, engines backfiring, marching troops. Sometimes you heard the squeak and grind of a rusty bike chain here as someone cycled past, or the shouts of the kids in the village school when they had their morning break in the playground. Occasionally a farm horse clopped by. That was it, really.

'Different from the town,' he agreed.

'What's that accent of yours, then?'

He flushed. Just occasionally he forgot and rolled an 'r' in an un-English way.

'Local,' he said. 'Perhaps you'll catch it too.'

'Bloody hope not.' But she grinned. Then her eyes became more watchful. She glanced at the man behind the counter. 'Want to go for a walk?'

Benny shrugged, feeling wary. But intrigued, too, if he was honest. And it would be something to tell Rainer.

'We're going to feed the chickens,' she called to the man, taking off her apron and throwing it onto a pile of potatoes.

'We're not really,' she confided as Benny closed the shop door. 'I thought we'd go into the woods.'

The dark, secluded strip of trees leading down to the brook, which Benny had rarely ventured into.

'You don't look like a Kraut,' she said as they strolled down the lane. Her arm swung close to his. Once or twice the little hairs on her arm touched his skin and he felt it like an electric shock.

'Is that a compliment?' he asked.

She tossed her head so that her hair bounced around her shoulders. 'If I hadn't known you were one of those Fairfleet boys, I'd never have guessed you were German.'

'What do Germans look like?' He forced himself to make the question sound casual. Perspiration ran down the back of his neck.

'In the news films they're always very blond.' She scratched her chin. 'Blue eyes.'

'Not like me, then.'

'No.' She laughed. 'Just as well. If they thought you were a proper Nazi they'd put you in a camp, wouldn't they? Or send you to Canada or Australia on a boat. But you're Jewish anyway, all you Fairfleet boys, aren't you? My aunt told me about you. So you're probably all right.'

He thought of Ernst and Richard. They'd been threatened with an internment camp purely on the grounds that they were from Germany and of fighting age. Lord Dorner had protested. Loudly and effectively. The boys had read about the *Arandora Star*, how the prisoners had drowned in the holds when the ship was torpedoed. And even if you weren't sunk you were stuck in a hold for weeks or months with sadistic guards who urinated in your food and stole your possessions. Ernst had heard the rumours and asked Dr Dawes if they were true. Dr Dawes hadn't been able to deny it, while assuring the boys that none of them would be deported.

They were under the trees now. Good. His emotions wouldn't be so readable. Insects buzzed around them. Benny blinked to make sense of the darkness.

She stopped. 'You're not bad-looking.'

Wasn't he? He had no idea how his looks compared with those of other boys his age.

'My boyfriend in London was all right. But I like you too.' She came closer. Her breath smelled milky. A band of freckles spread over her nose, as though someone had flicked a paintbrush loaded with gold paint against her face. Her hair was so light a blonde it was almost white. 'Want to kiss me?'

'All right.' Her mouth seemed suddenly to gain a life independent of its owner, fixing itself on his. The lips themselves felt nice: warm, soft. She pushed his mouth open and then her tongue was inside his mouth. He couldn't help springing back a little, as though she'd stung him.

'Don't you like it?' A hint of mockery in her eyes.

He put a hand to his neck. 'Insect bite. Sorry.' Vital to regain his dignity. He took her into his arms. She hadn't seemed curvy on top, but her little breasts jutted into his chest, like a pair of small warm animals.

'That's better,' she said. 'You're nice and tall, aren't you? I like tall ones. Want me to put my hand down your shorts? Or you can stick yours up my shirt, if you want.' She wriggled against him. He wanted to run. He wanted to stay. He didn't know what he wanted.

'What's your name?'

'Mona.'

'I'm Benny.' He stroked her face. 'You're pretty. I'm late.'

Late for nothing in particular.

'Meet me again?'

He smiled. The smile seemed to satisfy her because she took his hand as they walked back through the woods.

'Knew it wouldn't take me long to get another boyfriend.' Her voice hummed with satisfaction.

Benny thought of Rainer and felt guilty. For about a second.

~

'Fairfleet was so quiet during the war years, Rosamond,' Benny told me. 'Not only was it impossible to imagine there was a war on;

often it was almost impossible to think that there was anything at all happening anywhere on the planet.'

I knew that feeling, recalled it from childhood summers spent at Fairfleet: that dreamlike sense that we might be the last people left alive.

'I came back from the village and wondered what on earth I was going to do with myself,' he went on. 'The last thing I expected was that the day would turn out the way it did.'

12.

He was sitting on the stairs in Fairfleet, enjoying the cool quietness and reliving the encounter with Mona, when Lord Dorner came inside. They'd hardly seen him in the last eighteen months. Usually he stayed in a hotel in London, returning for occasional weekends if his wife was at home. Now there were so many planes piling out of the factories that Harriet Dorner was busier than ever; no more rubbish about women not flying *serious* planes. They'd even seen her photograph in the *Express*, standing beside a Spitfire. 'Society Hostess Does Bit for RAF', the caption read. Probably just a staged photo for propaganda, as it seemed unlikely they'd let women fly fighters, David said.

Benny stood up.

'Ah.' Lord Dorner looked worried. Probably trying to remember which one Benny was. The one who'd made a fuss about keeping kosher when he'd first arrived? One of the boys the police had wanted to inter on the Isle of Man? Or one of the more nondescripts? 'How are those poor ill boys doing?' Lord Dorner asked.

'David's a bit better, but they're worried about Rainer.'

'Poor chap.' A pause. 'And what about you . . . Benny? Finding things a bit dull, eh?'

'Not really.' He remembered his manners. 'Thank you, sir.'

'Fancy a drive?'

'In the Daimler?' He hoped he didn't sound like an overexcited kid. He'd never so much as sat in the shiny black car before. Since the early months of the war it had lived in one of the stables.

'It appears I am being encouraged to use it for . . . a particular bit of business. They've even given me petrol.' Lord Dorner looked excited himself. 'I've got a meeting in a factory in Slough. Meanwhile Harriet's touching down at an airfield between here and there.'

Probably White Waltham, near Maidenhead. The boys knew where most of the airfields in the south were located. David had stuck red pins onto a little map on the bedroom wall.

'I was going to say hello. She's delivering a Spitfire.'

'A Spit!'

'If the weather holds. So far as I know, conditions have been good across the whole country, so she should be landing in a couple of hours.' He checked his watch. 'I'm leaving in ten minutes. Ask Dawes if you can come with me. You'll have to stay in the car while I'm in the factory later on – security, I'm afraid. So bring a coat and something to read. And ask Alice Smith to make you some sandwiches.'

Benny decided to let the last suggestion slip from his mind. It wasn't worth risking more of Alice's frosty tone.

Half an hour later he sat beside him in the leather-scented Daimler, trying to look as though this kind of thing happened to him all the time. Benny had never spent more than an occasional hour with Lord Dorner and had certainly never been alone with him for more than five minutes at a time. He'd half expected Lord Dorner to have a driver.

'Bit of a treat for me to drive myself for a change,' he said, seemingly reading Benny's thoughts. 'My regular driver's off sick and they haven't replaced her yet. We don't often take out this beauty because of the petrol ration. But the ministry think it's worth it for this particular occasion.'

Sometimes Lord Dorner accompanied foreign visitors to factories, Benny'd heard, trying to persuade them to lend Britain money to build more weapons. Perhaps they'd be meeting Americans after they'd visited White Waltham, if that was where they were going.

The road wound slightly. The sun hit Benny's eyes.

'Pull down the visor,' Lord Dorner said, noticing.

There was a little leather tab you could pull up inside the visor, revealing a mirror. Presumably so that women could check their make-up. Benny regarded his reflection. He thought he could see his father in his features. He'd never noticed the resemblance before. The shock made him close the mirror and push up the visor. Had his father been handsome? Could he, Benny, really be so, too?

This had been a day of new experiences. Yet it had started mundanely enough, with Alice Smith placing his brown toast on a plate in front of him with her usual little sigh.

But he wasn't going to think about Alice Smith now. It was months since Benny had travelled anywhere further than the village. Winding roads skirted the northern side of the Berkshire Downs. In the fields below in the vale, they were raking hay. The sky was clear, pale blue.

'Perfect for Harriet's landing.' Lord Dorner glanced at his watch. 'She couldn't tell me exactly when she'd be touching down, but we should have timed it fairly well.'

Benny wanted to ask where she was flying in from, but had learned not to ask questions. So much had to be secret these days.

'Are you happy in England, Benny?'

The personal question made him straighten in the leather seat. How to answer? During the day the business of lessons, playing football, anticipating mealtimes and saving up for cinema trips swallowed him up, allowing no time for too much brooding.

Sometimes, just before he fell asleep, there'd be a slight pang, a memory of that kitchen drawer back in Germany that he'd open to find a bar of chocolate, bought just for him. There'd be a memory of his mother, laughing in a new hat, telling him that yes, he could have another ice cream, even though he'd probably *burst*.

'Yes, sir,' he answered Lord Dorner.

'I was a refugee myself, you know. Came over from Russia with my family as a baby.'

He looked at Lord Dorner in his well-cut suit, a pre-war purchase, still in good condition.

'My father was a silversmith. My mother took in washing. I grew up in Whitechapel and some say you can still hear it in my accent. When I stay up in the hotel in London, some of the admirals' wives and the lords from the shires murmur about Jews over their sherry. Not always out of my hearing.'

Benny couldn't speak.

'Things are changing, though, Benny. Society is more accepting of outsiders.' They were silent for a few minutes. The Downs dropped away. To the north the Chiltern Hills still sat green and blue, slightly hazy now. Lord Dorner turned off the road. 'We're going down here.'

Ahead of them Benny spotted hangars and a watchtower. If you lived around here, what sights you'd see. Sometimes living at Fairfleet was like being sealed in a beautiful bubble.

'Two planes stalled and crashed into bungalows near here only last year,' Lord Dorner said, just as Benny was thinking this. 'It can be dangerous living close to an aerodrome.'

Up in the sky a single plane circled, sun sparkling on its wings.

'That'll be my Harriet,' Lord Dorner said. 'In a Spitfire.' You could hear the pride in his voice. 'She's waited so long for this chance, Benny.' He slowed for the guards at the gates. When they stopped, he unwound the window and pulled something out of an inside pocket, ID or authorization or something, but the guard waved him on without looking at whatever it was, barely glancing at Benny. Perhaps they thought he was Lord Dorner's son. Which would also have made him Harriet Dorner's son. He wriggled on the leather seat at the thought.

Benny didn't need to have the plane identified. Every schoolboy in the country would have known the gravelly, throaty sound of its engine, and even if you were deaf you'd recognize a Spitfire. Benny couldn't pinpoint exactly what it was that made this particular combination of metal, glass and rubber more beautiful than any other plane. It was like trying to say why one girl's face was more beautiful than another's. Just a perfect blend of angles and roundness in feature, perhaps? But something more. Something about the expression in the eyes. Mona from the shop wasn't beautiful, but the memory of her body pressed against his and her lips pushing on his mouth made him feel a long tingle down his spine. He stood with Lord Dorner beside the car and half of him was in the woods with Mona and half was here at the airfield.

The Spit was coming in to land now, the light still bouncing against its metal surface as though a giant torch shone on it. The wheels came closer and closer to the runway. Benny could make out Lady Dorner in the cockpit. He heard Lord Dorner's intake of breath. They said landings and take-offs were the most dangerous times. Unless the Luftwaffe happened upon you while you were up there in the sky, as sometimes happened to auxiliary pilots, with no guns to defend themselves with.

The Spitfire was touching the runway now. Barely a bounce. Benny felt the warmth of relief, then a pang for Harriet Dorner. It must hurt, coming down to earth again.

'Light as a fairy,' Lord Dorner said. 'Complete control.' Pride oozed through his words. The plane came to a halt, resting so that its nose pointed skywards, keeping a lookout, Benny thought, in case it was needed again. The plane was smaller than he'd imagined it would be.

'Come on, Benny, let's go and congratulate her.' Lord Dorner strode towards the Spitfire.

Benny hung back. It felt like a private moment, as if Harriet Dorner had been showing off their newborn to her husband. She opened the cockpit and climbed down in what seemed like a few graceful movements. As she pulled off her helmet and gloves the sun seemed to turn its rays directly onto her, illuminating her. Her gold hair was tied in a bun against her neck. She wore a butter-coloured flying jacket over her uniform, which she undid. Her complexion was the unblemished honey gold he remembered. No freckles on Lady Dorner. The men's clothes and her scraped-back hair made her look even more feminine. Lord Dorner held her in a quick embrace and kissed her. Benny felt his own lips tingle as the middle-aged man's mouth brushed her lips. He knew what that sensation felt like now, thanks to Mona. But imagining his lips on Lady Dorner's, instead of Mona's, made him want to run away and hide. Lady Dorner was his guardian.

In an attempt to suppress his confusion Benny moved towards the Spitfire, half expecting someone to shout a reprimand. The aroma of fuel and hot grease hung around the open cockpit, which was almost perfectly designed for a woman of Lady Dorner's build. The engine ticked as it cooled. Above the exhaust vents warm vapours shimmered. He looked over his shoulder, saw nobody was watching him, and touched the aluminium body reverentially before returning to the Dorners.

Harriet was laughing, telling her husband all about it. 'Sitting in the cockpit's like wearing a Hardy Amies suit,' she said. 'And you only need the slightest touch and she'll turn like a sparrowhawk.' She noticed Benny. 'Benny! How wonderful to see you. I'm glad you're not ill too.' She put a hand to the bun of hair and released it so that the gold locks swung forward.

'I saw you land,' he said, feeling like an inarticulate chump. Only this very morning, out in the woods with Mona, Benny had imagined this to be the most exciting day he'd had in years. How low his standards had been.

'Wasn't I lucky to fly that beauty? I just pray they let me do it again.' She tucked one arm into her husband's and the other into Benny's. 'But tell me what's happening at home.' Her gaze was on Benny now. 'How are those poor boys?' She was studying him. He was expecting her to say how much he'd grown, but she didn't. The warmth of her arm in his was sending charges through his nervous system.

Lord Dorner told her what the doctor had told them. She listened gravely. Benny hadn't seen her look so solemn before.

'I've got some leave coming up,' she said. 'I was going to carry it forward in case they gave me more . . . But I think I'm needed at home now.'

'You need to rest, not nurse,' her husband said.

'I don't like to think of the boys being ill with just Alice to look after them.'

'You're always saying how diligent Alice is.'

'Yes . . .'

'There's Dawes, too. He's very good with the boys.'

'All the same.' She frowned. 'It's a lot to ask of him. I'll come home for a week.' She gave a last regretful glance over her shoulder at the plane. Perhaps taking leave now would prevent her from flying more Spitfires from airfield to airfield. A fresh batch of the planes might be lining up even now, waiting for pilots. But Harriet Dorner wouldn't be one of them.

Something of his sympathy must have shown because she gave him a sudden smile. 'Be good to see the gardens at this time of year.'

'I'm afraid the borders aren't up to their usual standard,' Lord Dorner said. 'More cabbage than delphinium this year.'

'Tell them to expect me at Fairfleet tomorrow.' She gave the Spitfire a last loving glance. 'I just need to make one last delivery, an old warhorse of a transport plane. Nothing like . . . this.'

Benny and Lord Dorner probably exchanged conversation in the car on the way to the factory. If so, he didn't remember it afterwards. Fog oozed through his mind, turning him into an automaton. He sat in the car while Lord Dorner went into the factory. On the way home he managed to reply to Lord Dorner's comments about the factory visit and the American guests but felt his benefactor's anxious gaze on him.

'You must still be worried about your sick friends, Benny.'

'Friends? Oh, yes.' He roused himself. 'But thank you so much for taking me out today, sir. I enjoyed myself.'

Trite words to express his emotions.

Lord Dorner nodded. For a second they seemed to share in a tacit yet complicit understanding of what they had both experienced on the airfield.

~

And so it was that Harriet Dorner returned to Fairfleet just before lunchtime the next day. A young man in RAF uniform dropped her off in a sports car. Apparently pilots could sometimes get hold of petrol. From the window of his new bedroom Benny watched her wave him a farewell. She wore the same flying jacket over a pair of riding breeches and sports shirt and carried a small suitcase.

'Take me to the patients,' she told Dr Dawes in the hall, their voices rising to the first floor where Benny sat reading. 'Poor things.'

Benny wasn't supposed to go up to the second floor since the diphtheria had struck. It hadn't been said specifically, but he'd sensed the tacit prohibition. But nobody said anything as he followed the adults upstairs. Harriet sat down on the end of Rainer's bed and talked to the boys softly. It felt like trespass, listening in, so Benny backed out of the room. Harriet was telling them about a trip she'd made to Austria, years ago, before the war.

'And all those cream cakes. Just as well we were doing so much walking.' She seemed to glow with the sunlight she'd attracted while flying through the heavens. Her edges seemed softer today, less those of the warrior-woman.

Rainer muttered something Benny couldn't hear.

She stood and pulled the sheet up Rainer's chest. 'I think your throat is hurting too much for you to talk. Let's chat again later.' She bent over the boy and kissed his forehead. Probably the first time anyone had kissed Rainer in years. Unless he too had sneaked off to the woods with a girl. Then she kissed David, too.

Harriet turned and saw Benny still standing there on the landing. He half expected her to tell him off, but she smiled. She closed the door softly behind her.

'I remembered Rainer once saying his family loved Alpine hikes.' Her brow puckered. 'I wish I could make him feel better, Benny.'

'You will.' He must have sounded reassuring because she looked at him as though their roles had reversed and she was the awkward youngster and he the adult. The strangeness lasted just a second. Then she was once again the cool and collected pilot.

~

Benny told me about my grandmother landing her first Spitfire and coming home the next day to nurse the sick boys. I saw her through his eyes: the female warrior in the butter-soft flying jacket, sun gilding her fair hair. Then Harriet, the gentle presence back here at Fairfleet, comforting a sick boy who'd no family to nurse him.

We sat in silence, both of us rewinding images and playing them through again, freezing frames to examine details. He seemed weary, picking up his paper as though he wanted to shield his face from me. I was only his nurse; there were emotions he didn't want me to see.

'Read me some more *Great Expectations*, Rosamond.' He laid down his newspaper and looked at me very intently, his eyes remaining on my face while I reached for the book.

I read a chapter and saw that Benny was sleeping. Perhaps in his dreams he'd gone back to 1943, to watching my grandmother land her Spitfire again.

I set the book aside. There were calls I needed to make, to the district nurse, who would want to visit in the next day or so. And to the nurses we had on standby for when Benny needed more night-time care. But I fell into a trance, still thinking of Magwitch, of interlopers, people who turned up where they shouldn't and upset everything.

An interloper had slid his way into this very house thirty years ago. I'd been a bit older than Pip when he'd arrived. Our interloper hadn't been a convict, not quite. But he'd caused damage and it had been irreversible.

The sunlight Benny's memories had brought into this bedroom seemed to dull. I might have been miles below the surface of the sea, where all was murky and dark.

I was Rose, not Rosamond, once again, nearly thirteen, living here with my mother, my brother Andrew. And my grandmother. My grandmother whom Benny had known as Lady Dorner.

And Smithy, too – Alice Smith, as Benny had known her – had still been here. Smithy was good with my mother. Her presence, an awkward, prickly one, occasionally illuminated by demonstrations of genuine affection, had provided ballast for Mum.

God knows, Mum had needed all the ballast she could get.

13.
ROSAMOND

My mother, Granny's daughter by her second husband, had moments when she was normal. Her light-blonde hair would be brushed and silky, her make-up applied discreetly to her apricot-gold skin. And she looked like Granny.

'Peas in a pod,' Smithy would say. 'Beauties, both of them.'

When she passed through this serene and radiant stage you'd never guess Mum was mental. That's what some of the children in my old school called her after she appeared at the school gate one afternoon wearing a silk evening dress paired with wellington boots, talking loudly about a letter she was writing to Margaret Thatcher, how it was already fourteen pages long and she hadn't finished yet.

But I'd left that school now, which was good, because over the last few months the fibres in Mum's brain had twisted themselves into even thicker knots. We'd come to Fairfleet for the summer because Dad had left home. He'd said he was going to work in the Middle East for a while, but both my brother and I knew it was because he found living with Mum so hard.

'You all need a holiday at Fairfleet,' Granny said. 'And your mother can rest.'

At first the change seemed to suit Mum. She hadn't rested, though. She'd fizzed with energy, rising early every morning to go out into the gardens and trimming the box-tree animals with a small pair of secateurs. When she'd done all she could outside she spent the afternoons sticking the photographs stored in shoeboxes into photograph albums for Granny. Smithy had observed the photo-sticking with approval.

'A place for everything and everything in its place.'

On one of these afternoons I admired a photo of Granny herself in a flying jacket, standing beside a fighter plane. Mum stuck it into the album and wrote '1943: Spitfire!' above it.

But a few days later Mum started spending more time in the four-poster bed in her room, sometimes drawing the curtains round it so that she was hidden from the world. She slept in until late and didn't get dressed until teatime. She was calm and gentle with Andrew and me, but her eyes looked flat, like torches whose batteries were running out.

This morning I hadn't been able to find her anywhere – not in her room, not downstairs, not in the basement. 'She can't be far away,' Granny said. 'We'll find her. Don't worry.'

Eventually I found her out among the box-tree animals, sitting on the still-dewy grass, propped up against the elephant.

'I'm sorry,' Mum said. Her hair was all limp over her brow and eyes and the buttons were done up wrongly on her shirt, as though she were a little girl just learning to dress herself. 'I just can't seem to cope.'

Granny rushed up now, slightly out of breath. She helped me lift Mum to her feet.

'Enough's enough, Clarissa,' she said, with a note in her voice I hadn't heard before. We led Mum back to the house. She shook as though she were an old woman, older even than Granny. Her arms felt cold in my hand. We met Smithy coming out of the kitchen door.

'You're heading for a fall,' Smithy told Mum. Unlike her to say anything less than flattering to my mother. Dad always said Smithy's devotion to Granny and Mum bordered on the fanatical, which apparently meant being too fond of them.

'All right, all right,' Mum muttered. 'Not now. I just want to sleep.' She lurched as we steered her through the kitchen door. Something in her pocket clinked against the kitchen table. 'I took this.'

She pulled out a large, ancient-looking key, which I didn't recognize.

'That's from the old garden door in the basement.' Smithy took it. 'That's how you managed to get outside without us seeing.'

'I needed fresh air and I didn't want to worry you.'

Smithy snorted.

'I'm calling the doctor for you,' Granny said. 'No ifs or buts this time.'

'If it makes you happy.' Mum grabbed the back of a kitchen chair as though she was on a ship lurching around in a storm. 'Oh, I'm sorry. I know you're right. I'll go down to the surgery today if they can fit me in.'

The family doctor sent her on to doctors with long titles in Oxford. Mum had to stay in the hospital for a few nights. She came home and packed a small suitcase but forgot to put in anything useful, so it was just as well that Smithy was there to remind her to take nightdresses, a comb and a toothbrush, not just writing-paper and pens.

Granny drove her in and returned a few hours later. She smiled at me and Andrew and we knew everything would be all right. 'The doctors are tinkering with the dose,' she said. 'We can pick her up on Wednesday afternoon.'

It was hot on the Wednesday. Andrew developed a headache. 'I want to go and collect Mum with you,' he complained.

'Stay here in the cool, darling.' Granny ran one of her manicured hands over his brow.

Mum was clutching a white paper bag outside the hospital entrance when we arrived, her face almost the same pale colour as the bag. But she smiled when she saw me. 'How lovely.' She hugged me. It was like being embraced by someone made of card.

'Where's your case, Clarissa?' Granny asked.

'Oh.' Mum's face crumpled. 'I must have left it on the ward.'

'I'll get it.' Granny pointed to a bench. 'You two stay here.'

Mum and I sat on the bench, next to a man reading a newspaper. Mum was still holding the white paper bag very tightly.

'Are those your tablets?' I asked. She nodded. I could see a labelled bottle inside the bag.

'*Lithium*,' I read aloud. '*To be taken three times daily*.'

'I'm sure it will be ghastly. But better than . . .' She glanced at the man reading the newspaper and fell quiet.

The newspaper dropped. I caught sight of a pair of dark-blue eyes, concerned-looking, conveying the impression that their owner knew how Mum felt and was silently wishing her well with her Lithium tablets. Then the man, who was about Mum's age or a little older, went back to reading his paper.

'There's Granny.' I stood up.

'Let's get back to Fairfleet, Clarissa,' Granny said, in that clear-as-a-bell voice of hers. 'I have work to do in the garden. Those lilies by the tennis court are starting to droop. They need staking up.'

Mum looked as though she needed staking up, too. Perhaps the tablets in the bag would act like Granny's bamboo sticks?

'You've got the charity tea party coming up.' Mum took the paper bag back from me. 'I must be well to help with that.'

'I don't want you wearing yourself out, darling,' Granny said. 'Just take it easy.'

Out of the corner of my eye I noticed the newspaper drop slightly. I felt the man with the dark-blue eyes watch us as we walked to the car.

Mum was quiet for the first few days. I almost preferred this reflective state to the times when she would say odd things and write her long letters.

~

Old friends of Granny's from her wartime flying job came to dinner a few days after we'd collected Mum from the hospital. Mum cooked vol-au-vents, rack of lamb and lemon soufflé. Nobody could cook like she could if she was in the mood. The soufflé smelled like a sweet citrus cloud. The night had stayed warm and I couldn't sleep. I sat by my open bedroom window. Granny and one of the guests, Reggie, came outside.

'Smell those tobacco plants,' Granny said. 'Heavenly, aren't they?'

An in-breath of appreciation. 'Forty years ago all this would have seemed like a lovely dream,' Reggie said.

'I know,' Granny said. 'Sometimes, during the war, it seemed hard to imagine that Fairfleet could still exist, just waiting for me to come back.'

A snap as Reggie lit Granny's cigarette with his lighter. 'Clarissa looks well.'

'She's making a huge effort. For the children.'

'So cruel, mental illness.'

'It's cost her so much already. I pray things won't go as badly for her as they did for her father.'

Mum's father; my grandfather Peter, whom I'd never met.

'They wouldn't do . . . that to Clarissa, would they?'

Granny seemed to cough on her cigarette. She was always saying she needed to give up smoking. 'A lobotomy? They're out of fashion now, thank God. I shouldn't have allowed it with Peter. He never recovered from the operation. The infection alone nearly killed him.'

'The medication's much better nowadays, anyway, isn't it?'

'Clarissa's on Lithium. I've heard things about it, but it must be better than the alternative, as you say.'

I remembered how Mum always twisted her mouth before she unscrewed the little bottle. Perhaps the tablets tasted bitter.

'And there's no prospect of Tony coming back to her?'

A sigh from Granny.

'I've read about expat life in Saudi Arabia,' Reggie said. 'It sounds a bit wild. I hope he doesn't become entangled.'

Granny made a sound like a gasp.

'I'm sorry.' Reggie sounded worried. 'I shouldn't have said that.'

'No. It's not that. Just a brief pain in my side. Perhaps I ate too much.' She laughed.

'Do you remember that night in the mess when you ate that vile meat pie and went down with food poisoning?'

'I thought I'd die! Shall we see if the coffee's ready?'

Their feet crunched along the gravel path towards the door.

~

Dad hadn't become entangled with some tanned woman in a small bikini, as I feared, having listened in to the conversation.

She was someone he met at a tennis tournament. Not very tanned and probably too large to look good in a bikini, I discovered much later when I met her. A few days after the dinner party he wrote and told Mum he wanted a divorce so he could marry this Marie person. When Mum read his airmail letter she let out a single gasp and went upstairs very slowly, leaving the letter on the breakfast table for Granny to read. She shut herself up in her room for the rest of the morning, then came downstairs to talk to Granny in the drawing room.

Smithy kept Andrew and me in the kitchen, making meringues, trying to distract us. It didn't work. Smithy didn't really like baking much anyway, and fretted over the egg white and oven temperature.

'The three of you will stay here at Fairfleet with me,' Granny said when they finally came out of the drawing room. 'In the holidays you'll stay with your father and . . . Well, we won't worry about the details now. All will be well.' She put an arm around each of us. 'We'll find you new schools, near here.'

'We'll manage.' Mum's smile looked as though it was hurting her. 'Your father is still your father. That hasn't changed.'

Mum, Granny and Smithy continued the conversation in the drawing room that night; Andrew and I were supposed to be in bed but crouched on the staircase, listening in.

'I thought it would all work out.' Mum sounded puzzled. 'That he'd come back to me when he finished the contract. I know I did silly things while I was ill, but I thought he still loved me.'

'You must keep on being brave,' Granny said. Smithy made a clicking sound that seemed to signify agreement.

'He wants the children,' Mum said. 'He says I'm not up to looking after them alone. He says I have to carry on living here if I want custody during term-time.' She sounded as though there was a stone lodged in her throat. 'I love Fairfleet, but it feels as if he's trying to make it into a kind of prison for me.'

'Fairfleet is your home, Clarissa.' Granny said. 'And you need to be here with me. Tony will be reasonable.' She sounded sad. She'd always liked Dad, his teasing about her flying exploits and his quick feet on the tennis court.

'Smithy looks after me and I will look after you and you will look after your children. You'll be back on your feet in no time,' Granny went on.

'Do what your mother says, Clarissa,' Smithy said. I pictured her pale green eyes moving slowly around the room, to the paintings, clocks and silver she dusted so carefully. Smithy regarded Granny and Mum as part of the fixtures and fittings: to be looked after. Smithy knew if someone had moved an ornament half an inch out of alignment. She liked things, and people, to stay in their places.

Granny went up to Mum's bedroom next morning to make sure she was still taking her tablets.

'My hair is coming out,' Mum said. The door was open. I could hear them from my own bedroom. 'And I have the shakes. And everything seems to take so much effort.'

'It'll be worth it to stay well, darling. Promise me you'll keep taking them?'

'I don't feel like me any more. But I promise.'

I crossed my fingers.

~

'Everything will be fine,' Granny said the very next day as she was leaving for the doctor's. 'Your mother is making good progress. I'll just get some pills for this silly ache of mine. I must have pulled a muscle weeding.'

The charity tea party was to be held in the garden in three days' time.

Granny didn't come back from the doctor's. He sent her straight up to hospital. Mum drove her in, returning to collect a bag for her. Just for a few days.

'What's wrong with Granny?' Andrew asked Mum.

'Appendicitis. They'll need to take it out.'

Smithy didn't say a word. She went up to Granny's room to find all the things that Mum wouldn't remember to pack.

Mum returned hours later saying that Granny seemed cheerful.

Next morning the telephone downstairs in the hallway rang very early; only Smithy was out of bed. I heard her feet running upstairs, the knock on my mother's door, Mum's cry.

I threw off my bedclothes and ran into my mother. Mum was sitting up in bed, her face as pale as the ivory sheets. 'No.' She shook her head. 'No.'

'I told her days ago it was an appendix.' Smithy's fingers clasped the front of her pinafore so hard they might snap. 'She said I was fussing.'

'What's happened?' Andrew was rubbing his eyes as he came in.

'It's Granny, she . . .' Mum's mouth stayed open, but no more words came out.

'The appendix burst before they could operate. They couldn't control the infection,' Smithy said.

Mum swallowed. 'I can't believe it. She was fine on Monday, pulling up bindweed.'

'She was never one for making a fuss,' Smithy said. 'Perhaps she should have been.'

Mum put a hand to her mouth. 'The charity tea. Oh God, it's tomorrow. What are we going to do, Smithy?'

'Leave that to me. I'll make calls.' Smithy stood straighter, releasing her hands. 'I'll take care of everything.'

~

Mum went into Oxford to see Granny's body. Smithy said she'd ring the funeral people and make arrangements.

'By "arrangements" you mean looking at Granny's body and ordering the coffin people to take her away until we can bury her?' Andrew liked things to be said plainly.

Smithy nodded. She sent us out while she made the call. When we came back into the house she was sitting at the telephone table with a list of all the people who were supposed to be coming to tea in the gardens the following day. She invited some of them to the funeral instead, seeming to know exactly which of them Granny would have wanted to come.

Granny couldn't be dead. Her body couldn't be going into a wooden box to be stuffed into a hole in the ground. I ran out of the house, into the topiary garden. If I ran quickly enough through the animals I'd catch sight of my grandmother, secateurs in hand, trimming the elephant's trunk or the wings on the beloved Spitfire someone had carved out of a box tree in the forties to commemorate her wartime flying.

My grandmother wasn't there. But she'd be out in the flowerbeds, dead-heading and clipping.

She'd be somewhere here at Fairfleet. She always said she never wanted to be anywhere else. I just needed to find her. Granny would laugh that amused throaty laugh of hers and tell us we were mad: here she was, full of life.

But Granny wasn't at Fairfleet any more. Eventually I stopped running through the gardens and up and down stairs, opening and closing doors, going down to the basement to check in all the rooms down there. She'd gone. For the next day or so I could still smell her Player's cigarettes in the drawing room, but then Smithy washed the sofa cushions so that they would look smart for the funeral tea and they lost the tobacco scent.

More people came back to the house after the service in the village church than anyone had predicted. Smithy nearly ran out of tea cups and I had to help wash them up as they became free.

'You'll stay at Fairfleet now, Clarissa?' a guest asked Mum, as I stood beside her at the dining room table.

'I suppose I will,' Mum said. She put a hand to her fringe, slightly damp, and pushed it back. Her skin was covered with a film of moisture.

'At least you'll have Alice Smith to help,' the guest said.

'Thank God for Smithy,' Mum said. 'I couldn't manage without her.'

14.

Mum finished constructing her daisy chain. It was only a few weeks since Granny had died and this felt like the first near-to-normal day. She hung it round my neck. 'You look like a princess, Rosie.'

'Not with those crumbs round her mouth, she doesn't. Fat chance of her marrying a prince in St Paul's like Lady Diana.' Andrew grinned at me. Nobody could be bad-tempered on a sunny afternoon like this. Even the sadness for Granny felt more like a kind of pet or old companion, creeping up to touch me unobtrusively.

From the garden came the scent of mint, rosemary and thyme. For the first time since Granny had died I felt it might be possible to enjoy summer afternoons again.

Andrew ran his fingers through the grass. 'It's getting long.'

'I'll get the mower out.' But Mum sounded doubtful. The mower was temperamental, spluttering out clouds of black, smelly smoke if it didn't like the way you handled it. Even Smithy couldn't manage it.

'When's the gardener coming back?'

'I don't know that he is. His back is still hurting him and gardeners need strong backs.'

But Mum seemed to put aside the worry about the long grass. She lay back so that a perfect shaft of clear light bathed her. If only Dad could see her now: despite everything, despite Granny dying, she looked beautiful. The tablets had made her put on weight, she complained, but her face looked better now, less thin. Mum was still taking them, because she'd promised Granny she would.

It was only the three of us here today. Smithy was visiting her niece on her afternoon off. Sometimes it was more relaxing when she was away. You could leave out a tea mug on the kitchen table without it being immediately removed for washing.

Don't move, I wanted to tell Mum and Andrew. Let's all stay here in the sun. If only Dad could come home now, this very afternoon, to see how well Mum was managing, how strong she was.

Being at Fairfleet was still doing her good, even now. Granny had always claimed there was magic in the air, benefiting everyone who lived here. During the war she'd opened her home to the refugees from Germany. On an afternoon like this I could picture the boys out here on the lawn, or perhaps plunging into the lake for a swim.

The view across the water would have been different all those years ago. Granny had sold a field adjoining the grounds six months ago and new houses were to be built on it. We had seen men with clipboards using strange instruments on legs to measure out the plots. In the spring Granny had planted a new hedge behind the lake, which would grow up and block the view of the new buildings.

Above the baby hawthorns something bright flashed. A man. White suit and a Panama hat. Too smart for a builder. Perhaps he was a surveyor. I felt proud of knowing that word. But he didn't really seem to be interested in the building site, standing with his back to the marked-out plots and gazing out across the lake towards us. When he saw me watching him he smiled at me and raised his hat, as though I were a grown-up. For a few seconds we stared at one another. Then he turned away.

'Who was that?' I pointed at the white suit as it retreated.

'Who?' Andrew squinted, but the man had gone.

'A man in a hat, staring at us.'

'What a nerve,' Andrew said.

'Thank heavens the new hedge will have grown up by next year.' Mum frowned in the direction of the building site.

But I didn't think that the man had been rude at all. Perhaps I had just imagined him, though. I lay back on the soft grass, watching the boughs of the oak sway as they picked up a breeze too light to be felt down here. Minutes passed.

The squeak of a rusty machine part made me sit up again. Someone was pushing a bicycle around the side of the house, past the tennis court. Whoever it was came closer. An intruder from the building site?

He stopped. I saw a man in his early forties, or so I guessed. Dark-haired. Tall. He wore old but clean cotton trousers and a short-sleeved t-shirt, revealing strong arms.

'Sorry to trouble you,' he said to Mum. 'I'm looking for work.'

'We've got nothing to do with the new houses.' Mum pointed down the drive. 'The construction site's back that way.'

'I'm not looking for building work. I can do gardening. Or clearing out guttering, cleaning paving stones. Odd jobs.'

'I don't need any help, thanks.' Mum gave a kind smile.

'I'd try my hand at anything. Weeding, perhaps?' he looked at the gravel, where weeds poked through. 'Or lawn-mowing?'

'I don't think so.'

I thought of how tired Mum had been recently, how she hated the mower with its bad-tempered ways. 'Let him,' I said. 'At least the grass.'

Mum's mouth opened as though she was going to say no again. Then she looked down at the long grass at her feet.

Andrew said nothing. Surely he could see how much Mum needed help.

'Let him,' I said again.

'Perhaps there are a few jobs you could look at.' She stood up. 'Mr . . . ?'

'Cathal.' He rested the bicycle against the steps and came towards her, hand out. 'Cathal Pearse.'

'Cattle?' Andrew said.

The man's dark-blue eyes twinkled. 'You don't pronounce the "t". My mother was a romantic. She named me after some Celtic chieftain, can you believe?' He sounded amused.

Mum and Cathal Pearse walked along the drive, Mum pointing out weeds, Cathal nodding his head every now and again. Andrew and I stayed on the lawn. It had only been fifteen minutes since we'd picked the daisies for the chain, but already the little white petals were curling up.

15.

That evening Cathal Pearse brought in a colander of raspberries, stooping as he passed under the kitchen lintel. He placed the raspberries on the table. 'You'll be wanting these for your supper.' He smiled at me with those eyes that were the colour of a new pair of jeans. 'Thank you,' he added. 'For putting in a good word for me.'

I felt my cheeks turn warm.

'Who is this?'

Smithy's sharp tones made us all turn round. She was wearing her best beige summer suit, the one she always wore to cycle over to her niece's, whatever the weather.

'This is Cathal,' I said. 'He will be helping out with the garden and odd jobs.' For a second I fancied there was a bit of Granny in my tone.

'I see.' Smithy's pale eyes scrutinized Cathal's open sandals and his faded trousers. He didn't look like the old gardener had. His fingers were clean and soft.

'Call me Cathal,' he said, smiling.

Smithy regarded him expressionlessly.

'Must get on,' he said.

He brought in more colanders of strawberries, redcurrants and raspberries, filling the kitchen with the scent of berries. 'Best to work in the cool of the day,' he said at about six. 'I'll be back tomorrow.' Mum looked up from the kitchen table, where she was hulling strawberries, ready to make jam.

'Would you like a cold beer before you go?' Mum looked at Smithy. 'There are still some down in the cellar, aren't there?'

'Just a glass of squash would do me.' I made him a glass and his long, strong neck pulsed with each swallow. The drink was quickly gone.

'What time should we expect you in the morning?' Smithy asked.

'About eleven,' he said.

She sniffed. I watched him cycle off, twiddling the almost-wilted daisies on the necklace around my neck.

Next morning Smithy and I stood at the window and watched Mum telling Cathal what she wanted him to do in the garden. 'Quarter past eleven, by the time he arrived,' Smithy said. 'And I need the rest of that soft fruit brought in.'

'He said *about* eleven,' I reminded her.

Smithy grunted. Cathal was tugging out bindweed from a honeysuckle bush, each movement firm, precise and graceful too. Mum walked away towards the lake. He stopped his work to watch her. When he returned to the bindweed his movements were slower. Perhaps he was feeling the heat.

I slipped out of the kitchen and upstairs to inspect the bottle of tablets on the dressing table. I counted them. Three fewer than yesterday. Mum was keeping her promise to Granny.

I went to find Andrew. He lay on his bedroom floor, a Meccano set spilled out in front of him in a grey-and-red metal heap. 'Don't step on anything.' Without looking at me he reached for a screw.

'I didn't know you had all this.' Surely there were enough metal pieces to build a full-size crane.

'Smithy brought it up from the basement. She says it's forty years old at least.'

'It must have belonged to the refugee boys.'

'Lucky things.' He tightened the screw and examined the joint he'd constructed.

'Not lucky to leave their homes and parents, though.'

His shoulders stiffened slightly and I knew he was thinking about Dad and how much he missed him.

I went downstairs again. Smithy was stirring another saucepan of bubbling fruit and sugar. Cathal came in with a colander of raspberries. 'Thought you'd like these, Miss Smith.'

Smithy blinked slightly at the title. 'Thought you were doing the bindweed this morning?'

'I like to move between tasks,' he said. 'I find it makes the work more interesting.'

She looked at him in a way that suggested he wasn't expected to find the work interesting. Cathal reached out to place the colander on the kitchen table. But before it reached the table, his hand twitched slightly. The raspberries trickled down to the lino. Smithy gasped. Cathal stared at the raspberries as though uncertain as to what they were doing on the floor.

'Well, don't just stand there.' Smithy slapped her spoon down on the worktop and crouched on the floor. 'Give me that colander.'

'What a mess I've made.' He pulled the colander back from her outstretched hand. 'I'll sort it out, Miss Smith, never you mind.' She straightened herself, leaving him to pick up the spilled fruit. 'They'll probably need rinsing.' He handed the colander to her and walked out.

'Don't worry about wiping the floor over,' she called after him. 'I'll do it myself.'

I listened to Cathal's footsteps echoing across the flagstones. They stopped. I went to peep out of the doorway. He stood at the table by the front door, examining the base of a blue vase, eyes screwed up in concentration. He replaced the vase on the table and made for the grandfather clock, reading the words on the face.

He turned.

I jerked myself back into the kitchen, but not before I'd seen him wink. He made me feel as though I'd sided with him, which was strange because until then I'd always really got along with Smithy; she let me help her make jam and tied old dusters to my feet when she was polishing the floor so I could skate on the surface and buff it.

But Smithy could make you feel you weren't living up to her high standards, as though you weren't living up to the shiny surfaces and perfectly dusted ornaments. Cathal seemed to suggest that it might be more fun not to try to be perfect.

~

Cathal came to Fairfleet most days. Mum would take him out a mug of tea, chatting to him while he drank it. Sometimes she smiled at his jokes. Seeing the lines crease around her eyes made me smile too.

'You'll grow roots if you keep standing at that window,' Smithy warned me, as I stood watching the pair of them. 'Go outside and play. Shame to waste the weather.' But she watched Cathal too. He was replacing stone slabs on the wall that separated the vegetable garden from the lawn. The slabs were large, but he moved them into place as though they were pieces of Lego. 'Bit of a navvy in that one,' Smithy said. 'I hope we haven't made a mistake, letting him ease his way in here.'

'What's a navvy?'

'An Irish labourer. They do heavy building, roads, railways, that kind of thing.'

But I couldn't imagine Cathal building roads.

Smithy was still frowning at him. 'There's more to that one than meets the eye.'

I felt as though she was accusing me of something. 'Mum was so tired,' I said. 'And the garden was becoming a mess.'

She put a wrinkled hand on my arm. Smithy wasn't usually one for making physical gestures. 'You're a good girl, Rose. You care about your family. But there are some in life that aren't as good.'

I went out and rode my bicycle around the lawn a few times, watching Cathal. Mum had left him with his mug of tea. He was preparing the lawnmower. The catch connecting the fuel container to the mower seemed to be causing problems. He swore gently, then turned as he heard me on my bicycle.

'Ah, Rose. You find me the victim of a recalcitrant piece of machinery.'

I didn't know exactly what he meant, but I liked the way he used grown-up words with me.

'Granny used to take off her boot and bang it on the catch.'

'I'd like to have met your grandmother.'

I wasn't sure what to say. It seemed surprising that someone who'd barely met us would want to meet Granny. Perhaps he was just being polite.

He reached down for the mug and took a mouthful of tea. 'You're all very kind to an old vagrant. This job is just what I need. And I know I've you to thank for it.'

'You like gardening?'

He placed his mug on the grass very carefully.

'Mine has been a funny old life. I've had some bad luck.' It was a kind of answer to my question, I supposed. He put a hand out to the stiff catch on the mower and snapped it down successfully.

His hands were strong, despite their smooth appearance. 'There, resolved without acts of violence against a defenceless machine.'

I laughed. 'My mum wouldn't say nice things about the mower. She hates it.'

He was watching me carefully now. 'A lady like your mother shouldn't be worrying herself about lawnmowers.'

'I know.'

'I feel at home here.' Cathal was looking over the gardens, the mower still rumbling beside him. 'Fairfleet reminds me of my old childhood home and your mother reminds me of some of the people in my own family.'

I wasn't sure whether I liked the idea of my mother reminding him of someone else.

'Although there's something very special about her, isn't there?' He nodded to himself. 'Not many people can be so strong when life is difficult. But she has you two to support her.'

'She misses my granny. And my dad.'

Cathal stretched his neck out a little as I said the last bit.

'Where's your father now?' He fiddled with the mower handle as he asked.

'Saudi Arabia.'

He pulled the brake lever, seemingly unbothered by its stiffness. 'I must get on. Wouldn't want . . .'

'What?'

'Well, I wouldn't want your mother thinking I was taking advantage. She pays me to do the gardening.'

I picked up his mug. 'She'd never think like that.'

Smithy would, though. As I approached the kitchen door I could sense her disapproving stare.

Mum seemed almost shy of Cathal over the next few weeks, letting me take out the tea to him. But on one of Smithy's Wednesday afternoons off, she took the tea mug from me. 'I'll do that.'

I waited until she'd gone out. 'He's very handsome,' I told Andrew, who was sitting at the table fiddling with some pieces of Meccano.

'He's only the gardener. He doesn't really matter.'

Andrew wasn't meaning to be snobbish; I knew that. He was just comparing Cathal with Dad, an oilman who travelled out to remote deserts or swamps to find petroleum to keep factories and houses heated and lit.

'Cathal makes her feel better.'

'Maybe.' Andrew looked out of the window too, his expression hard. 'Obviously you're going to see the best in him. You were the one who insisted that she give him work.'

'So what if I did?' Andrew was obviously jealous.

Mum and Cathal spent some time talking out on the lawn. When Mum walked back over she looked thoughtful. And a little flushed. She poured herself a mug of tea.

Something screamed in the garden. Mum's mug trembled and tea soaked her sleeve. 'What was that?'

I was already at the window. 'A peacock!'

'Really?' She came to join me. 'I don't believe it. There haven't been peacocks at Fairfleet for decades.'

But there he was, his blue tail displayed with the eyes staring out at us.

I was already making for the back door.

Cathal was leaning on his rake, observing the bird. 'Isn't he just grand, Rosie?'

I wasn't sure I liked him calling me Rosie, but I could overlook this for someone who shared my enthusiasm for this beautiful bird.

'Is he a stray? Can we keep him?'

'I haven't heard of anyone keeping peacocks around and about here. We could ring the police. Or the RSPCA. Tell them we've got him.' He made clicking noises at the bird. 'Tell you what: in the shed there's some bird seed someone must have put in the feeders.'

Granny. She'd loved watching the blue tits and chaffinches.

'Why don't you throw him a handful now?'

The peacock extended his graceful neck and picked at the seeds I sprinkled on the lawn. Mum came out to admire him. 'He's a beauty. I'll ring round, see if anyone's missing him.'

'Oh, I hope not.'

Smithy approached us from the washing line, carrying the linen basket. When she saw the peacock she stopped, eyes tightened. 'Where did that come from?'

'He's a he,' Cathal said lightly.

'I'm aware of the gender, thank you.' Smithy looked at Mum. 'You won't be keeping it?'

'Why not? If nobody claims him. Fairfleet used to have peacocks.'

'They were all dead by the time your mother and father had you.' She made it sound as though this was good news.

'Well, it's about time we reinstated the practice of keeping peacocks at Fairfleet.' Mum looked at Cathal. 'Can we make him somewhere to roost in the stable block? I think that's where they used to keep them.'

Tyres scrunched on the gravel. The post van. The driver got out, whistling admiringly when he saw the peacock. He handed Mum a brown envelope.

'Oh.' She held it gingerly. 'Better go up to my room. I've got all the paperwork there.'

Mum was still upstairs three hours later when I went to call her for lunch. She sat at the dainty walnut desk in the corner with papers strewn over the surface, frowning as she totted up rows of numbers. When I told her it was lunchtime she blinked at me.

Cathal came in for lunch too, padding through the hall in socked feet like a panther. He wore boots to work now, instead of the sandals he'd first appeared in. I couldn't remember how it was that he'd started sharing meals with us; he seemed always to have been sitting in the kitchen with us, telling us funny stories. In his hand was a single peacock feather.

'Poor fellow's about to go into moult, I suspect. We may be seeing the best of the display for this year.' He laid the feather on the table so that the eye examined us.

Smithy banged a bowl of soup down in front of him. 'You can get that out of the house for starters.'

'Smithy –' Mum began.

'Peacock feathers in the house are bad luck.' She twisted her hands. 'They give me the shivers. They look evil.'

Cathal sighed and rose, picking up the feather. 'I'll put it in the shed.'

'Thanks. I suppose I need all the luck I can get to finish these figures,' Mum said when he returned.

'Tax?' Smithy asked. Cathal looked from her to my mother.

Mum nodded. 'I think I'm getting somewhere then I realize I haven't included this or that. The accountant is very helpful, but I find it all hard.'

'Am I impertinent to ask whether I might help with those figures?' Cathal asked Mum. 'I'm not unfamiliar with this process.'

'Of course,' she said, looking less distracted. 'You've been through this yourself.'

'What figures?' Andrew asked.

'When someone dies you have to tidy up the money matters,' Mum said. 'Your grandmother left everything in good order. But it was sudden.' She pushed her half-empty bowl away. Cathal was watching her.

'I have been an executor several times,' he said. His dark eyes made it clear he knew what Mum was feeling.

Mum looked at Cathal as though seeing something in him she hadn't noticed before. 'Perhaps you could just check I've done everything.'

'There comes a point,' he said, eyes crinkling, 'when this stuff fills your head with sand.'

'That's it exactly,' Mum said. 'Sand.'

'You were always very good at maths, Clarissa,' Smithy said.

'It's not so much the calculations,' she answered. 'It's putting all the information together.' She looked very young today, with her blonde hair tied back into a ponytail and no make-up on her face. Almost like a little girl, looking for a grown-up to help with homework. I wriggled on my chair, finding the observation an uncomfortable one.

'Come on,' Cathal pushed his bowl back. 'Let's see whether we can't knock these devilish numbers into shape.'

Smithy watched them walk towards the stairs and shrugged. 'Perhaps he's more sensible than he seems.'

~

Next morning when Andrew and I came down to breakfast we found Cathal standing at the stove, stirring a saucepan of porridge.

'We worked very late on those figures.' There were grey rings under his eyes. 'Your mother said I could stay overnight.'

I wondered if he'd slept in one of the bedrooms on the top floor and hoped he hadn't woken Smithy, who also slept up there.

'Great view,' he said, nodding towards the garden, hung with a light mist that the sun was already piercing. 'They did the cook a favour when they moved the kitchen up here. In my childhood home there were about three sets of stairs between the dining room and the kitchen.'

Must have been a large house. 'Where do you live now?'

He gave the porridge an extra stir. 'I'm a wanderer. I find myself a berth here and there.'

Smithy came in, letting out a quiet gasp when she saw Cathal at the stove. 'What are you doing here so early?' A flush covered her neck.

'Making breakfast.'

'That's my job.' She walked towards him, holding out her hand for the wooden spoon.

He smiled at her. 'I like to finish what I start.'

Smithy snorted. 'I bet you do.'

He ignored her outstretched hand and served himself some porridge. He sat down, his back to Smithy. 'Better eat up. The working man must keep to his task.' His eyes twinkled at me. But he still didn't look like a working man. His shirt was too smart, even though the collar was frayed, and the corduroy trousers he was wearing now it was cooler looked as though they might once have been worn with a jacket and tie. But Cathal was one of those people who looked properly turned out even when they should have seemed scruffy.

Smithy grabbed his bowl as soon as he'd finished, carrying it off to the sink.

'Ah, Clarissa.' He was looking towards the kitchen door. Mum had pulled back her hair into a ponytail. She looked purposeful. Smithy and Mum exchanged a quick look. It was enough to tell me that Mum knew Smithy did not want Cathal here in the kitchen so early in the morning.

'I'm going to ring round some schools today,' Mum said. 'Then we can go and visit some of them.'

'Couldn't I just go to the comprehensive in town?' I longed to be with normal kids who lived with both parents, doing normal stuff.

Smithy was looking at me in that way that sometimes suggested she could read minds. 'There's more to education than having fun, Rose.' But there was a gentleness to her tone that wasn't always there.

'I could teach them here,' Cathal said.

'Teach? You?' Smithy said. 'What could you teach?'

Mum cleared her throat. 'Cathal used to be a teacher.'

'Did he now?'

'I must get on with the garden.' Cathal stood up. 'And let out Kronos.'

'Kronos?' Andrew asked.

'That's what I thought we might call the peacock. He is a bit of a god, is he not?' As he passed Mum he winked at her. She turned a bit pink and looked away.

Andrew waited until she'd left the room. 'I don't want him teaching me.' He said it quietly, but there was no mistaking the tone in his voice.

'He's not the type to stick to something regular like teaching.' Smithy blasted tap water into the sink. Andrew and I cleared the breakfast things. Outside the wheelbarrow bounced its way to the garden to the accompaniment of Cathal's whistling.

'Where does this man come from, anyway?' Smithy cut carrots into thin batons, like little spears. She always liked to prepare the vegetables early in the day, leaving them in bowls of cold water. 'What do we know about him?'

'His family are Irish.'

'Ah.'

'Oh, Smithy.' Mum picked up the tops and tails of the carrots Smithy'd cut and put them into the compost bin. 'They were propertied people in the South. Cathal grew up in a large house.'

'Did he now?' Smithy nodded to herself.

'We have mutual friends.'

Smithy looked at her as though she was about to ask who they were.

'Well, people we both vaguely know.'

'Vaguely know,' Smithy repeated. She pulled out the plug. 'We should start on the upstairs.'

They were clearing out the unused bedrooms on the top floor. Smithy picked up the strange navy turban she wore round her hair whenever she carried out dusty work. I trailed behind them as they went upstairs. Sometimes they found interesting things in those bedrooms, old toys and books. They opened the door of a room next to Smithy's own.

'Either we cover all this furniture with dustsheets or take it down to the basement.' Smithy ran a finger over the tallboy. 'It's too good to leave here gathering dust.'

'Perhaps it would be best to sell it. Especially if . . .' Mum glanced at me.

'You don't know it will be necessary yet, Clarissa.'

'What?' I asked. 'What's necessary?'

Mum sat down on the bed. 'Come and sit here, darling.' She put an arm round me. 'We have to pay tax on this house now that Granny's dead.'

'Death duties,' Smithy said. 'The chancellor wants his cut.'

'What does it mean?'

'We owe the government money, darling. Granny left me some money as well as the house. There may be enough to settle the bill. But if there's not . . .'

'You'd have to sell Fairfleet.' I stood up, shaking off Mum's arm. 'No. Not this as well. First Dad, then Granny, and now we're losing Fairfleet.'

I ran downstairs, the sob rising in my throat.

'What is it?' Andrew shot out of the kitchen. 'What's happened?' I shook my head.

Cathal brought in an armful of courgettes and aubergines. He looked at me and then glanced upstairs towards Mum, who was coming down after me. 'Perhaps we need to talk more about my idea,' he said.

'Your idea?' Andrew said.

'We should talk, yes.' Mum looked suddenly exhausted. 'Cathal had a plan for turning Fairfleet into a tutorial college.'

'Revision courses for O and A levels,' he said. 'Residential courses.'

Mum's attention was on me. 'Come back upstairs,' she said. 'Help us clear out the rooms. We can talk about this later.'

~

Smithy was on her hands and knees when I came back in, sweeping underneath a bed. 'You can check the drawers in that tallboy are empty,' she said. 'God knows, all this furniture must be worth a fortune. Those boys didn't know they were born.'

'The German boys?' I asked.

'The Jews.' Smithy looked as though there was more she might have said.

'Granny wanted them to have the best,' Mum said.

Smithy made a sound like a sniff.

I pulled a drawer open. It moved smoothly, almost soundlessly. Granny had once told me this was how you could tell furniture was well made. The inside of the drawer smelled of cedar.

'I'm going downstairs,' I said. Cathal was sitting in the kitchen. My socked feet made no sound as I came in and he didn't look up. His features were knotted into deep concentration, his brow puckered.

'Hello,' I said. He looked up and his smile was like the sun coming out.

16.

October lit Fairfleet's grounds with a honey tint. I smelled the tang of bonfires each time I went outside to help Cathal with the leaves. His rake moved in long, graceful sweeps and he hummed some folksong that might have been Irish to himself, hardly seeming to notice me. For someone who could pay people such dazzling attention he was surprisingly good at retreating into his own private world. I didn't mind because occasionally he'd nod at me, acknowledging my feeble efforts with the leaves.

Kronos had shed most of his tail feathers now and looked smaller and less important. Perhaps he needed a friend. I wanted to save his feathers, smuggle them upstairs where they wouldn't bother Smithy, but Kronos seemed to have shed them where I couldn't find them.

'We're getting stupider and stupider,' Andrew said when the leaves were neatly piled and I came back inside. 'It'll be half term soon and we're still not at school. We'll have to do menial labour when we grow up.'

'Like Cathal.' We were standing at our favourite spot by the kitchen window, looking out at him as he cut back the last of the summer growth in the flowerbeds. Smithy was in the kitchen, too, tidying up the cutlery drawer.

'Some people think teaspoons can go in any old place,' she'd said at breakfast, with a glance out of the window at Cathal.

'He seems to have made it work well for him, not having a proper job.' Andrew's lip curled. 'Living in a comfortable house.'

'Cathal doesn't live here.'

'He stays most nights.'

'That's because he's helping Mum with the taxes and they go through Granny's paperwork at night. Mum's an executioner.'

'What?'

'Executor,' Smithy said. 'Person who deals with the dead person's affairs.'

'It's taking so long.'

'I think he likes being here,' Andrew said. 'I think he's trying to string it out. Wiggle his way into Mum's affections.'

Behind us cutlery clattered onto the floor.

'My fingers are all thumbs,' Smithy said. Mum came in wearing an apron. Another one of her 'doing' days; there were more and more of them as the season progressed. She must be taking the tablets regularly.

'I think he's odd,' Andrew said. He cast a defiant look at Mum, daring her to dispute this.

Smithy banged the cutlery drawer shut. 'There. Let's hope the knives and forks and spoons stay in their right places now.' She looked at Mum as though indicating that what applied to cutlery should also apply to people.

Mum rolled her eyes. 'I'm going upstairs to clear out Granny's clothes. Want to help, Rose?'

I went up with her. Seeing Granny's old dresses and furs made my chest feel tight. We packed them into plastic bags according to whether they were to go to charity shops or downstairs to the basement. One of the dresses hanging up in dry-cleaning plastic in Granny's wardrobe was Mum's own wedding dress.

'Goodness knows how this got in here.' Mum took it out. 'I'll hang it in my own wardrobe.'

'It's too pretty to put away.' I ran a hand down the plastic-covered whiteness.

'Do you think so?' Mum sounded pleased. 'Let's take the plastic off.' The dress had long sleeves, with fabric-covered buttons running down them. The skirt fell from its fitted bodice in a neat ripple of silk.

'I prefer your dress to Diana's.' At the time of the Royal Wedding, just after we'd come to Fairfleet, I had longed for a dress like Diana's: a puff of silk. Remembering this made me feel disloyal to my mother.

'Perhaps if I put it on it will . . .' she said.

'Will what?'

But Mum shook her head. Perhaps she believed that if she wore the dress again it would act as a kind of lucky charm, bringing Dad back to her. Perhaps he didn't really love the tennis player as much as Mum. And Mum couldn't possibly be interested in anyone else apart from Dad. I struggled to push some thoughts about Cathal to the back of my mind.

'I was so happy when I wore this.' Her eyes had a faraway expression now. 'I didn't really want to change into my going-away outfit. I felt this dress was casting a spell over me.' She stroked it again. 'A bit like Cinderella in that Walt Disney film, wearing the wedding gown her fairy godmothers magic up for her. The dress that changes colour while she dances.'

I remembered the scene. 'But it was a ball-gown, the one the fairy godmother makes when she turns the pumpkin into the coach.'

She looked sad at having misremembered and I wished I hadn't corrected her.

Later on I remembered the scene in another Disney film, *Sleeping Beauty*, where the fairies change a wedding dress from pink to blue and back to pink again. I meant to ask my mother whether that was the scene she'd been thinking of, but I forgot.

Next morning when we came down for breakfast it was to find Cathal sitting beside Mum at the table. Both wore dressing gowns. Cathal must have borrowed an old one from the airing cupboard. He removed his hand from Mum's exposed knee.

'Hi, kids.' He gave us that quick smile of his. 'I was wondering about building a tree house in one of those oaks out on the lawn. What do you think, Andrew?'

I saw longing fight against distrust in my brother's face. He too had seen that hand on Mum's knee. 'OK,' he said gruffly, turning to the box of cornflakes on the table. After breakfast Cathal drove him in Granny's old shooting brake to the timber merchant. They returned with resin-scented planks, which Cathal and Andrew unloaded and carried onto the back lawn. Andrew's features were lit with the thrill of carrying out a man's task. The two of them spent the afternoon measuring and sawing. I took tea out to them. It had started to drizzle very gently, but the air was still mild.

'Pass me that tape measure,' Cathal said. As I handed it to him he seemed to misjudge the distance, closing his fingers in mid-air. The metal-cased tape measure dropped, hitting the side of Cathal's mug on the grass. The mug wobbled and a little chip came out of the rim. Some of the tea spilled out.

'For God's sake,' Cathal shouted.

'It was just an accident,' Andrew said.

Cathal was still staring at the spilled tea soaking the grass.

'I'll make you some more.' I heard the apology in my own voice even though it hadn't been me who'd dropped the tape measure.

'Don't you worry, Rosie.' His voice regained its usual warmth. 'We'll finish this tomorrow. Your mother wants me to move furniture down from the top floor to the basement.' He walked away, leaving the tape measure and mug beside the half-sawn planks. Andrew and I sat for a moment without talking.

'As I've said before, Cathal's a bit weird.' Andrew lined up a row of nails so that they all pointed towards the house.

I retrieved the tape measure and picked up the mug. It was an old one, so Smithy probably wouldn't tell me off too much for chipping it. 'What do you mean?'

'He says these things. There was this old woman in front of us at the lights. Her car stalled on the green and we missed our turn. He said we should bump her, just gently, to make her pay attention.' He shrugged.

We went inside and washed the mugs and put them away in the cupboard. 'A place for everything and everything in its place.' Andrew mimicked Smithy as he closed the door.

'Smithy really doesn't like Cathal,' I said.

'It's breaking my heart.' It was Cathal, standing in the kitchen doorway, looking relaxed, amused almost. He vanished before we could think of an answer. I folded the drying-up cloth into precise squares and hung it on the stove lid, as though Smithy-like attention to detail might somehow make things right. I didn't look at Andrew and knew that he wouldn't want to catch my eye, either.

Something thumped overhead. A chest or table falling over, perhaps. I walked out into the hall. Silence from upstairs. Followed by a laugh. Then a door closing.

Mum and Cathal didn't come down for over an hour. When they did, Mum's face was bright. Andrew bent his head down to the comic he was reading. I found a loose thread in my cardigan and wound it round and round.

Smithy came back from her niece's just as we were serving supper. She looked from Mum to Cathal, a slow, steady gaze that caused Mum to blush over the steaming dish of macaroni cheese.

'You know, Marcy would have me to live with her,' Smithy said. 'There's a spare room. I could help with the cooking and the little one.'

Colour fled Mum's face. 'You couldn't leave us, Smithy. We need you.'

Smithy leaving Fairfleet would be like removing November or February from the calendar: unthinkable, even though those months were chilly and gloomy.

~

'I call him Cattle,' Andrew said when we talked about the day's events later on, sitting on my bed and whispering. 'Because he's stupid like cows.'

I didn't think he was stupid at all. I'd seen him with Mum, standing patiently with her while she ummed over the relocation of a piece of furniture. Helping her re-hang paintings. He was good at that: able to see how moving a frame an inch this way or that changed the look of a wall. He'd suggested relocating a red Persian rug from the dining room into the drawing room and had transformed a dull room into one you wanted to spend all day in.

Smithy had observed the relocation of objects through half-closed eyes. 'I suppose nobody minds that the dining-room carpet has holes in it and we can see them now the rug's gone?'

Next morning Cathal was quiet as he ate. When we were clearing the plates he spoke. 'I've said it before, but we should teach the children ourselves, Clarissa.'

'Isn't that against the law?' Andrew asked.

'The law says you have to be educated, but it doesn't specify that it has to be done in a school,' Cathal answered.

'So *you'd* teach Andrew and Rose?' Smithy had been listening intently to the conversation as she washed up.

'I would.'

'Miss Smith is doubting I'm up to the task, aren't you?' He was watching her with his amused expression.

'Of course you're up to the task.' Mum sounded almost brusque. 'But why would you want to do it, Cathal? There are enough good schools in the county. We just need to get on with looking for one.'

'What do they really teach them, though? They're examination factories. They knock the curiosity out of children. Look at me – full of intellectual beans as a child.'

'Which school did you go to?' Smithy asked.

'It was in Ireland. You wouldn't have heard of it. But I have taught in this country.'

'Where?'

'I'll write you down a list if you want.' He sounded jovial. 'The point is, these two could do better. Fairfleet is full of books.'

'You're certainly the best-educated person I've ever met,' Mum said. 'But it's a big undertaking, Cathal.'

'It buys us time. By next academic year they'll be really up to speed, ready to thrive in a truly excellent school. Probably ahead of their peers.'

'Ahead,' Mum murmured. 'Yes, I suppose they would be.'

I noticed that he had moved position very quickly and smoothly, from claiming that schools were examination factories to stating that some of them were excellent.

'I'll drive you into Oxford and we can buy the books you need,' Mum said. 'We shouldn't let any more time pass.'

'You children can spend the morning clearing out the old classroom so we can use it,' Cathal said.

Smithy stared at him.

'What old classroom?' Andrew asked.

'The room beside the stairs.' Mum was hunting for the car keys. 'That's where the Jewish boys had their lessons during the war. But Cathal thinks it's a shame not to –'

'Where Smithy keeps her things?' Andrew interrupted. Smithy stored mops, dusters and the ancient vacuum cleaner in the room, along with some of her own possessions. Sometimes she made herself a cup of tea and sat down in an old armchair with a copy of the *Mail*. I had never thought of it as a proper room. But it had windows, I remembered.

'I'll move my things.' Smithy spoke in a tight voice, as though reminding us that she knew she was only a servant, paid to live here, not part of the family. But she was more than that, surely?

'We'll help.' Andrew pushed aside his plate and stood up.

'I wanted to go to the comprehensive,' I told Andrew as we moved buckets and mops out of the room.

'Perhaps he'll get bored with the whole teaching thing.' He stretched up to remove a cardboard box of laundry soap from a shelf. 'Where shall we put this?'

'Down in the basement.' Smithy held out a hand. 'I'll take it down.' We heard her trudge towards the steps.

I remembered something. 'There's an old blackboard down there. We could bring it up.' A small thump of excitement hit me. It felt disloyal to Smithy to feel excited about Cathal teaching us.

'What's that?' Andrew nodded at a dusty flat object lying on its side on the shelf where the soap had been.

I stood on tiptoe to pull it down. 'A photo.'

A rare colour photo from the war. Granny in flying jacket and trousers, smiling, at the centre of a group of young men, recognizable despite the mannish clothes and forties hairstyle. They looked fondly back at her. One of the younger ones, hardly more than a boy, stood out from the others because of his fine features and height. And the expression he wore on his face as he smiled back at Granny.

'He really liked her, didn't he?' I pointed at the boy.

Andrew sneezed. 'God, that's dusty. Yes, he fancied her all right. Let's get that blackboard up. And there might be some old desks down in the basement, too. Granny never seemed to throw anything away.'

I wiped the photograph on my jeans and replaced it on the shelf. It seemed a shame for such a happy picture to be stuck down here where nobody could look at it.

Smithy came back in. She looked hollow, as though the clearing out of this room was somehow sucking the spirit out of her.

'I'm sorry about your things, Smithy,' I said. 'Perhaps they'll send us to school soon and you can move back in.'

'I expect I'll manage.' Smithy looked around the room with something approaching a smile, a very cool smile, like sunshine on a frosty morning.

Cathal was silent when he appeared at lunchtime following the shopping trip. He sat with a sheet of paper and pen, writing out days of the week and subjects to be studied.

'I wonder if he ever goes home,' I said to Andrew when we went outside after the meal. 'He seems to spend all his time here now.'

'What do you mean, go home?'

I didn't understand.

'He lives here now. Haven't you got that yet?'

'But where . . . ?'

'Where does he sleep?' He laughed, not in a particularly cheerful way. 'Where do you think, Rose?'

Not in Granny's room; I'd seen the quilt still pulled tight and creaseless over the bed, untouched since we had cleared out the room. And not on the top floor, in the rooms next to Smithy's, because those beds had been stripped.

He slept in Mum's bedroom. I couldn't let myself say it.

Andrew kicked the side of the stone steps leading to the front door. 'Yup. God, it makes me sick, just thinking about it. And now he's going to teach us too. He's just squirming his way into our lives, Rose, like a worm.'

Mum cooked dinner that night, roast lamb and potatoes. She brought up a bottle of Granny's wine from the cellar. Cathal put his hand over his glass.

'Need to keep my brain sharp to deal with these youngsters in the morning.' His eyes glittered.

'It's very good claret.' Mum poured herself a little. She didn't drink much alcohol these days, said it didn't go well with the Lithium.

With an intense look of concentration Cathal watched the dark red liquid flow into her glass.

~

In the morning when we went down to lessons, a Cathal greeted us whom we hadn't encountered before. He wore a shirt I hadn't seen and what looked like new cord trousers, neatly pressed. On each of the desks sat a maths textbook, exercise book, pencil, compass and protractor.

'I'll be setting Andrew more advanced work as he's older. But I'll stretch you, too, Rosie. You've a sharp brain on you.' His eyes still twinkled, but there was sharpness in them this morning. Cathal the teacher might not be as easygoing as Cathal the gardener and general handyman.

'You're both starting with geometry. Let's just run through what you know.'

Triangles, acute angles, rectangles, pi, circles. He asked questions and probed. Drew shapes on the blackboard. Asked us questions about football pitches and circus rings. He had a way of making me believe I knew the answer, that it was buried somewhere inside me and I only needed to extract it, that I was far better at maths than I could have dreamed and it was only the stupidity of earlier teachers that had prevented me from discovering this fact.

Andrew learned how to do all kinds of fancy things with triangles, using a small book of mysterious numbers called logarithms. The three of us measured and multiplied for an hour and a half.

'Enough now.' Cathal looked at his watch. 'Sit back, close your eyes and just listen.'

He started to read us a poem about someone arising and going now to build a cabin. The words didn't seem very clever, but there was something about the rise and fall of Cathal's voice that made me want to listen to the next word and the next.

'W.B. Yeats,' he said, when he'd finished. 'We will be looking at more of his poems. Some people say they're too advanced for children, but Rosie would disagree, wouldn't you, Rosie?'

I nodded, pleased he'd noticed my appreciation of the poetry.

'Off you go then. Go and run around outside for ten minutes. We'll do some geography then before lunch. That'll be enough for today.'

We sat out by the lake eating the Garibaldis Smithy had left out for us. 'Well,' I said.

Andrew grunted. I knew what he was feeling. It was hard to admit it, but Cathal was good.

'We'll study French this morning,' Cathal said, next day at breakfast. 'There's more to learning a language than memorizing nouns. French is the language of philosophy.'

'Most children need to be able to ask for a glass of water or directions,' Smithy objected.

'I'm not teaching these two to be just like any other children,' he said mildly.

'They still need to start with the basics. That's what Dr Dawes did with the Jewish boys. He taught them to ask for simple things in English: an apple, what the time was, where the railway station was. And he made them learn the rules.'

'Oh rules, rules,' Cathal answered carelessly.

'Rules are there for a reason.'

It looked as though Smithy and Cathal were about to lock themselves into one of the arguments that flared up between them. I slipped out of the kitchen. Still an hour until we started lessons. I went up to my mother's room.

Mum was getting dressed. Today she was going to wear a very simple navy wool dress. She was looking much smarter in the last few weeks; Cathal had encouraged her to put aside the old trousers she'd preferred before. Dad had never seemed to notice what Mum was wearing, but I'd heard Cathal suggesting she might swap one shirt for another, this cardigan for that jacket, add this belt or that scarf.

I looked for signs of Cathal in the room. He didn't appear to have many possessions at all, but I spotted a comb I didn't recognize on the bedside table on the other side of Mum's bed. And a pair of his shoes under the dressing table. Perhaps he was keeping the rest of his things in one of the upstairs bedrooms.

'Can I look at your wedding dress?'

Mum took it out of the wardrobe for me, laying it on top of the unmade bed. It felt strange to think of Cathal sleeping here too.

I wished the covers had been pulled up over the bottom sheet so that I didn't have to think of his long body asleep on it beside my mother's. I touched the buttons on the dress sleeves through the plastic film. But this morning the dress didn't seem to be exerting its influence.

In search of further reassurance I looked at the dressing table. Mum must have found some little candles. She'd arranged them in a horseshoe shape on the dressing table. In the middle was a photograph of Granny and Mum herself, with Andrew and me. Dad must have taken it years ago; Andrew and I were tiny.

'I find it reassures me,' Mum said, following my gaze. 'I feel the presence of something more powerful than me when I light the candles and sit there. It calms me.'

'What does Cathal think about all this?' It felt strange, almost grown-up, to be having a conversation of this kind with my mother.

Mum laughed. 'He teases me. But it helps me, it really does.' And she gave an embarrassed half-shrug.

But there were already more important things on my mind. I scanned the dressing table for the bottle of pills. There it was, towards the back, along with some discarded hair pins and cotton wool puffs. Mum saw me looking at the bottle.

'I've already had this morning's.' She nodded at her shrine. 'It's as if Granny is encouraging me. But Cathal doesn't think I should take drugs.'

Questions burned in my mind.

'He thinks I can heal myself, with his support. He says it's my soul that is hurt and it doesn't need drugs.'

'You promised Granny you'd do what the doctors say.'

'I know.' Mum bowed her head.

The following morning Mum complained of having a cold. She stayed in bed. Cathal continued with the day's lessons. History.

He told us the story of Henry VIII and the break with Rome, of Cardinal Wolsey and Thomas More. When Cathal taught you history it was like listening to a really good story. Even Andrew had stopped frowning when Cathal was explaining something and listened, his head resting on his arm.

'So there you have it, a huge religious change brought about by one man falling for one woman. And that wasn't the end of Henry's marital adventures. These are all the women he married.'

Cathal turned to the blackboard and started writing the names of all the wives. The chalk snapped.

The expression in his eyes turned to that sudden frustrated anger that I had noticed before, when he'd spilled tea on the grass. He said something under his breath, then saw me watching him and switched back to his composed-schoolteacher manner.

'There's a new box of chalk in my front jacket pocket, on a chair in the kitchen. Go and fetch it for me, Rosie.'

The kitchen was empty. Smithy must be upstairs. I found Cathal's tweed jacket. The front pocket was empty. Something was stuffed into the inside pocket, however. I unzipped it. Inside was a newspaper cutting, folded over. It seemed to burn in my fingers. I looked over my shoulder. Nobody was watching me. I unfolded the paper.

It was an article from the *Oxford Mail* about Granny's death and the funeral, with photographs of the house and a description of the estate. I scanned it quickly: . . . *one of the first women to fly a Spitfire . . . Fairfleet House . . . example of Palladian architecture . . . Lord Dorner . . . survived by her only child, Clarissa Madison . . . now inherits . . .*

Why had Cathal cut this out of the newspaper? Granny's funeral had happened before he'd come to Fairfleet, so why had he taken such an interest in a stranger? I refolded the cutting and put it back in his pocket. Then I changed my mind and took the cutting out again and stuffed it under the band of my trousers. The box of chalk had fallen out of his jacket onto the kitchen floor.

For the rest of the morning I tried to concentrate on Henry and his wives, and then on the first part of *Hiawatha*, which Cathal read to us in that expressive voice of his.

Everything was fine, I told myself. Mum would take her pills. Cathal was helping her with the money. Andrew and I were having lessons again, doing really well, Cathal said.

After lunch I stuffed the newspaper cutting under my mattress, on top of the metal springs on the bedstead, being sure to push it out of the reach of Smithy's fingers when she came to change the bed linen.

17.

A low beam of sunlight emerged from behind a cloud and illuminated Benny and me where we sat, thirty years after I had found the newspaper clipping in Cathal's pocket. In the space between us bright motes of dust glittered briefly like half-lost memories. I gave myself a mental kick and reminded myself that I needed to count out Benny's tablets, refill the water jug, check the oxygen cylinder.

Benny blinked at me and turned his head away from the light.

'Shall I close the curtains?' I asked.

'No.' He looked back at me. 'Just for a second . . .' He shook his head. 'I'm seeing things that aren't there. Is it part of the illness?' His features crumpled.

'Possibly. I can't be sure.' It was best, I'd learned, to be honest about what I did and didn't know. 'Sometimes people tell me that they see things. Sometimes they don't mind. If they do, I have a word with the doctor.' I passed him his water glass. 'Drink this.'

'How did you know I was thirsty?' He sipped the water. 'You're very good at this, Rosamond.'

'I like my work.' It was the truth. I'd come here with another purpose – an obsession, others had said – in mind. And a need to run away from what had happened to me more recently. It was easy to forget all this when I was with Benny. I thought he'd be interesting, but I hadn't expected to relish his company so completely. I needed to be careful, on my guard. He was still observing me as I replaced his glass on the table.

'You can leave me now.' He glanced at the laptop beside him on the pillow. 'I'll ring the bell if I need anything. Go for a walk or read the paper or talk to Sarah. You know I have visitors later on?'

Old work colleagues, Sarah had told me.

'I'll look in again in twenty minutes.'

'I'm not a bloody baby.' He folded his arms and came close to scowling at me.

'And I'm not a maternity nurse, either.'

His lips twitched as he reached for the laptop, but his concentration was on the screen, on whatever it was he was writing. I noticed that there was a yellow tone to his face now. Jaundice. The cancer was working away on him.

As I walked across the landing the window above the stairs showed me clouds massing in the sky to the east, tinged with yellow and beige. Snow. Probably by evening. Possibly heavy. I shivered. We'd been snowed in that last winter I'd lived at Fairfleet, isolated from the rest of the world. Our enchanted refuge had become a beautiful prison.

Sarah was washing up in the kitchen. 'I'm popping down to the shop with Max,' she said.

'I'll keep an ear open for Benny,' I said. 'You shouldn't delay your walk: look at those clouds.'

She frowned. 'Snow. I always worry that the doctor won't be able to get up the drive if it's too heavy. Or the extra nurses for the nights, if and when we need them.' Sarah took off her apron and whistled for the dog, who appeared from underneath the table.

'Could you get me some more Clementines?' I asked. I'd been making tiny ice-lollies for Benny from the juice. He liked them when his mouth was dry from the medication.

She put on Max's lead and found her boots and coat. I watched them stride out round the side of the house to the lane, the dog almost beaming with the joy of an excursion.

Time alone in the house, except for Benny upstairs. I felt a tingle of anticipation.

I knew where I needed to go now. Down into that basement. I gave another quick glance through the window at the clouds and felt myself again becoming a young girl. Thirty years ago snow had brought events at Fairfleet to a head. At the time, I'd felt its arrival as a pure thrill.

~

When December came that winter of 1981 the weather forgot this was England, not Russia or Canada.

I opened my curtains one morning and saw the snow. My heart leaped. The lake might freeze, a rare but wonderful occurrence. The skates would still be down in the basement, waiting for us to use. Outside everything would sparkle. And the topiary animals would be giant Christmas biscuits frosted with icing sugar. I banged on Andrew's door.

'Snow!' We were pulling on wellington boots and scarves and running across the white lawn within minutes.

The lake hadn't frozen yet. 'Another day or two.' Andrew peered at it from the small landing jetty. We scrunched back to the kitchen, blowing on damp, woollen-gloved hands.

'I always forget how really cold snow is.' I shook my wrists.

'Idiot.' But his smile was kind. The snow had cheered him up.

Cathal met us on the landing, eyes bright. 'We must all go sledging. Have you a sledge, Andrew?'

'Ours was left at home – where we used to live with our dad, I mean, when we moved here,' Andrew said.

'I used to have a sledge,' Mum called out from her room. 'I doubt Granny threw it out. It's probably down in the basement.'

'Damn lessons for once,' said Cathal. '*This* is a lesson. A geography lesson and a physics lesson and all kinds of other lessons too, if I put my mind to it.' He turned to Andrew. 'Find that sledge. Clarrie, pull on waterproofs. Fun shall be the order of the day.'

Perhaps Cathal was getting a bit above himself, ordering us around like this, but even Andrew didn't seem to resent him this morning. Smithy, however, was having none of it. She stood on the staircase to the top floor, arms folded.

'It's a long walk to the nearest hill,' she said.

Cathal's face fell, but only for a moment. 'I'll tie the sledge to the back of the car and pull it up and down the drive. The kids'll love it.'

'Come on.' Andrew was already running downstairs. 'I'll find the sledge.' I had never seen him respond so enthusiastically before to any of Cathal's suggestions.

'The runners will need waxing,' Mum called after him. 'Ask Smithy for some beeswax.'

'I'll go and find it for him.' With a sigh Smithy followed Andrew down. Mum caught my eye.

'Boys, eh?'

'Will you come out too?' I asked. 'Please?'

Mum hesitated.

'Of course she will, won't you, Clarrie?' Cathal put an arm around her. 'It'll do you good. You've spent too much time worrying about money.'

Mum smiled back at him and looked suddenly years younger.

A series of thumps from below told us that Andrew had located the sledge and was bringing it up from the basement. I rushed downstairs to look at it. Smithy was already polishing the metal runners with the wax. She always preferred to use her dusters herself, not trusting other people with them.

'Mind you take care.' She put the lid on the polish. 'That drive's not as smooth as it looks. Don't go too fast.' She addressed the words to Cathal as he came downstairs, without looking at him.

Cathal winked at Andrew. He was wearing a smart ski jacket and carrying a pair of boots specially designed for snowy weather and looked a bit like James Bond. He even had sunglasses folded up in a top pocket, ready to put on. I hadn't noticed him bringing his possessions into Fairfleet, but clearly this had happened at some point.

'Where did you go skiing?' Mum asked.

'Switzerland,' he said.

'Oh, when?' she asked. 'I used to love Verbier.'

'Some years ago,' he answered casually.

The jacket looked fairly new.

'Isn't skiing awfully expensive?' Smithy asked. I knew she was wondering how someone like Cathal could have afforded that kind of holiday and all the clothes and equipment.

'A friend treated me.' His eyes were on the sledge. 'She looks grand. Let's go.'

Mum had put on wellingtons, old waterproof trousers that Granny had used when she cleared algae from the lake and an old fur jacket that must once have been Granny's too. A scarf was wound around her neck. She looked very young this morning.

Cathal fetched a length of rope from the car boot, left over from the timber-buying excursion. He tied the sledge to the rope in a neat knot and then fastened the rope to the tow bar.

'Someone taught you sailing knots,' Mum said.

'We had a boat when I was a boy.' He looked at her more closely. 'Where's that other scarf, the blue one?'

'Upstairs. This one is cashmere, warmer.' She snuggled her neck into it.

'But the blue one matches your eyes better.' He put down the rope. 'I'll get it.'

'But I'm happy with this one.'

'It's no trouble.' He flicked off his boots at the front door and ran inside past Smithy, returning quickly with the scarf. She started to protest but then shrugged, removing her scarf and replacing it with the blue one. Smithy watched from the stairs, eyes narrowed, silent.

'Now, who's first?' he said.

'Me!' begged Andrew.

'You and Rosie can share the first ride.' Cathal opened the car door. Andrew and I clambered onto the sledge. At first it didn't seem to want to glide through the snow as it ought. Snow clogged its runners as the car towed it so that it jerked, threatening to snap its rope, throwing wet shards into our faces. Then the rope tautened and we shot forward again. The journey to the bottom of the drive was a disappointment.

Cathal slowed to a halt at the end of the drive and wound down the window. 'It'll be easier on the way back,' he said. 'We've compacted the snow down. Jump off now while I turn the car.'

On our return the sledge seemed to know what was expected of it. We flew down the drive, little pieces of ice flying into our faces, the snow swooshing cleanly underneath the runners. Andrew laughed, a sound I hadn't heard for months.

'This is brilliant,' he called out to Mum. 'You've got to try it.'

I jumped off. 'Have a go.'

'Oh, I don't know.' Mum eyed the sledge. 'I'm happy just watching you two.'

'I insist,' Cathal called from the car.

'Watch out for potholes,' Smithy said from the steps, where she stood with arms folded. 'And don't drive too fast.'

Cathal rolled his eyes at me. Mum climbed on behind Andrew, holding him round the waist. Andrew, my serious, critical brother, was grinning with the fun of it.

Cathal released the handbrake and the car moved forward, pulling the sledge. Mum let out a laugh of delight. As they approached the oak trees on the left of the drive he accelerated.

'Yippee!' Mum called out. A pang of envy filled me; Cathal hadn't driven as fast when I was on the sledge.

'Careful,' Smithy called out from the steps.

The sun came out and flooded the scene with white light that bounced off the snow, shining on Mum's and Andrew's smiling faces. This snow had achieved something quite unexpected: made us all happy together at last. I could still hear them laughing as they reached the end of the drive. Just as he had before, Cathal made them dismount while he turned the car. The return trip back towards the house was taken at speed. Andrew whooped. I moved towards them, ready to claim my turn. The sledge was only yards away from the house now.

Its nose shot up. Andrew and Mum were flying through the white light, an untidy jumble of limbs and scarves, before they sprawled over the snow.

I ran to them. Andrew stood up, beaming. 'That was the best bit.' He rubbed snow out of his eyes. Mum sat up very slowly, holding her left wrist. Her face was twisted with pain. 'I think I might have done something.' She tried to straighten her leg and let out a yelp.

18.

Broken wrist. Badly sprained ankle. She can't drive and she can barely walk, either.' Smithy glared at Cathal. 'I warned you about that drive.'

'It wasn't his fault,' I said. 'It was just an accident, Smithy.' Cathal gave me a quick, appraising glance, mixing surprise with something else: relief, perhaps.

'Just when she was starting to pull herself together.' Smithy slammed a bowl of soup onto a tray. Mum was resting upstairs after the trip to accident and emergency, which had resulted in her left wrist being x-rayed and plastered. 'How's she going to manage?'

Cathal opened his arms, seeming to accept both blame and responsibility.

'At least she didn't break her neck,' Smithy said.

Cathal had hardly spoken since he'd driven Mum back from casualty. I remembered how he'd looked as he helped her into the house, supporting most of her weight as she struggled over the snow on the crutches, her broken wrist strapped. His face had been illuminated by an emotion so strong it had been uncomfortable to look at him. He must feel so sorry for her, so worried. Perhaps he blamed himself. Lucky for Mum he was so tall and strong. When they came to the steps he'd scooped her up and carried her in his arms with one of his powerful yet graceful movements.

Later, as I was going to bed, I heard him talking in Mum's bedroom.

'Clarrie, my darling.' His voice was very deep and low. 'Don't worry about a thing. Leave it all to me.'

I couldn't hear my mother's reply, but I felt relief that Cathal was here to look after things.

And yet there was something in his tone, something I couldn't define, that worried me. Didn't he sound almost happy to be in charge? He came down again and I heard him in the dining room. Glass clinked. He must be pouring himself some of the brandy or whisky left in the crystal decanters from when Granny was still alive.

~

When I went to see her in the morning, Mum was propped up in bed. 'Hello.' Her eyes brightened as I approached.

'Are you still hurting?'

'They've given me painkillers.' She yawned. 'They make me a bit sleepy.'

I looked at the other tablets on the dressing table.

'I'm running out,' Mum said, following my gaze.

'Ask Cathal to get you some more.'

Mum lowered her head towards the quilt.

'What's happening downstairs?' she asked.

'We're going to do the future tense in Latin this morning. And then some history. Elizabeth I.'

'He's a good teacher,' Mum said. 'Perhaps his plan is a good one.'

I remembered. 'Turning Fairfleet into a school?'

She nodded. 'A tutorial college. One way or another I'm going to have to make some hard decisions soon.'

'For the tax?'

'Oh, I've paid that now. But it's left me without much money.' She smiled. 'But I shouldn't be bothering you with this, Rosie. Go and do your homework. And then perhaps it's time to decorate this house for Christmas.'

Christmas! I had almost forgotten about that.

Cathal hadn't. After lessons had finished he went down to the basement and returned with the cardboard box of decorations.

'Your mother told me where to find them.'

'I could have done that for you,' Smithy said. He ignored her.

'I'll bring in the tree I bought yesterday.'

'You've already got it?' Normally Andrew and I went to help select the tree. But Cathal wasn't to know this.

'We'll make it look beautiful. It'll cheer up your mother.'

'Glad you're trying to make it up to her,' Smithy said.

He stiffened. Poor Cathal. His feelings must have been hurt. But he didn't look put out for long. He dragged the tree into the room. When it was standing straight in its metal bucket he took his time over choosing baubles from the cardboard box, laying them out on the hearth rug and examining each one, rejecting some because they were the wrong colour or shape. I climbed up onto the sofa arm in order to stick the fairy in her usual position on the top of the tree. Cathal shook his head.

'Not that tatty old object. Let's use this instead.' From a paper bag he extracted a large silver star. 'A lucky star. I bought it yesterday.'

Although I felt sad about putting the fairy back in the box with the other discarded ornaments, I had to admit that the star looked just right when it was in position. Perhaps it would brighten the new year.

Smithy came in to draw the curtains. 'That little tree looks a bit lost there,' she said. 'Why don't you move it next to the piano?'

'The tree's not little.' Cathal spoke softly.

'And where's the fairy?'

'The tree is just fine as it is.' He banged the arm of the sofa.

Smithy took a step back. 'Someone's tetchy today,' she muttered.

For a second the anger stayed on Cathal's face. But by the time Smithy had left the room he looked composed again. He tacked lengths of ribbon from the picture rail and showed me how to peg the Christmas cards onto them with special metal clips he'd bought in town.

'And for God's sake, put the hideous cards somewhere where we don't have to look at them.'

'Like this one?' I showed him a card with shiny embossed red-and-gold candles.

He made a face. 'Tie that horror to the very bottom of the ribbon over there.' He pointed to a dark corner.

Smithy returned with another batch of cards. 'Your mother opened these and gave them to me for hanging up.' She watched me pin the candles card where Cathal had directed. 'That card is from one of your grandmother's old air auxiliary friends. She came to the funeral and she's known your mother since she was a baby.'

I paused, card in hand.

'We can't all be top of the ribbon,' Cathal said smoothly.

'The bottom is where you put tradesmen's cards and cards from distant acquaintances,' Smithy retorted. 'Family and old friends go on the mantelpiece.'

It was easy to roll my eyes at Cathal when Smithy walked out, but when I went up to see my mother later on I felt a pinprick of guilt. Smithy might be annoying, meddling and old-fashioned, but she was part of Fairfleet, just like the old furniture and the pictures. Cathal sometimes encouraged me to laugh at her. That wasn't right.

I went up to see Mum. She was out of bed, hobbling around the room. 'So gloomy in here this afternoon. Light the candles on the dressing table, darling,' she said. 'I can't do it with one hand.'

I took the box of matches from her and did what she asked. Immediately the room looked more Christmassy.

'That's better.' Mum sat down on her bed with a grunt of discomfort. 'Tell me what's happening downstairs?'

I told her about the tree decorating and the spat about the card. Mum smiled, but the smile was only fleeting and replaced by a frown. 'I need to get down there. Trouble's brewing between those two.'

'Can you manage the stairs?'

'Cathal doesn't want me to try. He says it'll put too much strain on the ankle. He'll carry me down later.'

I looked away from her.

'Rose, you mustn't think it's like that between us.' My mother took my hand. 'Cathal and I . . . well, he's just helping out until we're back to normal.'

What was normal? I wondered. Life as it had been when Granny was still alive? That time was gone.

'What about the tutorial college?' I asked, to distract myself from thinking about my grandmother.

She looked down at my fingers. 'I don't know about the college. He's keen, but I'm not sure. It's quite a commitment to take on when you don't really . . .'

'Really what?'

She shrugged. 'Know your business partner that well.'

Strange that she should say she didn't feel she knew Cathal. He certainly seemed to know her. I'd seen him watching her, learning about her: how she liked her tea and coffee, books she liked, television and radio programmes she enjoyed. He studied her with those eyes of his that showed so little expression unless sudden anger flooded them.

Perhaps Mum was worried that she hadn't been paying such close attention to him.

~

The postman came when I was alone in the kitchen, during the morning break from lessons.

'Your drive's like the Cresta Run.' He handed me more Christmas cards. At the table I sorted them into piles for Mum and for Smithy, who received a couple each year. Andrew and I only had the one: from Dad. Camels in a desert.

'Very nice and appropriate.' Smithy came in and nodded approval. 'That card must go on the fireplace. Cathal or no Cathal. Where is he, anyway?'

'In the basement.' I'd seen him go down there earlier on.

Smithy looked out of the window. 'He must have slipped out through the hall without any of us noticing, then. Probably listening in to our private conversation.' Her mouth pursed up. 'Anyway, he's outside now.'

The thought that Cathal had walked past the kitchen door without us seeing him made the back of my neck feel weird.

Hop, skip, thump came from the hall. I turned to see Mum, looking triumphant. 'I'm trying to move around a bit more.' She hobbled to the table and sat down, resting the old walking stick we'd found for her in the basement against the table. 'It's hard work for you and Cathal, Smithy.'

Smithy said nothing.

'He must have found it hard yesterday,' I piped up. 'He had a drink. Just like Daddy when he had a bad day in the office.'

'Cathal doesn't drink,' Mum said.

Smithy gave her a sharp look but said nothing.

'He's still planning to run his school from here, is he?'

'I need to talk to him,' Mum muttered.

'Yes.' Smithy folded the dishcloth over the taps. 'I'm going to do some more upstairs. Then I'll make the mincemeat.'

'Oh, leave the upstairs until after Christmas, for goodness' sake.'

'Best to keep on top of things,' she said, as she left the room. We heard her footsteps, very heavy-sounding for someone who wasn't large, trudging upstairs.

'Your grandmother would be worried that we're exploiting Smithy.' Mum sighed. 'She needs more help. It's hard work sorting out all the old furniture. She isn't as young as she used to be.'

Talking of Granny reminded me of something. 'Stay there,' I told Mum, as though she were capable of running away. I dashed upstairs to find the newspaper cutting I'd taken from Cathal's pocket and hidden under my mattress. 'He had this in his jacket.' The words came out in a gasp. 'He must have cut it out before he came here looking for work in the summer.'

Mum read it and shrugged. 'Perhaps he just happened upon it and thought it was a good time to come to the house and ask if we had jobs for him. There's so much to sort out when someone dies.'

But something was still playing on my memory. I couldn't pull it out, not now. It would come to me, later.

Mum looked at the kitchen clock. 'Shouldn't you be starting lessons about now?'

Andrew came into the kitchen. Approval flashed over his face as he saw Mum back downstairs again. 'Cathal must be running late.' He sounded scornful.

'Why don't you help Smithy with the furniture while you wait?' Mum glanced down at the cutting in her hand as though she wanted to read it again.

He went up to the top floor. We heard his voice and Smithy's from upstairs. They were carrying something heavy; every now and then Smithy would caution Andrew to take care. Something bumped on the landing. A series of further thumps came from the staircase down to the ground floor.

'Let's stop for a moment,' Smithy said, panting.

The front door closed. Cathal walked into the downstairs hall.

'Oh good, you can give us a hand,' Smithy called, hearing his footsteps.

He hesitated. 'I was just coming in to get water for the car windscreen washer.'

'The car will have to wait. We need you to help us carry this bookcase over the wooden floor. It'll scratch it if it catches.'

'Could you give me just a minute?'

'Oh don't mind us,' she hissed. 'Doing all the heavy work. Thought you were due back in the classroom, anyway?'

'Smithy . . .' Mum put the cutting into her pocket and hobbled out of the kitchen now.

'I'll help.' I ran up to them.

'Come on,' said Andrew. 'Let's just get it done.'

It took some minutes to manoeuvre the bookcase over the wooden floor and down the stone steps to the storeroom in the basement where old furniture was stored.

'You've done enough.' Smithy wiped her hands on her apron. 'Go up and get five minutes' fresh air before your lessons. I'll just cover this up with a dustsheet.'

Andrew and I were almost out of the front door when we heard Smithy scream. Looking at one another in horror we ran back inside. She came upstairs, her face putty-coloured.

'In the pantry down there.' She pointed to the basement steps.

'What is?'

She shook her head. 'In a vase by the sink.'

We went downstairs again. On the stone draining board in the pantry stood an old chipped Wedgwood vase that nobody liked, but nobody could bring themselves to throw out. Empty.

'There's nothing in the vase,' Andrew called to her.

'It was full of peacock feathers.' We heard her tramp down the steps.

She came into the pantry, eyes almost bulging, and picked up the vase, as though the peacock feathers might be hidden inside its depths. 'He's playing jokes on me. Where's he hiding?' She ran to the full-length doors that housed the old larder and pulled them back. 'Where are you, you devil?'

'There's nobody in here, Smithy.'

'He must have gone upstairs.'

'We'd have seen him go past us,' I said.

'Then he's still down here, hiding.' She looked at Andrew. 'You mind the steps, so he can't slip out. Rose, come with me.'

But she marched me out of the pantry and we walked from one basement room to another, opening dusty doors and closing them. Cathal was nowhere to be seen.

'She must have imagined it,' Andrew whispered as we went back upstairs, leaving Smithy standing in smouldering silence in the pantry.

In the classroom Cathal greeted us as though nothing at all had happened earlier. 'Geography until lunchtime. We're going to look at different climates in the British Isles and their effect on types of farming.'

He drew a map of Britain on the blackboard in what seemed like a few easy lines and curves. I noticed that the bottoms of his cords were damp from the snow outside.

'Look at your geography books and the atlas, if necessary, and write me a paragraph on each of the following areas.' He wrote them on the board: *East Anglia*, *The West Country*, *The Lake District*. He walked to the door. 'I'll be back shortly.'

Andrew and I were not in the mood. I managed to scribble something about hills making it hard to use combine harvesters in the Lake District, and lack of rain meaning grass wouldn't grow to feed cows in East Anglia.

Andrew flicked through the pages of the geography textbook. He snorted. 'Daft cattle! Look.'

He showed me the photograph. One of the cows had stuck its neck through a fence and the other one was observing it with gums pulled back so it looked as though it was laughing at its companion.

'Stand up.' We hadn't heard Cathal coming in. He towered in the doorway, his face tight.

Andrew stood, looking puzzled.

'What did you just call me?'

Surely it was obvious from Andrew's blank expression that he didn't know what Cathal meant? But I did.

'He said "daft cattle".' I held up the textbook to show him the cows.

A half-smile flickered over Andrew's face. 'Oh, you thought I said –'

Cathal was in front of him in a few strides. 'Don't you dare!'

'I didn't say that, I –'

Cathal banged the desk so hard that pencils and pens jumped off it. 'I know boys, sonny, I know them very well. I know what they're like and I won't stand for cheek. Understand?'

Andrew blinked. 'Yes.'

Cathal took a step back. 'Lessons are over for today. Finish your work later on.'

We wandered out, too shocked to say much to one another. Smithy gave us searching looks when we came into the kitchen, but didn't ask why we'd finished early.

Cathal returned just before lunch. 'Rosie,' he said, poking his head around the drawing room door where I was hanging the latest Christmas cards. 'You're doing a great job there.'

I nodded, trying hard not to make eye contact.

He sniffed. 'Smells like vegetable soup for lunch. Shall we?' He stood back to let me through the door first. Cathal could be so polite, as though his only wish was for you to feel comfortable. Perhaps he was sorry about his loss of temper this morning.

Smithy narrowed her eyes as we came into the kitchen. 'Why did the children finish early?'

'We're now in the Christmas break.' He poured himself a glass of water. 'As of this lunchtime. Rose and Andrew, you're at liberty.' I wondered whether that meant we didn't need to finish the geography.

'So you'll be writing them reports?'

'You have a very outdated, formalistic view of education, Smithy.'

'Miss Smith, to you.'

'Miss Smith.' The corners of his mouth turned up in a smile. 'Nobody ever try to make you a missus? Ah, well.'

'That's that.' She untied her apron. 'I've had enough. I know what you're up to.'

'Oh, Smithy.' Mum was making calming motions with her hand. 'I'm sure –'

'He didn't mean anything, you're going to say.' Smithy hung the apron on the peg behind the door. 'There's none so blind as those that cannot see, Clarissa.'

Mum turned white. She started to say something, but Smithy held up a hand.

'It's just not right, what's happening here.' She nodded at Cathal. 'It's not what your mother would have wanted, for you or your children. I've stayed on to try to look after you all, but it's pointless if you won't pay attention.'

'Smithy, it's not for you to tell me how to lead my life.'

'No? Who else will if I don't?' She looked at Andrew and me and her eyes grew softer. 'Perhaps it is just me. Perhaps I'm old-fashioned. But this isn't what I'm used to. Strange men moving in and throwing their weight around. Shouting at children. Playing practical jokes.'

Mum looked at Cathal. He shrugged. 'I don't know what she means.'

'There were no peacock feathers down there, Smithy,' I said. 'Honest.'

Cathal was now watching Mum intently, hardly seeming to notice Smithy at all.

'Marcy wanted me there for Christmas anyway. And she's still on at me about moving in. They could do with my help.'

'But, Smithy –' Mum's face was growing paler by the second.

'I'd like to go tomorrow, if that's all right. That way I can help them get ready for Christmas. You don't need to pay me for this week as I haven't given proper notice.'

Mum looked as though Smithy had struck her. We'd all forgotten that Smithy wasn't really family. She worked at Fairfleet. For money.

~

It only took Smithy the rest of the day to pack up her life. How was it that someone who'd lived here for so long had so few possessions, filling only a large suitcase, a cardboard box and a holdall? After breakfast the next day Smithy brought her things down with Andrew. She pointed at the holdall.

'I can take that with me on my bicycle. Marcy's husband will drive over for the box and suitcase.'

'Smithy, you can't cycle in all this snow. If you really feel you have to go now, let Cathal drive you.' Mum was very pale this morning.

'I'm happy to cycle.' She put out her hand to Mum in farewell. 'The plough's cleared the main road. Goodbye, Clarissa. You take care and don't let . . .' She shook her head.

'Oh, Smithy.' Mum embraced her. 'I wish you'd stay. Have a good rest over Christmas with Marcy, but come back in the new year.' She released her reluctantly. 'This is for you.' She handed her a cheque.

'That's too much.' Smithy tried to pass it back to her.

'I've paid you until the end of February. It will give you time to think.'

Smithy placed the cheque in her holdall. 'Goodbye, Rose.' She hugged me as well. It was like being embraced by an oversized coat hanger with the coat still hanging on it. She let me go and held out a hand to Andrew.

'Take care of your mother.'

Mum, Andrew and I watched from the front door as she cycled down the drive, using the car tracks and making slow and upright progress on her old-fashioned black Raleigh, the holdall strapped to a carrier on the back. She wore a black coat and beret and looked like a large dark insect against the snow.

'I need a drink.' But surely Mum still wasn't supposed to be drinking?

'I'll pour you a sherry,' Cathal said, retreating back into the house. No mention of having one himself. But he'd been fiddling around with the decanters, I remembered. I couldn't think about that now, though. My concentration was still on Smithy as she cycled down the drive. I was unable to avert my eyes until she turned into the lane, out of sight.

19.

Smithy had been a servant, not a member of the family. I reminded myself of this harsh fact as I stood in the kitchen where she'd been such a fixture all those years ago.

But the reminder still didn't sit right, not now, not even to the adult me. She'd been part of us, part of Fairfleet, a house she'd dusted and polished and vacuumed and cherished. I'd returned here myself in a similarly ambiguous position to hers. Benny's nurse, close to him but not family.

I ran lightly upstairs and picked up the pile of Benny's laundry I'd left outside his door. The key to the basement was kept in a jar in the kitchen, just as it always had been.

At the basement door the key turned easily in my hand. I hesitated. Still time to abandon this plan. I told myself not to be ridiculous. Nobody could lock me in. But I was no longer the calm professional in her early forties.

I was twelve, going on thirteen, again.

No, I wasn't. I forced myself to return to the present, to the adult me. The only other person in this house was a very sick elderly man, bedbound upstairs. Nobody could imprison me down there.

'I'm doing this for you, Mum,' I whispered, pushing the basement door open.

I was doing it because I'd failed so completely to help her before. More than failed. And there must have been a moment before the very end when I could have told her more directly what I feared, forced her to confront Cathal, told her that Smithy was right to suspect him.

~

Do something about it, I'd wanted to scream at my mother as Smithy went. *Stop her from leaving. Smithy's prim and proper and snobbish and she hates anyone moving an ornament a quarter of an inch out of position. But you know she's right about Cathal.* Again that little bit of hidden memory about Cathal inside me had seemed to flash for an instant so that I felt I could retrieve it. Then it was gone again, dissolving in my fingers.

I didn't quite know what to do with myself now that Smithy had gone. I went back into the kitchen, which still smelled of the cleaning fluid she used to wash the floor; I stared at her apron, still hanging on the peg behind the door, at the dishcloth neatly folded over the taps. I put on my coat and went outdoors, standing by the lake, staring at nothing. It was too cold to stand still, so eventually I walked on, finding myself by the oak tree where the unused planks of wood still lay buried under the snow.

'He'll never finish it.'

I jumped at Andrew's voice.

'No?'

'The hospital just rang. Mum has missed an appointment.'

The hospital. Again the memory vibrated in my mind. But it wasn't the hospital itself. I looked at the clear blue sky. It had been clear and blue that day, too, but hot. Mum and I had sat on a bench in the shade, waiting for Granny to collect Mum's prescription. And something else had happened on that bench, something apparently insignificant. We hadn't been alone.

There'd been a man on the bench too. Reading a newspaper, but not so interested in the paper that he hadn't paid attention to what Mum and I said. I remembered his eyes on me, full of concern, even though we were perfect strangers. He'd listened to every word. I broke into a run towards the house.

'Rose?' Andrew ran after me. 'What's up?'

'I know why Cathal wanted to come here. It wasn't just chance.'

'What are you talking about?' He tugged at my sleeve, trying to stop me, but I ploughed on through the snow.

'Cathal. He was at the mental hospital, back in summer. He overheard us talking about Fairfleet. And about Mum's tablets. He knew she was ill.'

Andrew looked doubtful.

'He read that newspaper article about Granny dying. There was a photo of the house.'

He let me go. I reached the house, kicked off my boots, made for the stairs, was reaching for the door handle to Mum's room when I heard it: deep, rhythmic breathing from inside, slightly disjointed. Not one person; two people. Someone gasped. I stood still, listening.

'So you feel better about things now, Clarrie?' Cathal said eventually. 'My poor darling. You've been through so much.'

'I don't know,' Mum said. 'We should get up. The children –'

'Are safely outside, playing in the snow. And that meddlesome old woman isn't in our hair any more. We're free, Clarrie. Free to make plans.'

'I suppose so.' Mum sounded faint. 'I feel so sleepy. I don't want to rush into things. We need to think it all through.'

'Indeed we should. But now you need to rest, sweetheart.' I heard him move towards the door.

I shot away down the landing to stand behind my own partially closed bedroom door as he came out. He looked like a big, sleek, powerful cat this morning. His clothes looked smarter these days, too. Perhaps Mum was buying them for him.

He turned as he reached the stairs. 'Rosie?'

I shrank back into my room. It reminded me of how it had been that first day he'd been here, when I'd caught him scrutinizing the base of the blue vase and he'd known I was observing him.

Cathal stood at the top of the stairs, stiff-backed, frowning. He looked at the window above the stairs as though reassuring himself that I was still outside with my brother. He seemed to reassure himself because he carried on downstairs.

I lay down beside my bed and crawled underneath it. I hadn't done this since I'd been a tiny child, playing hide and seek with Andrew. I felt safer here. For the first time I could admit something to myself.

I was scared of him.

20.

Mum limped downstairs for breakfast the next morning. She sat at the table looking almost puzzled, as though there was something she wanted to say but couldn't quite think what it was. Cathal buttered her toast and poured her a cup of coffee.

'We need food.' She sounded exhausted. 'I should write a list, go through the cupboards. Smithy used to tell me when we ran out of things.'

'I'll manage the shopping,' Cathal said. 'Goodness me, I managed for myself for so many years, I'm quite able to sort out these domestic details.'

'And Christmas is so close now.' She put a hand to her head. 'I need to wake up properly and sort things out.'

'Leave it all to me.'

I thought of asking if I could go with him to the supermarket. It had been weeks since I'd left Fairfleet. Even crowded supermarket aisles and harassed shoppers stocking up on Christmas goods would be a change. But something about Mum, her weakness, her sense of confusion, made me anxious not to leave her.

'And I'll post this.' He picked up a foolscap-sized white envelope.

'Oh yes.' She sounded flat.

'If you're sure?' He lowered his voice. 'Want to talk about it some more?'

'I know you've explained it to me before.'

Andrew was looking from one of them to the other, eyes creased up into a frown.

'He's made her sign something,' he said, when we were alone together on the landing upstairs. 'I don't know what, but it's something to do with this house.'

'His school idea, perhaps.'

Andrew's frown became a scowl.

Cathal brought in two carrier bags of groceries when he returned. Mum hobbled into the kitchen while he was unpacking. I was sitting at the table eating a piece of bread and butter I'd helped myself to for tea.

'Foie gras?' She examined a tin in one of the bags. 'For Christmas Day?'

'I thought we'd have it tonight. On toast. Delicious.'

He pulled out a bottle of olive oil. Mum looked at it. She seemed more awake now. Earl Grey tea, Bath Oliver biscuits, Stilton, a tin of white peaches, lobster bisque, a bar of plain chocolate. I didn't even know what some of these foods were.

'Did you buy milk and bread?' She peeped inside the second bag. 'Eggs?'

'I'm sure I can go back if necessary.' He sounded more clipped than normal.

'We're short on rice as well.'

Cathal slammed a can of smoked oysters onto the table. 'I was trying to buy you some treats. To tempt your appetite.' His face was white. 'Do you want me to drive back through the ice now and get the damn milk and bread? Is that what you want?'

Mum blinked. Perhaps it was the first time she'd seen Cathal's rapid changes of mood. 'I was just saying . . .' Her cheeks were pink now. 'Look, you've been doing all the work. Sit down and relax.'

He allowed himself to be fussed over, Mum hopping round the table on her good leg and bringing him one of Granny's best china cups, brewing a pot of Earl Grey and putting out the Bath Oliver biscuits on a plate.

I slipped out and went up to Mum's bedroom. It was neat, the bed made. I opened the wardrobe, breathing in the sandalwood scent, and took out the wedding dress, laying it out on Mum's bed. I undid the plastic film and turned the dress over to look at all the little buttons up the back.

When Mum had worn this dress she must have felt safe, beautiful, cherished, as though nothing bad could ever happen, as though she were a Disney princess who'd been rescued. And some of that hope must have transmitted itself to the dress. Happiness must still be woven into its fine silky threads.

I stroked the front of the dress as though it were a cat. My fingers were small, pink invaders of the pure white surface. I was trespassing on my mother, on the private part of her life that Cathal hadn't yet invaded.

I snatched the dress up from the bed and rewrapped the plastic round it before closing it up in the wardrobe. I was on my way out when I was drawn to the little shrine on Mum's dressing table. Tempting to light one of the candles, but the shrine was Mum's special place, where she found the strength to get well and cope with all the bad things that had happened to her: Dad leaving, Granny dying, Smithy walking out. And Cathal? But Mum probably still regarded him as a good thing.

I resisted the candles, but couldn't promise myself that I wouldn't succumb in the future. The little pill bottle was empty when I shook it. How long had Mum not been taking her pills? I tried to remember when she'd last gone to the hospital to see the doctors as she was supposed to do regularly. Since Smithy had left I'd found it hard to remember the day of the week. It must be four days until Christmas. Three. Or perhaps five. Funny, only this time last year I'd known exactly how many hours there were until we'd open our stockings.

I was still standing there, empty pill bottle in hand, when a creak behind me made me look round.

'If I didn't know you better, Rosie, I'd think you were snooping on your mother.' Cathal smiled a smile that lit his denim-blue eyes very briefly and walked away.

'Please,' I begged the photograph on the shrine, 'please make him leave.'

~

'She needs to see what he's really like,' Andrew said. It was the following morning and we were standing at the frozen lake. He threw a stone at the ice. 'He's got her under a spell or something. And she doesn't care about us any more. It's nearly Christmas. Do you think she's even bought us a single present?'

Andrew threw another stone and it cracked the ice around it, splintering it into dozens of pieces so that it no longer reflected the pale sunshine.

'Mum does care about us.' I tried to inject conviction into my voice. 'She'll get presents.'

'She does what *he* wants.'

'It's not her fault.'

'He wormed his way in here and he can worm his way out.' Andrew was frowning. 'What did she say when you told her?'

I explained about my failed attempt to talk to Mum by herself last night, saying Cathal had interrupted us. 'They were making . . . noises,' I said.

Disgust washed over his face. 'We need to show her what he's really like,' he repeated. 'Then she'll listen.'

I tried to think of how this might be achieved.

'I'll think of something,' Andrew said, touching my shoulder lightly. He was a self-contained boy, rarely showing emotion or affection, but I knew then that he was feeling what I was feeling, wanting to show me reassurance, wanting to be the big brother. His eyes narrowed. 'Look.' He nodded over my shoulder. 'He's going out.'

I turned to see Cathal walking down the drive. Probably going down to the shop.

'Let's have a look upstairs, shall we?'

Cathal slept in Mum's room, as we knew, but kept some of his possessions in a bedroom on the second floor. We found a plastic carrier bag and an old brown suitcase underneath the bed.

'Bottles,' Andrew said, opening the bag. 'Vodka and gin. So much for him not drinking.' He pulled the suitcase out and tried to open it. Locked. Andrew gave a grunt of annoyance. But I'd seen something.

'What's that?' I pointed at bright blue fronds protruding from the side of the case, like a fringe. 'A feather. A *peacock* feather.'

We looked at one another. I tugged the fronds and little by little the eye became visible.

'There are more.' Andrew pointed at the tip of another feather now protruding underneath the lid. 'So he did fill that vase to bait Smithy. And then took the feathers out to make her feel stupid.'

'But how? We searched the whole basement. He wasn't down there. And he couldn't have got back up the steps without you seeing him.'

'He went out through the basement door to the garden.'

I must have looked puzzled.

'That old door that's kept locked, remember?' he explained. 'There's a key somewhere. Bet he's got it now.' Andrew stiffened at the sound of someone climbing the steps to the front door and shoved the suitcase back under the bed. 'Quick.' We took the feather we'd pulled out of the case and went downstairs, managing to get to the kitchen before Cathal came inside. Andrew hid the feather in the cupboard under the sink, where Smithy had stored the washing-up bowl and spare rubber gloves.

~

An outsider wouldn't have known Andrew was plotting. His expression was as impassive as ever. At lunch we sat in the kitchen. Cathal drank his soup, his eyes on Mum.

'The grey jumper would go better with that skirt,' he said.

'This one is easier for me to put on.'

'I'll help you put on the grey one after lunch.'

'I'm happy with this one, thank you.'

Cathal's features remained unmoved, but I saw him clench the soup spoon.

When we'd cleared the table Cathal asked Andrew to carry in logs from the woodshed to charge the stove in the drawing room. Andrew folded his arms.

'I'm tired.'

Mum stared at him.

'We're all tired, sonny.' Cathal looked amused. 'We only need an armful.'

'You do it, then.'

'I beg your pardon?' Some of the joviality fled from Cathal's face.

'I said *you* could bring the wood in.'

Cathal stood up. 'We need to talk. Outside, Andrew.'

Andrew looked at Mum. She said nothing.

'No.' Andrew sat back in his chair, folding his arms. Part of me wanted to cheer him; the other was horrified.

'Outside with me now, please.' The sharpness must have worked well when Cathal was a schoolteacher.

Andrew ignored him.

'I'm asking you for the last time.'

Andrew shrugged.

The blow fell so quickly that it took me a second to realize that Cathal had hit my brother with the back of his hand. A red mark already throbbed on Andrew's cheekbone. Andrew put a hand to his cheek, not seeming to understand why it hurt. Nobody was looking at Cathal.

I jumped up and ran the drying-up cloth under the cold tap. I'd seen Smithy do this before, when we'd been younger and had bumped into things or fallen.

'Hold this over it.' I pressed the wet cloth against my brother's cheek. Still nobody else had said anything. 'You shouldn't have done that,' I told Cathal, voice shaking.

Dad had smacked us on the backs of the legs once or twice when we'd been smaller. Rarely. Nobody in our family had ever hit anyone around the face. Never.

'How dare you?' Mum's words were like little splinters of ice. I wanted to cheer. She pulled herself up and hobbled round to Andrew. 'Let me.' She took the drying-up cloth herself and held it to his cheek. 'Fill the washing-up bowl with cold water and bring it over here, Rose.'

Cathal's mask of easy confidence crumpled for a moment when he heard her. Then, just as quickly, it returned. 'I'm so sorry,' he said. 'I lost my temper. Unforgiveable. Can I tell you how sorry I am, Andrew?'

Andrew was silent.

'Leave us,' Mum said.

Cathal hesitated. What would happen now if he refused? Mum was unable to walk at more than a slow, painful pace. Andrew appeared stunned by the blow. That left me. I knew I couldn't make Cathal Pearse, with his height, his strong hands and broad shoulders, leave the kitchen.

But he walked out.

'Tell her, Rose,' Andrew hissed. 'Tell her now.'

I explained about the hospital, how I'd seen Cathal there, how he'd listened in to our conversation. I worried that Mum wouldn't believe me, that it would sound like one of those memories that aren't really memories at all, but things you think of afterwards that seem to fill in the gaps in a story. She sat speechless as she pressed the cloth to Andrew's cheek. I couldn't read her expression.

'Go out to the telephone table. Look in Granny's address book. Smithy's niece is called Marcy Edwards. Ring Smithy. Tell her I need her. Ask her if her nephew will drive her over.'

I went into the hall, listening out for Cathal. The old burgundy leather address book was in the drawer underneath the Bakelite receiver. I found the number and dialled it. I hadn't used the telephone much to ring adults, apart from Dad. Ordinarily I'd have felt awkward, but today it felt normal. A young woman answered the phone. I asked for Miss Smith.

'She's taken my little one to Santa's grotto,' Marcy told me. 'Who's speaking?'

When I'd explained, Marcy promised that Smithy would come to the house. She was saying goodbye when the call ended abruptly, as if she'd put the phone down without meaning to. I returned to the kitchen and reported back to Mum.

'Good girl.' She removed the cloth from Andrew's face. 'The worst of the swelling has gone down. Thank God he didn't break the skin. I'd like to . . .' She stopped. 'This is the end now. Cathal has to leave.' She frowned. 'I think I know now why I always feel so tired. It's not just the tablets the psychiatrist gives me: it's sleeping tablets.'

'I didn't know you took those as well.'

'The doctor gave me some when Granny died. I didn't use them all. Cathal brings me a hot drink before I go to bed at night. I think he puts the tablets in the drink to make me feel woozy. Sometimes I know there are things bothering me, but I can't drag them out of my brain.' She rotated the sprained ankle. 'But last night he didn't notice that I hadn't drunk the cocoa. I think he'd been drinking. He says he doesn't touch alcohol, though.'

'He does.'

We told her about the bottles under the bed.

'There are other things I need to know,' she said. 'Calls we need to make. Rose, go and fetch the telephone directory.'

I brought it in. She flicked through the pages. 'Here's the solicitor's number.' She pointed at a name with a manicured finger. 'But I need to make the call; you can't make it for me. Can you take a chair out to the telephone so that I can sit down out there?'

'I'll do that.' Andrew stood up. The mark on his cheekbone still glowed, already taking on different hues. But when the chair was taken through and Mum sat down and picked up the black receiver she scowled.

'The line's dead.'

I remembered how my call to Marcy had ended so abruptly.

'He's cut the wire,' Andrew said. 'He must have gone outside to do it.'

Her eyes widened and she seemed to lose all colour from her face.

'There's a phone box outside the village shop,' she said. 'I'm going to write a number for you to call, Rose.' She tore a page from the telephone directory and scribbled it down, along with some other points.

'Ring him and tell him to expect a letter from me in the next few days. I know it's Christmas the day after tomorrow, but tell him it's important. In the meantime, ask him to find out anything he can about Cathal Pearse. Say he's been violent towards us and I don't want to go through with the college plan for Fairfleet.' She looked at me. 'Andrew will have to stay here, Rose. He's . . .'

Bigger than you, she meant. Andrew's voice had already broken and he was tall. Not large enough to pose a real challenge to Cathal, but more of a threat than I was.

Something about her decisiveness now told me that this morning's events hadn't come as a complete surprise to my mother. She was wearing a thick cardigan. I bent over her arm and rolled up the sleeve.

'Rose . . .' She tried to stop me.

On her arm I saw bruises. They were still red: fresh. I recalled Cathal's fury when he thought Andrew had been rude about him in the schoolroom, his anger when the chalk had snapped and all the other instances I'd not paid attention to.

Andrew stared at the marks without saying anything. I knew he wanted to find Cathal, to make him pay for doing that to Mum. 'Rose should ring the police as well,' he said.

'And what should she say?' Mum smiled gently. 'That a man I invited into my house has hit you and ill-treated me? They will expect to see more than bruises. They'll say it's just a domestic dispute.'

'*Just,*' Andrew muttered. Then he looked at me. 'Go to the phone box,' he said. 'Do what Mum says. Hurry.'

'Yes, hurry.' Mum spoke with composure, every bit Granny's daughter. But I could see the fingers of her uninjured hand clenching themselves together. 'But, Rose, mind how you go.'

'I'll go through the shrubbery,' I said.

The ghost of a smile played on my mother's lips. 'I used to do that, too, if I wanted to go and buy sweets without Granny knowing.' She looked more serious again. 'My bag's up in my room. You'll need to get some ten-pence pieces for the telephone. Everything you need to say's written down on that piece of paper.' She explained how to use the telephone.

I slunk upstairs, ears open in case Cathal was still around. At the bedroom door I stopped, placed my ear to the wood before tapping very softly on the door. No answer. I pushed the door open. He wasn't in there. Mum's black bag sat on the dressing-table stool. I took the purse and crept out again.

Downstairs in the hallway she emptied the purse of its few bits of silver. 'I'm sure I had some money in here.' She looked surprised. 'Never mind, it's enough for the telephone box.'

I was almost out of the front door when she called me back. 'I know I've been a useless mother,' she said, clutching my hand. 'That's all going to change now.'

I squeezed my way through the shrubbery and into the lane, finding it impossible not to look over my shoulder at intervals, in case Cathal was tracking me. How had it happened that this man had gained so much power over all of us? I asked myself this again and again as I crunched through the snow.

I'd never used a public telephone box before and studied the instructions carefully, glad Mum had explained it all to me first. The phone rang and rang. I was about to hang up when someone answered.

'They're all out at the firm's Christmas lunch,' a woman replied when I asked for Mum's solicitor. 'Doubt we'll see them back here this afternoon. I work in the next office. May I take a message?'

I tried to give her the details, but in the telling the story became garbled.

'So your Mum's boyfriend hit your brother and now he can't walk because his ankle is fractured?'

I explained that it was my mother's ankle that was fractured.

'And your mother's boyfriend caused the injury because your mother doesn't want you to go to school?'

'She doesn't *not* want us to go to school. She doesn't want him in the house. He's dangerous. Once he drove into someone. On purpose.' The pips went. I froze. Just in time I inserted more ten-pence pieces.

'There was a car crash?' the woman said. 'And you're truanting? Have the police been round to see you?'

'No.' I sighed. 'Perhaps it's easier if I call back tomorrow morning.'

'I'll tell the partners when they come back. You look after yourself. And call the police if you're worried.'

She sounded kind, but I knew she wouldn't pass on the message the way Mum had intended. My fault.

Meanwhile the document Mum had signed would still be on its way through the post alongside all the cheerful Christmas cards, giving Cathal the right to run this residential college at Fairfleet. And I hadn't even told the woman I'd spoken to about our own telephone not working any more. Perhaps I should just call the police right now, ask them to send a car to the house. Even if they couldn't do anything, it would show Cathal that we were on to him. Maybe he'd leave of his own accord if he thought the police were showing an interest.

The shop door opened. A middle-aged woman came outside. 'I'll bring those cabbages in before they turn to ice,' she said. I hadn't noticed the vegetables stacked outside the shop.

She looked at me. 'You're from Fairfleet, aren't you?'

I nodded.

'Haven't seen much of you since your grandmother passed away. I've seen your stepdad around, though.'

'He's not my stepdad.' The words sounded almost fierce. The interest on the shopkeeper's face grew more marked. I knew she'd be telling other shoppers that there was something odd about that Fairfleet family.

The door opened again. A woman a bit younger than Smithy stood shivering on the doorstep. 'Want me to help with those veg?'

'I'm all right, Mum, you keep in the warm.'

But the older woman's attention was on me. 'You're Clarissa's daughter, aren't you? What's happening up at the house? I used to know some of the boys who lived up there during the war.'

For a second I was tempted to tell her everything. This woman might be a way of communicating with the outside world. Then I looked again at the sharp curiosity in her eyes. I couldn't tell her about Cathal and the way he'd eased his way into our family. How to explain Mum's weakness? How to explain that she hadn't always been like this, but that separation from Dad, her illness and Granny dying had worn her down? It would be disloyal to tell this woman those things, to let her imagine Mum and Cathal lying together in Mum's room, making those noises.

'We're keeping ourselves busy,' I said.

'You heard from Alice Smith? She left sudden, didn't she?'

I nodded.

'Those were good times, those war years,' the woman said, sounding wistful.

'Get inside, Mum,' her daughter ordered. 'You're letting all the heat out of the shop.'

I made my escape, walking as quickly as I could through the snow. I wished I'd thought to save some of the coins.

As I reached Fairfleet I remembered to squeeze back through the hole in the fence. I emerged from the shrubbery, shaking snow off my shoulders, cold, uncertain that I'd achieved anything helpful at all.

The sky was a mink-coloured wash behind the house. More snow was on its way; now it would be even harder to make contact with people outside Fairfleet. I broke into a run.

My brother met me by the shrubbery, brandishing an envelope. 'He's back. But Mum wrote this, though, to the lawyers, telling them she's changed her mind about the legal agreement.'

I looked at the letter. 'There's no stamp.'

'Have you got any coins left from the phone?'

I shook my head.

He looked white.

'There must be more coins somewhere.' Hadn't Smithy retrieved ten-pence pieces from under sofa cushions when she was cleaning? And we could search the pockets of our summer clothes.

'What should I do with this in the meanwhile?' He waved the envelope. 'We can't let him get hold of it. It's got other stuff in it, all about what she suspects Cathal has been up to in the past. It's probably not the first time he's tried to wriggle his way into people's families and take over their property.'

I scanned the house mentally, disregarding cupboards and drawers. Then I thought of Smithy lugging furniture down to the basement, those chests of drawers and bedside tables.

'I'll hide it in the basement.' I held out my hand for the letter. 'Until we can post it in the morning.'

He looked as though he wanted to argue, but I knew I would be lighter on my feet, that I could creep across the hallway and down into the basement without Cathal hearing me.

I took a circuitous route back to the house, hugging the garden wall until I reached the topiary garden. I hid behind the overgrown box-tree elephant with its white mantle of snow, peeping through the kitchen window. Cathal was with Mum. She sat pale-faced at the table listening to whatever it was he was telling her. I'd have to creep past the doorway and pray the basement door had been left unlocked. If it hadn't been, I'd have to hide somewhere until Cathal left the kitchen and I could retrieve the key from the jar.

The front door had been left on the latch and opened quietly. I removed my coat and boots slowly and deliberately, placing them on the mat without a sound. I could hear Mum and Cathal now. She was telling him that he had to go, that she wanted no more to do with him. His reply was a low rumble I couldn't hear clearly. I stuffed the letter up my jumper.

My socked feet moved me towards the kitchen. The door was open. He'd hear me. But still they kept on talking. His back was to me. Mum was out of sight. Good: she wouldn't show any reaction at my appearance.

The couple of feet of open doorway felt like a thousand miles as I inched my way past. Once, Cathal stopped talking and I froze. But then I heard liquid pouring into a glass.

'You said you didn't drink,' Mum said. 'Remember? When you first came here?'

His reply was inaudible. I hurried on a bit, reaching the basement door. The key was in the lock and the door opened to my touch. I almost sobbed with relief. I knew it would emit a slight squeak if I pushed it all the way open, so I squeezed myself through the narrowest gap I could manage, taking my time, not letting myself rush it.

I looked longingly at the light switch on the wall. The short winter day was almost over. Too risky: Cathal might see the beam shining beneath the door. I crept down the stone steps, one hand out in front of me. At the bottom I stood still, listening. I made out the deep, melodic tones of Cathal's voice in the kitchen as I padded along the flagstone floor. The room where Smithy had stored the old furniture was right at the end of this passageway. If only there'd been time to find a torch. Eventually my eyes adjusted to the gloom. I made out the white oblong of the door I needed.

Something crashed above me. Someone shouted. Andrew? Mum? And then Cathal raised his voice in a deep bay of anger. I hurried towards the door. Inside, the dark shapes of the discarded furniture greeted me like silent friends. I squeezed myself between a cupboard and a bedside table, hands feeling for drawers. I found one and pulled it open. The lining paper rose as I poked underneath it. Something was preventing me from lifting it up completely, something dark and heavy, like a leather bag or pouch. I pushed the letter underneath the lining paper and pulled the unidentifiable leather object back over it. I wriggled my way free of the furniture and was almost out again when I heard the basement door open. I held my breath and crouched down behind the cupboard.

Cathal's footsteps came down the stone-floored passage. Lights turned on and off as he went from room to room. There was just space for me to squeeze to a safer position between the tallboy and wardrobe. I told myself not to rush, to move carefully, there was time.

I slid in between the two bits of furniture, feeling their solid presence as reassurance. Cathal was in the doorway now. The light came on. I was still, my breath coming very light and slow. He couldn't hear me.

He switched off the light again. I waited until he'd reached the cellar steps before I stood. As I moved, I caught the side of the bedside table on my thigh. I let out a gasp.

'Rosie?' He turned back and I heard his footsteps returning to me. 'I know you're in there. If you like this basement so much you can stay down here. All night.'

I heard him shut and lock the door. Then I was alone with my fear and frustration.

21.

Fear and frustration. That's what this basement smelled like now to the adult me, the nurse Rosamond Hunter. Decades later the bitter note overcut the scent of the apples they'd once stored down here. A note that even Benny's benign ownership of Fairfleet for the last thirty years hadn't smoothed away.

I made myself take a few more steps until I was standing on the flagstone floor. This was mad. The furniture would long since have been cleared out of the storage room. Mum's envelope wouldn't still be stuffed inside the drawer of a chest stored down here. But still I walked down the basement steps, telling myself there was just a chance that the letter might have stayed down here during all the years of Benny's ownership of Fairfleet. Benny hadn't thrown much out, Sarah had told me when I'd arrived, just stored discarded furniture down here.

I trod along the passage, keeping my eyes focused ahead of me as though afraid that demons lurked just out of sight, still feeling the childish hope that if I didn't actually make eye contact with them they wouldn't bother me. I reached the laundry room. The familiar outlines of washing machine and dryer, the soap-powder box, the bundling of the washing into the machine – all these things soothed me for a few minutes. When the machine was on I was tempted just to go back upstairs again.

But on I went down the passage, half expecting, half hoping the storage room would be locked. Then I'd have an excuse not to go in. But the door opened.

Inside stood a collection of furniture. Chairs, tables, chests of drawers. Standard lamps. Desks. All jammed together. I didn't recognize most of it. It would take me ages to move the things around so that I could open drawers. And there was no way that this could be done without a lot of noise. I stared at the objects and it was like staring at a projection of my own mind: a collection of unrelated objects, dusty yet throbbing with old emotion. Anger, mostly; bitter anger that, even as an adult, I could still taste in my mouth.

Cathal had meant it when he said I'd be locked in the basement all night.

I emerged from my hiding place between the old pieces of furniture in the storage room to slump on the stone staircase, my face resting against the cellar door, almost comatose, legs numb, fingers blue from cold. I covered myself in a fur-lined coat I'd found in the storage room and lay on an old velvet curtain. Nightmares punctuated my sleep.

A devil materialized through the wall of the basement corridor. It stalked the rooms, finally coming to stand over me and stare down at me as I lay there. I felt the hatred in its red eyes scorching me. I was down in hell and I would suffer worse pain.

I woke, a scream on my lips, to find myself alone, with just the hint of a draught from the corridor behind disturbing me. An open window in one of the rooms, I told myself. Sometimes Smithy opened them, even in winter, to prevent damp. Just a draught.

Eventually I slept again. But the devil figure turned into a different monster with a smooth, handsome face like Cathal's. I could have sworn that he had descended to the basement to mock me, but my head was still resting against the basement door leading into the hallway and I knew he could not have come in without standing on me. Granny came to me as well, briefly, and told me I shouldn't have unlocked the door, but I didn't understand what she meant.

I heard the devil or the monster moving around in the storage room, but as long as I didn't wake up properly to look at him he couldn't harm me.

When the putty-coloured dawn finally broke I woke properly, my neck aching. Nobody came to help me. Mum couldn't have known what was happening. Or if she did, she was somehow powerless to help: I didn't like to think about what Cathal must have done to her to prevent her from coming down and letting me out. At some point in the morning I thought I heard voices above me in the entrance hall, but couldn't make out whom they belonged to. Wheels scrunched over the snow-topped gravel in the drive. Not a car, something smaller and lighter – a bicycle? Footsteps ran after it, followed by shouting. A brief silence, then an engine turned over and a car swooshed through the snow. I hoped someone would come for me then, but nobody came near the cellar door.

I found an old bucket in the scullery and peed into it when I couldn't hold off any longer. The cold crept up the stone floor and into my bones. I put on a pair of boots I found in a chest, lined with sheepskin but chewed by mice. Probably Granny's old flying boots from the war.

A sudden yellow light made me blink. A tall shape stood in the bright rectangle where the closed door had been. I quivered in front of his pale gaze. He smiled at me. I knew I must look small, grubby, defeated.

'Had time to think, have we?'

I said nothing. My mouth felt dry and my legs hurt as I tried to stand up. I lurched against the wall.

'Didn't your mother tell you lying was wrong, Rosie?' His voice was gentle. 'Perhaps she doesn't really know that herself.'

'Where is my mother?'

He hesitated. 'Sleeping.'

'What have you done to her?'

'She needed to rest.'

'You're lying.' I tried to wriggle away from him as he took me by the shoulders.

'Your mother's not really one for discipline, is she? But someone has to take responsibility. Sometimes that means punishing a child. For its own sake.'

'You're not my father,' I said. 'You've got no right to punish me. We don't want you here.'

He took one hand off my shoulders to open the kitchen door.

I eyed the expanse of hallway leading to the front door, wondering if I had enough strength to sprint there while he was distracted. I pulled away from him. But not quickly enough. He swung round and yanked me by the hair. 'Don't make me furious, Rosie. I'm trying so hard to be patient.'

22.

I trembled where I stood now, a woman of forty remembering the scared child she'd once been. Gathering my self-control, I peered around the storage room again. Surely this was fruitless? Someone would long ago have cleared out all the drawers and cupboards.

I pulled out the top drawer of a tallboy. It squeaked as it opened and I could only see a few inches inside because the chest was so closely placed against a wardrobe. A dark, squashed leather object met my gaze, smelling of old leather. I tugged it out. Some of the leather had decayed or been the victim of mice. Letters were embossed onto the surface, worn away now so that I could only make out an O, D and N . An old bag? No, a ball. Nothing else in the drawer. I replaced the ball.

I opened a second, third and subsequent drawers, then turned to the two drawers at the bottom of an oak wardrobe, again finding nothing. Examinations of a bureau and bedside table yielded nothing except a screwed-up piece of lined paper with faded pencil writing on it that I couldn't read. By now my hands were covered in a film of dust. I shut the bedside table drawer and the handle came off in my fingers. I spent precious minutes replacing it.

This was insanity. Andrew was right. If Benny had found an envelope addressed to what was obviously a professional firm of some kind he would have passed it on. I already knew him well enough from sitting by his bed to be sure that he wouldn't have thrown the letter away or left it in the drawer. He'd talked to me of his work as a journalist, of the notebooks he'd kept, of how he'd eagerly welcomed computers as an efficient way to file notes and maintain databases of contacts. He was a meticulous person, Benny.

My patient, Benny. Alone upstairs.

I blew the dust off my hands. I hadn't needed to come down into this basement at all, but at least I had faced my old fears. Perhaps that was why I'd needed to come back to the house.

Time to return to Benny. It was almost a relief to know that I wasn't going to look any further for the letter. I'd text James, tell him he'd been right about the futility of my mission. I would concentrate on being the best nurse and companion to Benny I could be.

The telephone rang upstairs. I was locking the cellar door when Sarah came out of the kitchen. I hadn't heard her footsteps. A quick glance at her told me why: her black cashmere coat was covered in snow; it would have muffled the sound of her feet across the garden.

'Just checking none of Benny's washing needed to go into the dryer,' I told her.

The phone rang again and I followed her into the kitchen.

Another of Benny's friends. 'Keep in touch,' she said to whoever was calling. 'I'll tell him to call you on his mobile. He loves hearing from you.'

'So many calls.' She replaced the phone on its holder. 'So many people wanting to know how he is, wanting to send him books or magazines. This weather makes it so hard.'

She looked out of the window. 'I hope Benny's friends can get here safely. That snow's settling now.'

'It's certainly cold enough.'

'I'll have to find someone to clear the drive and paths.' She reached for the pad she kept by the telephone and wrote a note to herself. 'It was like an ice-rink out there last year. If we had an emergency it would be impossible for them to get up here.'

'I'd better go up to Benny now,' I said. 'Get him ready for his guests.'

She finished her note and nodded at me. I thought I could make out traces of curiosity in her well-groomed features. Perhaps she guessed that I'd been nosy, snooping down in the basement.

I opened Benny's door gently. He was dozing in his chair. I removed the laptop from his lap and placed it on the dressing table. The screen had gone into sleep mode. I covered him with a blanket. Beside him on the floor lay a large album of press cuttings. I put it on the dressing table. He'd been looking at some of the articles he'd written years ago, at what must have been the very beginning of his journalistic career. A short piece on a spate of burglaries in Kingston upon Thames. A longer article on a spaniel that had saved a family in New Maldon, Surrey from burning to death in a house fire. I turned the pages. By the late fifties and early sixties he'd been writing longer pieces for local and regional papers. After that he'd moved to the nationals. I scanned a report on the Six-Day War for *The Times* before closing the album.

I could tell by looking at him that his sleep was troubled, dreams buffeting him. The doctor had changed his drugs. I checked the notes again to make sure I knew exactly what I was to dispense from now on.

He stirred in his sleep. Muttered something. I moved closer to hear.

'. . . shouldn't be on the train. Someone else. Don't tell Vati.'

Vati was German for *Daddy*, I remembered. Why wouldn't he want his father to know he was on a train? I reminded myself that dreams seldom make much sense.

He said something about some little children who seemed to be in the carriage with him. Of course. In his dream it was 1939 and he was trying to leave Germany, but he seemed so worried, so unsure he should be there.

'Take someone else,' he muttered again. 'Hurry up. It's almost too late. Here are the travel papers. And hide the vase. It was Rudi.' And with that he opened his eyes and looked round the room and then at me, appearing to relax as he woke up properly. I watched as he shook away the dreams and the sophisticated persona of Benny Gault slipped back into place.

'Hello, Benny.' I poured him some water and handed it to him. His mouth was always dry when he woke. 'You've been dreaming,' I told him. 'About travel papers and trains.' A guarded look came over his face.

'What did I say?'

'You told someone to hurry up. Something about a vase? And you mentioned your father. And someone called Rudi.'

At the mention of the name his eyes widened. Who was Rudi? A friend? A brother? I didn't like to ask. So many of Benny's close childhood circle must have perished. I remembered what Sarah had told me about Benny's avoidance of the subject.

'What nonsense goes through my mind while I'm asleep.' He grinned. 'Could you help me get freshened up and dressed?'

When he was ready and I'd tidied his room, I went back down to the kitchen. I knew I had aroused suspicions in Sarah's mind and I was determined to quell them.

She had cleared the kitchen of baking ingredients and trays. We ate at the table, the air fragrant with the scent of Christmas. I felt a faint thrill; it had been years since I'd been excited by the arrival of the feast, but the smell of the mince pies drew me back to an earlier, more innocent age. I remembered Granny making Christmas food for us: boiling up puddings, stirring up cakes. My mother had loved

Christmas too and passed on the affection to me. But I would have no child to whom I could transmit the old traditions of baking and decorating. My hand went to my lower abdomen.

'Just in time to sample this.' Sarah took a freshly baked mince pie off a cooler and placed one on a plate for me. Her face was as friendly as ever as she added a dollop of double cream. The pastry dissolved on my tongue and the fruit filling was rich and moist. I praised it. 'Not long till Christmas now,' she said. 'I just hope he can hang on. On the other hand, I don't want him to feel that he has to be here for Christmas for my sake. Not if it's too . . .' She turned her back for a moment. 'Sorry. I've known him a long time. I was with them when his wife Lisa grew ill and died, and now this.'

My self-pity dissolved.

'He might make Christmas,' I said. 'Let's tempt him with one of your pies later, get him into the festive spirit.' Perhaps he wouldn't manage a whole one, but a little bit of the melting pastry and luscious filling might be irresistible, even to a man as sick as Benny.

Hope flickered in her eyes.

'And you should try to rest during the day,' I said gently. 'The nights will start to become more demanding.' Last night Sarah and I had operated a rota: one of us on until midnight, the other taking over until six in the morning, sitting in the armchair beside Benny's bed, dozing while he slept, waking when he woke.

I looked around this expensively furnished kitchen, with its stainless-steel appliances and the oak unit doors. I remembered the mismatched pieces of furniture in here in Granny's time. Mismatched, but beautiful and kept spotless by Smithy. Granny hadn't had to cook as a young woman. Even Smithy wouldn't have been expected to cook when she'd started working here in the pre-war years: it hadn't been her job. They'd both had to learn how to exist in the new world.

Thinking of old family history made me think of Benny and his bad dreams. Not surprising, given what had happened in Germany just before his departure. Kristallnacht, when the Nazis had set synagogues on fire and smashed the windows of Jewish businesses, must have been only a month or so earlier.

'The last weeks in Germany must have been a time of great panic,' I said. 'He dreams about it, doesn't he?'

'It might be the drugs,' Sarah said. 'But God knows, he had plenty to be panicked about in Germany. He rarely talks about that time.' She picked up an orange from the bowl on the worktop and started grating its zest onto a plate.

I made a note to myself to talk to the doctor about the morphine.

'Who's Rudi?' I asked. 'Did Benny have brothers and sisters? It must have been awful for him to leave people behind.'

She looked surprised. 'He was an only child. He's never mentioned a Rudi.'

Sarah yawned. 'I might lie down with my book for half an hour when Benny's guests have arrived. I love the preparations for Christmas, but they take it out of me.'

'You've been working hard,' I said. 'And not getting as much sleep as you should.'

'I like to make a bit of a splash. And there's not long to go now.' For a moment she looked like a small, excited girl. The doubt I'd seen in her expression when she'd caught me coming up from the basement had gone now.

I wondered who would come to Fairfleet to share Christmas Day with them. I'd probably be here. James was spending the holiday with his daughter, Catherine. So he'd be fine. The thought made me feel lonely. Not for the first time I promised myself that when I'd finished this job, I'd devote more time to him. While Sarah busied herself with weighing out ingredients I checked messages on my phone.

As I'd expected, there was one from James, asking if things were still going well. I texted a quick affirmative reply.

We'd met at a charity event in London nearly two years ago, before I'd gone to Singapore. James was a widowed English and drama teacher at a secondary school in southeast London. Neither of us particularly enjoyed white-wine-and-canapé events and it had been a relief to start chatting to him and find that we shared the same sense of humour and a love of Victorian novels. Endless school plays kept him busy during term-time and he liked spending time in second-hand bookshops during holidays. We seemed perfectly matched, enjoying time together but relishing days spent apart. All the same, I hadn't expected the relationship to last my two months in the Far East.

When I'd returned from Singapore, though, we'd picked up the relationship again. He'd rented out his old marital home and moved into my apartment, so convenient for the new teaching post in east London he'd recently taken on. We had almost become a proper unit, a little household, a family. Almost.

My running away to Fairfleet probably hadn't been the best way of nurturing our relationship. And it was, as people had persistently reminded me, a high-risk strategy. If Sarah found out who I was she might terminate my employment. No danger of that for now, though. Who'd remember a pale, thin girl who'd lived here for a period of months back in the early eighties? The old woman in the shop? Perhaps. But she wouldn't be able to link Rosamond Hunter, forty-something nurse, with Rose Madison, not yet thirteen.

When we'd recovered from the immediate fallout of what had happened here at Fairfleet, Dad had settled us in schools in another county. There'd been no time to say goodbye to the few people we knew locally. When I'd abandoned my medical career, I worked in Europe: Italy and France, mainly, teaching English and looking after children. I hadn't stepped foot anywhere near Fairfleet until now.

There was another message on my phone, from my brother: *Hope you're all right. Still worried about why you're doing this. Nothing that happened back then was your fault.*

All going well at Fairfleet, I replied.

A noise outside the kitchen window made me look up. A man was shovelling snow off the path.

'Did I tell you?' Sarah asked. 'I found someone to clear all the paths and the drive. It may snow again, I know, but at least we'll be ahead with the job.'

I watched the man, who brandished the shovel in jerky movements, a balaclava over his face. I wondered how cold it was out there now. I hadn't been out today. The sun was appearing, weak and pale, but a welcome presence. This might be the day's last half-hour of sunshine.

The front doorbell rang. 'That'll be Benny's friends.' Sarah went to let them in.

I bundled myself up in scarf, hat and boots. The air was harsh on my skin to start with, but as I walked I could feel my head clear. I made for the lake, admiring the effects of the low-lying pink-tinted sun on its icy surface. The water rarely froze all the way over like this. I could only remember a couple of occasions in my lifetime when it had happened. A heron flew over the water, very low, as though hunting out a break in the ice but finding none. The bird continued on to the shore, perching on the small jetty.

Once, when Mum, Dad, Andrew and I had been staying here with Granny, we'd found old skates in the basement and gone out onto the ice. I'd been very small, perhaps only four or five. We formed a line, Andrew and I in the middle, with Mum and Dad skating on the outside, all holding hands. Mum balanced on her skates with perfect poise, holding my hand and keeping me upright.

The heron watched me from the jetty as I remembered all this. But it was too cold to stay still for long, so I made a loop of the lake, striding out to make my blood run warm, passing beside the hedge and fence separating Fairfleet from the houses built in the eighties. From this position the house looked blood-stained by the sunset. I walked more quickly.

I was almost back at the kitchen door when the snow-shoveller shuffled into view. All I could see of his features through his balaclava were his eyes: red-rimmed but still very blue. I noticed that the hand holding the spade shook. He moved stiffly, as though the cold had eaten into his bones.

'Are you all right?' I asked. 'Would you like a hot drink?'

He shook his head hastily, muttering something, but continued to stare at me for a moment. I put a hand to my arm, rubbing the scarred skin through the layers of winter clothing.

'He must be frozen,' Sarah said when I came into the warm kitchen. She must have watched the exchange. 'But he was very keen to take on the work. I was surprised by his quick response. I suppose people are eager for any kind of work these days.' She was loading a tray with tea cups, saucers and a plate of mince pies for the guests.

I peered outside. The man was shuffling off, holding the spade awkwardly, as though it hurt his hand. Easy to forget that there were people in such need of cash. Especially this time of year. I was fortunate; I had money. Work in a warm and comfortable house with an intelligent and likeable client. People in my life who loved me.

'Shall I draw the blinds?' I asked, keen to block out the dying afternoon.

23.

'Tell me more about yourself.' Benny sat back, observing me. His friends' visit the previous afternoon had boosted his spirits but wearied him. I'd heard them all laughing in his room and felt a moment of near-envy. Now he was sitting up in his armchair, looking as alert as he had in his television days, but very gaunt. His hands shook as he placed his newspaper down beside his laptop. 'Where did you live as a child? Did you have brothers and sisters?' He rolled his eyes and the professional in me noted how yellow the whites had become. 'Listen to me. I'm back in investigative mode. Or just being plain nosy, as my wife used to say.'

I was prepared for this and had composed an edited version of my life, jumping straight from Mum and Dad's separation to us going to live with Dad, mentioning Mum's death only in passing. I said nothing about Fairfleet.

I talked about the times spent away at boarding school, or working in Lyons for six months before university so that I could learn to speak French fluently. I told him more stories about my working life in France and Italy: the families I'd loved and those I'd struggled with. I described the Milanese family who'd tried to marry me off to an errant nephew because they thought I'd straighten him out, and the family who fed me one small meal a day, forcing me to subsist on croissants from the bakery across the road. I didn't mention my original career choice and what had brought it crashing to a halt.

His expression was sharp as he listened. I finished and ran my fingers over the cover of *Great Expectations* lying in my lap.

'Is your father still alive?' he asked.

I told him about Dad and his second wife, the tennis player, Marie, who'd become a loved stepmother, and their house in the French Alps.

'And you have a flat in Docklands?'

I nodded. He was silent for a moment. Probably wondering how my job financed a property of that kind.

'Sometimes I think I've seen you before,' he said, matter-of-factly.

I stared back at him, meeting his eyes, not flinching.

'You weren't in a studio audience for one of my TV interviews, were you?'

I shook my head. 'Perhaps I've got a doppelganger.' I smiled breezily, but it struck me that I well might have: a ghost version of my old self hanging around Fairfleet. Perhaps Benny had glimpsed this alternative me: the me who might have evolved if Cathal hadn't turned up, the adult version of the girl who'd lain out there on the sunny daisy-covered lawn with my brother and mother.

Then memory shot me an image so sharp that I almost cried out. I prayed Benny hadn't noticed my shock. He *had* seen me before. He had entered my childhood briefly. It had happened on that summer afternoon out on the lawn.

Just before Cathal's bike had squeaked its way towards us I'd spotted a man in a white suit, with a Panama hat. Standing across the lake and staring at us. He'd smiled and waved at me. The day had been perfect: warm air shimmering over the lake, the smell of flowers from the overgrown flowerbeds. Cathal had still been whole minutes away from reaching Mum. If I could only travel back in time and poke a stick into his bicycle wheels to prevent him from cycling up the lane.

But surely Benny couldn't link me to a thirteen-year-old he'd glimpsed briefly? There must be something about me that reminded him of my grandmother.

I needed to be on my guard. I didn't want to be guarded, though. I wanted to tell. My mouth was opening.

Someone knocked on the door. Sarah came in. 'The doctor's here,' she said. 'He was passing and thought he'd come early to avoid the snow that's forecast later.'

With a mixture of relief and regret I stood up to fetch Benny's medication and notes.

The doctor, a tired-looking man nearing retirement age, listened to Benny's heart and took his blood pressure. He asked Benny some questions about his eating and what he termed outputs and whether he was in pain. Benny answered in curt sentences.

'I hate all this, you know. Oh, not you, doc,' he gave his sudden dazzling smile. 'But the whole business of dying. Not the thought of death itself. That I can handle.' He glanced at the photograph of his wife, perhaps acknowledging that she'd gone this way before him and he'd be following her. 'But everything that might come first.'

The doctor touched his arm. 'I promise you, Benny, that as a team we will do all in our power to make sure you're never frightened or in pain.'

'I promise, too,' I said, the words coming out more vehemently than I had expected. The doctor and I exchanged glances. I knew we were thinking the same thing: death was coming closer.

'It's not that.' Benny sighed. 'Though obviously not being in pain is good. It's the damn dreams.'

'It might be the medication.' The doctor was examining Benny's notes.

'They're real,' Benny muttered. 'The things I see. They happened.'

The doctor studied him silently. 'I know only very little about the circumstances of your leaving Germany as a young boy. It doesn't surprise me that it might come back to haunt you. Would you like to see a –'

'No priests or shrinks, thank you,' Benny said quickly.

'I can prescribe something to help with the agitation,' the doctor said.

'I don't want sedatives either. My subconscious and I will just have to find some way of getting along together.'

It was a comment lightly made, but I sensed that Benny was rattled. Whatever it was that was haunting his sleep needed driving away, exorcising. I wondered whether he'd confide in me, whether it would help him if he could.

'Let me know how it goes over the next day,' the doctor told me as I showed him out. 'He's going to need the pump soon, for the morphine.'

We discussed painkillers, delivery methods and antipsychotics. I wrote notes and asked questions.

The doctor gave me an appraising look. 'You're very well informed on pharmaceuticals.'

I smiled, saying nothing. I went back to Benny and saw he was sleeping again, tranquilly enough, it seemed now.

My first husband hadn't understood why I enjoyed the closeness I built up with patients. James, I felt, had an inkling of why this aspect of the job appealed. Perhaps because he also had a job that required trust from people: teenagers, in his case, some of them troubled, difficult young people.

James still didn't know I'd given up on the search for my mother's letter. I went to my bedroom to ring him, but his phone was on voicemail. I sent him a text instead.

All well. Seem to be building rapport with Benny. No sign of Mum's letter, but this doesn't matter any more. I've put demons behind me now.

I felt better having sent the message. The snowfall had slowed. Fitful sunshine lit the garden, though more clouds clustered, threatening a fresh snow dump. I decided to take a few minutes' fresh air and wrapped up to go outside.

A few minutes out in the garden revived me. It was impossible not to respond to this winter perfection. Someone would need to shake branches and bushes free of their white drapery before they were damaged, but it would be a shame. The box-tree shapes were particularly enchanting. I took photographs on my mobile. As I went back inside snowflakes were falling again.

Benny's room was tidy and there was nothing that needed doing, so I sat watching him until he woke. I showed him the images on my phone.

'Winter perfection,' he said. 'I do miss the topiary animals, though.'

I knew what he meant. I also missed my childhood friends: the fox, the elephant, the pig. And the Spitfire.

'You've still got rosy cheeks, Rosamond.' He handed me back my mobile. 'Can you help me to the window? I'd like to look at the trees in the front with the snow on them. I'm fond of those old oaks and chestnuts.'

I wrapped his dressing gown around his shoulders and helped him out of the chair. He winced as he stood, looking irritated when he realized I'd noticed. We stood at the window looking out at the white trees. The snow was covering the tracks in the drive left by the doctor's car. I tried not to replay my mother's sledge ride down the same route, when Cathal had driven too fast and she'd fallen off.

'I hope Sarah doesn't need to go out in the car today,' Benny said. 'But she's sensible.' He shook his head. 'So sensible I was surprised she didn't throw me over when I became ill, go and work somewhere more fun. We used to have dinner parties here. Weekend guests. People coming and going.' He smiled, remembering it. 'Sarah and Lisa spent hours planning menus and preparing bedrooms, poring over every detail. Sarah always worried they'd missed something.'

Yet sensible Sarah *had* missed something when she'd let me into Fairfleet. I shivered, imagining her response if she found out who I was. James and Andrew had probably been right: if I'd been open at the beginning they might have let me come to Fairfleet as a nurse anyway. My hidden identity would look much more suspicious if the truth eventually slipped out. They might think I'd come back to make some kind of claim on Benny. I hoped he'd forgotten about the conversation we'd had earlier.

Benny stood there for nearly five minutes, probably learning the scene by heart in case it was the last time he saw such snow.

'It reminds me of Germany,' he said.

'You probably had proper winters out there every year,' I said. Only that one particular English winter thirty years ago really stuck in my memory.

'I remember being out in the garden with a friend one snowy night. The moon was out and the white bushes and lawn shone with light. It was almost like daylight. We had to hide because . . .' He stopped. Perhaps another memory he couldn't face was surfacing. He stared at the snowy scene for another moment.

'I'd like to go back to bed now,' he said. 'I don't think I'll get up again today.'

I helped him lie down and returned to the window to draw the curtains. Sarah's snow-man was pushing a wheelbarrow full of salt and grit across the front of the house. He stopped, rubbing the top of his arm. Heavy physical work like this in freezing air must make his muscles ache. And he wasn't young, either, I could tell. He moved on stiffly. His hand rubbed the side of the balaclava, as though his head was aching in the cold.

I turned back to Benny. He seemed older this morning, sicker. I didn't want to leave his side and sat quietly with him. He passed through a dreamless sleep into a more agitated state.

Benny said, quite clearly: 'Tell them it was a mistake.' His face, even in sleep, was full of concern for this friend of his.

'What was?' I whispered to him, not expecting that he would respond to the question. But his eyes flicked open for a moment.

'I couldn't make them understand.' He sighed and closed his eyes, seeming to jerk back into his uneasy sleep. 'Rudi was just trying to help.'

I placed the laptop next to him on the bedside table in case he needed it when he woke up.

24.

Benny was dreaming, he knew that. Real life was back with that nurse, Rosamond Hunter, who couldn't be whom he sometimes felt she might be, because Harriet Dorner had been dead for thirty years.

'Harriet had appendicitis and it killed her,' he told the boy who sometimes stood beside his bed. Benny supposed the boy, dressed in the short trousers of their childhood, was a manifestation of the dream, not real at all. It didn't matter; his silent company was comforting.

'But Harriet dying was years later. Let's go right back to the beginning.' Back to that small town in Germany where he and the boy had grown up. 'Things weren't too bad when we were very young, were they?' Benny remembered Christmases, days out in the garden in summer when the sun never seemed to go in and his parents had laughed and played with him.

Before things had become complicated.

'It was the broken vase that started it,' he told his companion. 'Grown-ups get so angry and that leads on to all kinds of other problems.'

His friend nodded.

~

Benny watched Rudi come across the snowy lawn at the back of his house holding the shards of what looked like a smashed vase. Rudi was trembling as he approached the shrub behind which Benny waited.

'Did you break that?' Benny asked.

Rudi nodded. 'I kicked the ball at the wall beside the window.'

And obviously missed. 'Whoops.'

Rudi's father would be furious. Benny could just about remember when accidentally breaking something and getting into trouble was the worst thing that could happen. In the last few months it had become acceptable to smash other people's possessions on purpose. The angry uniformed youths were particularly keen on breaking windows.

But poor Rudi, all the same. It wasn't his fault his father was the way he was. Or that he wasn't Jewish and couldn't understand the bigger fears life might bring you.

'What should I do?' Rudi whispered.

'Shove the pieces in a box and throw them away. Perhaps they'll think a burglar pinched it.'

There weren't as many burglaries these days, though. Not unless you were a Jewish household, Benny's mother said. In which case, the state itself robbed you.

'Good idea.'

While Rudi ran inside to find a box, Benny reassessed his position. Exposed on the white lawn like a beetle on a sheet. He moved behind a tree while he waited.

Rudi returned, his face losing its tension. 'I found a shoebox. Vati won't be back for a few days anyway.'

'Don't worry about it until then.'

You just had to worry about the immediate things: what you could eat, whether your boots would keep the snow out, whether your mother could find a doctor prepared to see her.

But for the moment, all that mattered was kicking the ball around in the garden with Rudi, pretending for a brief time that everything was normal again. Benny took a last look around to make sure nobody was watching them from the neighbouring houses, but Rudi's house wasn't overlooked. Reassured, he rolled his brown leather ball across the snow. His mother had bought the ball for him last birthday. How she'd managed it, he didn't know. She'd even somehow had his name embossed on it in small gold letters.

Benny drop-kicked the ball and managed to strike the narrow trunk of the cherry tree. Rudi tried the same shot. Failed.

A window on the second floor squeaked open. Benny froze. If you stood quite still people sometimes missed you. He'd learned to keep each muscle motionless, except for his eyes: they darted from side to side, looking for places to hide.

'Just Olga,' Rudi said. 'She doesn't mind what I do out here and she probably isn't wearing her glasses anyway.'

The elderly housekeeper shook a duster out of the window and banged it shut again. Benny hoped his friend had shoved that shoebox well under his bed. If the housekeeper found the broken vase she might feel obliged to tell Rudi's father. People in this town liked telling on other people.

He scooped up his ball and looked at it, reminding himself what he'd promised he'd do. 'Here,' he tossed it to Rudi. 'You'd better keep this.'

'Don't you want it?

How could Benny *not* want his beautiful ball? Rudi meant well, but even he didn't understand how things were. Benny managed a shrug.

'You're moving, aren't you?' Rudi asked.

'We're moving in with my aunt tomorrow.' No point hanging onto a large house with a frontage of smashed glass they couldn't replace, even if the house had once been a perfect example of modernist architecture, according to Benny's mother.

Benny felt suddenly exhausted. Only now did Rudi seem to notice.

'You look strange, Benny.' He squinted at him. 'You've got grey shadows under your eyes and your lips are blue.'

'My throat's a bit sore.' Now he thought of it, it felt more than a bit sore. He coughed and the coughing seemed to go on a long time. He felt hot, too. Probably just from running around.

'What's your aunt's place like?' Rudi asked when the coughing subsided.

'Two rooms for three of us. But my mother's going into hospital. Best place for her, my aunt says.' Benny pulled at a loose piece of stitching on his sleeve. 'At least there aren't many windows at the new apartment. So if they get smashed again it won't cost much to fix them.'

All that modern glass his father had taken such pride in, shattered.

'There's more.' Benny spoke in a whisper, his eyes still darting round the garden in case of listeners-in. 'They're sending me away.' This was the big news, the news he hadn't been able to comprehend himself until he said these words.

'Away?'

'To England.' Benny slumped down onto the garden bench. How could he be so tired after so little exertion?

'On holiday? With the enemy?'

'They're not the enemy yet.'

'But they will be soon, Vati says.'

Rudi's father knew a lot about things because of his job at the railways. Herr Lange had to approve the closure of whole lines to allow troops to move on exercises. He knew about engine sizes and track-sizing issues when engines moved from one country to another. He took calls in his study in the evenings, voice raised as he told the caller that the solution to a problem was impossible. Rudi sometimes told Benny bits and pieces he'd overheard, even though they both knew it was reckless and silly to share information like this. They could put you in a camp for less. That's what they'd done to Benny's father, who wasn't even a practising Jew. No one in their family was.

Benny concentrated on the loose thread on his sleeve. 'England will be safer for Jewish kids, my aunt says.'

Rudi seemed to be focusing on the gold lettering on the football, but Benny knew it was just that he couldn't think of a reply.

'Do you have any food?' Benny hadn't known he was about to ask this question. Rudi looked startled. 'Just there wasn't much breakfast. My mother's found it hard to find a shop that'll . . .'

That would serve them.

'So if you had some bread or a bit of cheese or something,' he went on, keeping his voice casual.

Rudi ate well, Benny knew. Despite the meat shortages he still had veal and pork a couple of times a week. With a nod Rudi crept back into the house. Benny hoped Olga was still busy upstairs. But even if she caught Rudi in her kitchen she wouldn't guess he was feeding the Jewish boy who'd once been his friend.

Sometimes Benny wondered how Rudi reacted during racial theory lessons. Rudi probably turned his eyes down towards his wooden desk so that nobody could see his expression. Or perhaps he just laughed with the others when the teacher showed them pictures.

The boys always played in Rudi's garden while Herr Lange was at work. The park was too dangerous. If it was snowing, Rudi and Benny sat in the garden shed on empty upturned terracotta pots in a space they'd cleared between garden tools and the lawnmower.

The shed was too cold now that it was winter. Benny thought, daringly, of asking Rudi to smuggle him into the house while he ate. If he could sit by the stove for just ten minutes the heat would ease its way into his cold limbs.

Too dangerous. The housekeeper might see him. They needed to stay in the cover of the trees and shrubs.

Rudi returned.

'Here,' he pushed a plate towards him. Two cutlets, a chunk of bread and an apple. Benny stuffed the bread into his mouth.

'I'll save the rest for later.'

'Bring the plate back tomorrow and I'll find you something else.' Rudi was watching him. 'Are you going to London? There're some good football clubs there.'

'Think I'll be staying in the country somewhere.' Benny rubbed his mouth with a grubby sleeve.

'Will you be gone for long?' Rudi asked.

Benny shrugged.

'And your mother?'

'Not fit to travel. Even if they let her out of hospital in time. The English won't take her unless she takes a job as a servant or something. She's never worked.' Another fear enveloped Benny. 'I'm not even sure I'll be able to go.' He coughed again. 'I have to pass a medical and get a health form signed.'

'Olga told me about this disease that starts in your throat and tries to strangle you.'

'Thanks.'

'Sometimes they cut your throat to release your airways.' Perhaps Rudi could tell from Benny's face that this was not reassuring. He stopped talking.

'I'm sure I'll be better by tomorrow.' Perhaps he was already feeling a bit better. Must be the food. But another cough broke in his chest. He slumped back on the bench.

'You'll have to do better than that.' Rudi looked concerned. Probably worried that someone would hear the coughing.

'I'll be fine.' If only his throat didn't hurt so much. 'I'll bring the plate back in the morning.' He thought of something. 'Be careful yourself, Rudi.'

~

They'd resumed their friendship cautiously after a chance meeting in the street. Rudi had mentioned the back lane that bordered his family's garden. 'Come over at about ten. Kick your ball over the wall. When I see it, I'll let you in through the gate. Nobody'll notice.' Rudi lived just outside the town centre, where the houses were less crowded together, with more trees and shrubs to hide behind. Benny's own house was equally spaciously located, but with open lawns around it. So Rudi's garden it had to be.

They'd been diffident with one another to start with, feeling all the differences, seeing them too. Benny knew the clothes his mother had bought for him from the smartest department stores in Berlin were now shabby, outgrown. But ten minutes of kicking the ball around had ended any awkwardness.

'You know it's big trouble for you if they catch me here?' Benny had said when they finished their first game.

Rudi'd given a casual shrug. 'My father's always at work and our housekeeper's short-sighted. Nobody can see us if we stay in the garden.'

And from then on, Benny had appeared in Rudi's garden once or twice a week. Except for that time in November when he'd stayed at home for a fortnight. After that his mother had grown sick. And she'd started talking about England for Benny.

Rudi had almost reached the back door, Benny's ball under his arm, when he stopped and came back.

'I could go to the doctor's for you tomorrow.'

'What?'

'You've been healthy until now, haven't you? Haven't needed to see the doctor?'

'I've been fine.' And he had, until this morning. 'But we don't really have a doctor any more. He's left.'

'And we've both got brown hair and eyes. You're not like . . .' Rudi stopped, blushing.

'Not like one of those cartoon Jews with a long nose and black greasy hair,' Benny finished for him.

'I don't see our doctor, either,' Rudi went on. 'He left as well.'

Benny watched him. 'So?'

'So who'd know if I went to this medical for you tomorrow?'

'There's a form. With my photo on it.' Benny thought about it. 'But you're right, we don't look that different.' They stared at one another. Rudi's face was fuller and he wasn't as tall as Benny. His hair was straighter and finer. But looking at a small black-and-white photograph, who would really notice these differences? And, as he'd said, Rudi's chest and throat were clear. Nobody would look at a boy like Rudi Lange and not imagine him fit to go to England.

'They'll just stick one of those cold metal stethy-things on my chest and a wooden stick down my throat,' Rudi went on. 'Make me cough so my balls drop down. Then they'll sign the paper and you'll go to England. My thank-you for giving me the football.'

How could anyone be so dim? But Rudi meant well. 'If they look at your bits you'd never get away with it,' Benny said.

Rudi flushed. 'I don't understand . . . Oh.' He turned pink. 'Can't I just say I didn't get . . . done?'

Benny shook his head. 'We're all done as babies.'

'Perhaps I was really ill? The doctor told my mother to wait until I was older.'

Benny thought about it. 'But then the Nazis came to power and she decided not to.' He hoped he sounded more confident in this story than he really felt. 'Or she didn't know she was Jewish. Only found out when you were older.' People liked sniffing around birth records, didn't they? Uncovering things about people's families.

Voices came from the house. Rudi stiffened. 'My father's back early. Quick, what time's the appointment and where is it?'

Benny dug out a pencil stub from his pocket. He had no paper, but Rudi found a handkerchief that could be written on.

'Put the medical form on the plate when you bring it back tomorrow morning,' Rudi whispered, already making for the house, probably scared stiff his father was going to notice the missing vase.

'*Danke*,' Benny called after him, softly.

Rudi's father hadn't always made his son so scared of him, Benny remembered as he climbed over the wall. Benny had a distant memory of Herr Lange taking the two of them on a train, onto the engine itself, so they could help the engineer shovel coal. Benny had pulled the whistle and everyone had laughed. Herr Lange had ruffled his hair.

It had become a habit to tuck good memories away. Benny folded this one up with those he had stored of his own father.

The walk back to his house took longer than normal. Not just because there were more youths in uniform out on the street this afternoon: Benny knew how to dodge *them*, knew the alleyways and back streets, the dark corners where you could wait until they'd passed. No, it was the pain in his throat that slowed him. It felt as though someone had replaced the lining with an old leather sole. He couldn't easily draw a breath. He stopped outside a shop to rest, doubling over to breathe. He must have looked dreadful because an old woman stopped and asked him if he was all right.

That kind of thing didn't happen very often now.

25.
PRESENT DAY

Rosamond

'What was I talking about?' Benny asked. 'In my dreams? I need to know.'

'About someone called Rudi and how he helped you.'

Benny shifted in the bed. I went to rearrange his pillows.

'They're fine.' He put a hand out to stop me. 'Rudi tried to help, yes. But he couldn't have understood what was going on, not really. Nobody who wasn't Jewish could have. But he did his best.'

'What do you mean?'

'If you were sick, badly sick, you weren't allowed on the train to England. You had to be healthy. That's what Rudi did, went to the medical instead of . . .'

'You,' I prompted.

'Rudi went to the doctor's,' Benny said. 'And the doctor didn't notice that he wasn't Jewish.'

I had to think about it for a moment. 'Rudi wasn't circumcised, you mean?'

'No. But the doctor apparently just saw a fine, healthy boy and didn't feel he had to examine him in detail. Rudi was quite pleased with himself. He'd done something good for his friend.'

Benny had a dispassionate way of talking about Rudi, I noticed. 'He must have been sorry when you went to England?'

He reflected on the question. Perhaps because Benny Gault had once been the interviewer he had a way of analyzing everything I asked him as though looking for the catch.

'He liked playing football with me. But boys that age don't reflect on relationships much. It's all about doing things together.' Benny nodded to himself. 'Say what you like about the Nazis, they were quite good about providing healthy boys with opportunities for male bonding. If you didn't mind uniforms and obnoxious marching songs.'

'Ghastly. At least you left Rudi the football as a souvenir to thank him for helping you out with the medical. What happened to him? Did you ever look him up after the war?'

'No.' He said it very quietly.

'Benny, may I ask you something?'

He looked surprised.

'Do you feel guilty about Rudi taking your place at the doctor's?' His eyes flashed. I bit my tongue.

'Guilty?'

'You sound as though the swap was bothering you.' Perhaps he felt that he'd been allowed into the country under false pretences. 'You must have been well enough by the time you arrived in England, or they wouldn't have let you in. So no harm was done really, was it?'

'No harm done,' he repeated, sounding weary.

'We've talked too much,' I said.

'No.' The word came out with force. 'I want to tell you what happened. There's more.'

'Why me?' I asked, startled.

'I think I know who you are, Rose.'

His eyes were those of the interviewer, shrewd and piercing.

26.

I'd dreaded this moment, rehearsed my lines. But now they deserted me. I was flailing on the end of a line, knowing I couldn't escape.

'It's been thirty years,' Benny said. 'Why come back here now, Rose?' We'd switched so abruptly between the roles of interrogator and interrogated. 'You could have returned before now. I'd have let you see the house, with pleasure. I would have been delighted to meet you.'

I couldn't say anything at first.

'The job came up. I knew I shouldn't take it, but I couldn't resist Fairfleet. It seemed like it was meant to be.' Again, my hand went to my lower abdomen. 'That it was the right time to return.'

I expected him to look shocked or angry or just sad. He looked none of these things, still the interviewer he'd once been: interested, alert.

'Meant to be? My dying was the chance you needed?' he said humorously.

'No! Not that. Something else.' I prayed he wouldn't push me.

'I know that your mother died in a fire and afterwards you and your brother went off to live with your father. There was another man in the house at the time of your mother's death, wasn't there?'

'Cathal Pearse.' Even saying the name made my body feel tense.

'I remember hearing that name. He had a reputation for preying on women, didn't he?'

'He'd had relationships with several rich women. He moved from one to another, waiting for them to get tired of him, or growing tired of them himself.' Dad had uncovered more about Cathal after the fire.

'Poor Clarissa.' Benny said it softly to himself. 'I never met her, only saw her once.'

'At the lake, one summer afternoon.'

'Just after your grandmother died. I had this urge to see the house again. To say goodbye to her at her beloved Fairfleet.' His eyes were closed now, as though he was seeing the summer afternoon again. 'I should have gone over and said something. I saw the three of you there and you looked so complete, so untouchable. I felt almost shy, like an intruder. So I dithered. I hung around for a while, but when I took another look across the lake there was someone else coming towards you. I thought you had a visitor, so I left.'

'That wasn't a visitor,' I said. 'That was him, Cathal.' I spat out the name.

Cathal the interloper. But it was still my fault, what happened to Mum. 'I still blame myself,' I whispered. 'I told her to give him a job and then he came to live with us. But that wasn't the end of it. The fire was my fault, too.'

'Tell me, Rose.'

~

Cathal had released me from the basement after my night spent alone down there in the cold. And now he was dragging me across the floor towards the kitchen. I could smell something on him, some kind of alcohol.

'Rose!' Andrew came out to meet us, his face a white, anxious mask. 'We thought you'd . . . He told us he'd looked everywhere for you. Where were you?'

'Locked in the basement.'

'You said you'd looked in there.' Andrew glared at Cathal.

'I need to make her understand a few things.' Cathal's words were slurred.

'Leave my sister alone. Leave us all alone. I've already called the police from the phone box.'

Cathal straightened his back, like an animal preparing for a fight.

'I crept out while you were still snoring like a pig.' Andrew sounded triumphant.

'What are the police going to do, sonny? This is a family matter.'

'You're not family.' I wriggled in his grip. 'This is our home, not yours. Mum wants you out.'

Cathal twisted my wrist so that it hurt. 'I'm going nowhere, Rosie. This is my home now, too. Your mother and I are partners. With a legal agreement. When we start the new tutorial college in the new year there'll be changes around here.'

'She won't start a college with you.' I looked up the stairs. 'Where is she?'

'Sleeping.'

'He probably made her take more sleeping tablets,' Andrew said.

I shook my head. 'You can't make her unknow what she knows about you, Cathal.'

He gave my wrist another twist before releasing me. 'Your mother's fine. Go up and see her, why don't you?'

I rubbed my sore wrist and ran upstairs, legs still numb and slow. The bedroom door opened to my touch. Mum was sitting on the bed. She turned, blinking, to me as I came in. Astonishment and relief flashed across her face. 'Rose. Thank God, you're all right.'

I told her where I'd been.

'He said he'd looked down there and you weren't there. He made Andrew search the gardens, walk round the lake. I thought . . .' She put a hand to her throat.

That I had fallen through the ice.

'I went outside to look for you, but I didn't get far.' She looked down at her foot. I saw a fresh bandage round it. 'I slipped and I couldn't get up.' I pictured my mother trying to scramble to her feet using her uninjured hand, wincing as she finally stood up on the damaged ankle.

She brushed something from her eyes. 'I've been so pathetic. Forgive me, Rose. It's all going to change.' She dropped her voice. 'Did you hide the letter?'

'It's in a drawer in the storage room,' I whispered.

I sat beside her. She drew me into her warmth. I knew it was going to be all right, that we would rid ourselves of Cathal now.

'Smithy came to the house,' she said. 'While Andrew and I were outside. Cathal must have sent her away, told her we were all out shopping. Andrew saw Smithy cycling away from the house, but ran after her, calling to her, but she didn't hear.'

I remembered the noises I'd heard: Smithy's bike, slipping and sliding on the icy gravel. And the car following her.

'Why didn't you look for me in the basement?'

'By the time I got back to the house Cathal had the key in his hand and said nobody needed to go down there again. Andrew tried to find the key for the garden door, but Cathal had taken that too.'

My mother's voice shook. I realized that it wasn't with fear. It was fury.

'Smithy will know something's wrong.' Mum squeezed my shoulder reassuringly. 'I know her: she'll have rung the police. She'll get her niece's husband to drive her back over here this morning to see what's going on.'

Mum was right. Smithy wouldn't have been convinced by whatever lies Cathal had told her. She'd persist in finding out what was going on here.

'It won't be long now, Rose. We just have to hold on for a bit longer and someone will come to help. Let's get Andrew up here with us and I'll lock the door. Cathal's still drunk. He must have finished off the whisky and the brandy. God knows how much he's had.'

'Andrew rang the police too.'

'If they get two calls they'll take it seriously.' She gave my shoulder another squeeze.

Someone knocked on the door. 'Will you come out or shall I come in and say what I have to say in front of the child, Clarissa?' Cathal sounded calm, reasonable. 'Let's just talk first. If you want me to go, naturally I shall go. No need to involve the police.'

We looked at one another. 'Don't believe him,' I whispered. She was standing now, grimacing as the ankle took her weight.

'Let's see if we can't come to some agreement,' Cathal called.

'Lock the door,' she whispered to me. I did as she asked.

'Andrew is with me now, Clarissa,' said Cathal. 'Shall I tell him that you're not going to come downstairs?'

Mum turned even paler. I knew she'd be worrying that Cathal would hurt Andrew again. She looked at me.

'It's fine,' I whispered. 'I'll just wait up here until help comes. Go downstairs.'

'I don't like to leave you.'

'Go,' I hissed.

She hobbled to unlock the door.

I lay back on the pillow. A slight scent of Cathal remained on the pillowcase. It made me feel sick. I threw the pillow at the wardrobe. It hit the door, releasing the lock. The door swung open.

I could see Mum's clothes hanging there, the wedding dress a long white presence at the side.

I needed to feel that silky material between my fingers again. I pulled it out of the plastic covering and held it up in front of me at the mirror, feeling like a ghost from a happier past. The December light showed me my pale face and the dark rings around my eyes. I thought of the candles. I should light them to see if I could cast a spell to evict Cathal from Fairfleet.

The matchbox still sat beside the candles. I put down the dress on the bed and struck a match. The five candles were quickly lit. Immediately my reflection looked warmer, brighter. When I again held up the white silk against myself it no longer leached my pale features of colour. I closed my eyes.

'Make him go away. Today. Let it just be us again.'

I wished hard, so hard I could almost feel the wish push its way out of my heart and diffuse into the air around me. I pictured my prayer, for that's what it was, drifting downstairs, enveloping Cathal so that he was forced to gather up his few possessions and walk out. I saw him trudging down the snowy drive, never looking back, leaving us alone forever.

'I will give you anything if you get rid of him for us,' I said aloud, not even sure whom exactly I was begging or what I was promising. 'Anything.' Even if Mum and Dad never got back together again, it was a price worth paying.

I let out the breath I'd been holding. I needed to put the dress away in the wardrobe. I turned from the dressing table. As I did, the right sleeve brushed a candle. I felt only a mild sensation of warmth, almost pleasant on such a cold day. I dropped the dress. But when I looked down there was an orange flower already bursting open on the sleeve of my woollen jumper. I felt the heat on my skin.

I screamed for my mother. God knows how she managed to get upstairs so quickly on that ankle, but she was in the room, crouching beside me, pushing me to the floor, grabbing at the folded quilt on the end of the bed with her left hand to put out the fire. But the quilt was heavy and her left hand too weak to manage it alone. She gave a grunt of frustration and pulled harder.

The quilt fell to the side of the bed, just out of reach, behind me. She moved forward to grab it and as she did, her own sleeve brushed the flames on the discarded wedding dress. Fire ran up her arm.

'It's all right.' Even then, she was reassuring me. 'I'll put it out.'

But the combination of the ankle and the wrist injuries made her movements clumsy. She tried to stand, slipped and fell back onto the carpet.

'Andrew,' I shouted at the same time as I tried to reach the fallen quilt. 'Help!'

Nobody came. I pulled myself up, the flame running up to my shoulder. Mum's room had a hand basin in the corner. I ran the tap into her tooth mug and poured the water over my shoulder and chest, knowing I couldn't help my mother unless I first helped myself. Smoke, thick and acrid, choked me. The first mugfull of water made little difference. I held my arm under the tap. Steam hissed.

Behind me Mum moaned.

Under the hand basin hung a towel. I soaked it under the tap and wrapped it round myself. My jumper no longer blazed, but flames were running up the sheets dangling from the bed and onto the drapings and headboard, trying to lick the bedside tables, too, and the dressing gowns hanging on the back of the bedroom door. I bent to Mum.

Strong hands were on me, pulling me away. I smelled the whisky-soured breath. 'Leave this to me.'

Cathal. He pushed me out of the room. 'Go downstairs, Rosie.'

'But Mum –'

'I'll take care of this. Go downstairs now.'

His strong arms were too much for me to resist. I fell out of the burning room, lungs hacking up smoky air.

Andrew was running upstairs. 'Where's the fire? Where's Mum?'

'In her room. Cathal's with her.'

He seemed to notice the burnt sleeve, the way I was holding my arm. 'Rose?'

'I'm fine. Call the fire brigade. Hurry.'

Smoke was curling its way downstairs now like a lock of thin grey hair. I jumped the last steps, making for the kitchen.

'Rose.' I turned. Mum must have pushed past Cathal, pain giving her a desperate strength. She came downstairs so slowly, almost calmly, arms out in front of her, orange flames still flickering along the sleeves of her jumper.

The smell. Burning fabric. Burning hair and skin. Always the smell.

Now the fire rippled down Mum's torso, cackling like a goblin.

I ran through the hall to the kitchen to fill the washing-up bowl with water, flung myself back to the staircase, water sloshing over my feet.

I'd only been gone seconds, but already Mum's face was lost to the flames now licking the banisters. I threw the water at her. For an instant the fire died down and I could make out Mum's face again, twisted, teeth bared. She was screaming, but I couldn't hear it: the world had gone mute. I yelled something back at Mum, some promise that I'd stop the fire, and ran to refill the washing-up bowl, my scorched arm protesting.

But the water only hissed as it hit her. I grabbed the Persian rug from the hall and pushed Mum down to the floor. Then Cathal was behind me, shouting something, pulling me away from her, his powerful body overpowering me, just as he'd overpowered our family since the moment he'd cycled down the drive. He muttered something I couldn't hear.

I grabbed the blue vase from the console table by the front door. And then Cathal was down on the ground, blood oozing from his head. I looked at the vase I still clutched and dropped it on the parquet floor, where it cracked into pieces. Andrew was back in the hall, shouting that he could hear sirens now. Too late. Smoke whirled over the floor where Mum and Cathal lay motionless.

'Go outside,' Andrew screamed. 'Tell them to hurry.'

I turned my back and staggered through the hall and front door. A coughing fit ripped through my lungs. The skin on my arm felt heavy, as though it had come unstuck. I touched it and the heat of the skin hurt my fingers. The stench of burning flesh was everywhere: inside my clothes, my hair, inside my body. Blue lights flashed, throwing up reflections on the white snow.

'I was just doing what she showed me.' My words were a plea, to whom I didn't know. I'd lit the candles on the shrine, praying for a miracle. But I'd made a mess of it. Far from helping my mother, I'd brought fire down on her. I should have burned instead of Mum. The fire should have torn into my flesh, not hers.

An ambulance, fire engine and police car slooshed to a halt outside the door.

My arm now felt like a glowing cinder. I heard someone screaming and realized it was me.

27.

Benny said nothing, but waited, knowing there was more. He might have been a priest in a confessional. This had been his job, interviewing people, getting them to expose more of themselves than they had ever intended.

'It was my fault. I was careless. I started the fire.'

'Remind me again how old you were?'

'Nearly thirteen.'

'And Cathal? What on earth was his game?'

'It looked as though he was trying to stop me from helping her. The police interviewed him in hospital, but he claimed he didn't remember anything about the fire because of the head injury I'd caused him.'

'Why would he have stopped you?'

'He was furious that Mum had ended the relationship and he was going to be booted out of Fairfleet. But he was just plain drunk, out of his mind.'

'He sounds psychopathic as well, from what you've told me of his mood swings and violence.'

'We never found the letter Mum wrote to the solicitors, cancelling the legal agreement she'd made with him. I also wondered whether there was more she knew about him. Or suspected.'

'Shame you couldn't find what she'd written,' Benny said. 'If she'd left some good evidence you might have had him in court.'

~

It was the arrival of a letter from Cathal's solicitor that prompted the search for whatever it was Mum had written to her own lawyers.

A month had passed since the fire. We were settled in with Dad and Marie, in the house they had hastily rented in Abingdon to provide us with a home. The letter from Cathal's lawyer was addressed to Dad as the parent of Rosamond Madison, a minor who'd caused serious injury to Cathal Pearse.

Cathal was making a civil claim against Mum's estate for injuries received at my hands and for loss of earnings resulting from the fire at Fairfleet. The letter also told us that the police were making investigations into possible arson, in which case criminal charges might follow the civil case.

I concentrated hard on the torn-open white envelope sitting on the kitchen table.

'This is madness,' Dad said. 'Blaming Rose, claiming against the estate. Don't you worry, sweetheart.' He pulled me into a bear hug. I'd missed my father's physical presence while he'd been away. Now I just wanted to melt into his arms. 'I'll speak to Meadows.'

He was the lawyer Dad had appointed for Andrew and me to help with the winding-up of Mum's estate.

'Meadows is a property lawyer,' Marie said. 'He won't be able to fight this kind of claim.'

'He may know someone else in the firm we can talk to.'

'If we could just find Mum's letter, that would show them what Cathal was like,' I said.

'What letter, darling?' Dad asked.

'Mum wrote it all down: everything Cathal had done.' I didn't know how to describe the way he'd wriggled into Mum's affections and taken charge of things. 'I put the letter in the chest of drawers down in the storage room in the basement. That's what I was doing when Cathal locked me in down there.'

Marie squeezed my arm. I instinctively started to move away but felt real warmth in the gesture. 'Your mother was acting very sensibly and calmly.'

Dad made a sound with his tongue. Marie gave my father a look that told him to mind what he was implying about Mum's state of mind. 'She did what she could with a fractured wrist and sprained ankle,' Andrew said.

'We'll look in the basement.' Dad put a hand over mine.

Dad and Marie returned to Fairfleet. They searched the basement, and indeed every other part of the house, for the letter, filling a van with our clothes and possessions.

'Cathal's already been back to the house to collect his things. Apparently a policeman came with him, but obviously he wasn't watching him very closely. He's helped himself to some bits and pieces.' Dad slammed the van door. 'It was like Kim's Game: going into a room and trying to work out how many ornaments and clocks there used to be there. No doubt he helped your mother make an inventory of the house contents after your grandmother died. He knew what was worth taking.'

'Where is he now?' I tried to make it sound casual, but Marie gave me one of her sympathetic looks.

'Apparently he's undergoing further surgery. He discharged himself from hospital to return to Fairfleet for his stuff. Then collapsed in the bed and breakfast he's rented.'

'Good,' Andrew said.

'Did you find the letter?'

'I'm sorry.' Marie squeezed my hand.

'There's something else.' Dad glanced at Marie. 'We found out quite by chance, from the woman in the village shop actually, when we stopped for cigarettes. It's Alice, Miss Smith. I'm afraid she was in an accident.'

'Smithy?' I hadn't thought about her much, if at all, since the fire. The loss of my mother had pushed other losses out of my mind.

'Knocked off her bike.' Dad shook his head. 'I thought it was odd she didn't come to your mother's funeral. She was nuts about the family.'

'Smithy's dead?'

'I'm so sorry.'

'When did she die?'

'Just a week or so ago. But she'd been in a coma for a while. Head injury.'

Poor, poor Smithy – she'd loved the house and my mother and grandmother.

~

Dad and Marie fought for us to keep the house. The lawyer Dad found wrote back to Cathal's solicitor rebutting his claims. The police showed no interest in pressing arson charges against me.

But Andrew and I owed the government the death duties on Fairfleet: tens and tens of thousands of pounds. Dad sat in his office with bank statements and a calculator, trying to see if he could raise the money so we could keep the house.

'But I can't,' he said. 'Not all in one go like this. I'm so sorry. I know how much it meant to your grandmother and your mother that you should have Fairfleet.'

So my mother's executor, a local solicitor, briefed a land agent. And Fairfleet was sold.

'Mum's letter wouldn't have made any difference.' Andrew tried to cheer me up. 'Whatever happened, we can't afford to keep Fairfleet.'

'Writing it all down mattered to Mum.'

~

'The letter she wrote to you mattered because it showed she was trying to undo the damage,' Benny said, sounding as though he really understood what had been going through my mother's mind the day before her death. 'I've never found anything like that in Fairfleet and I know every inch of this house.' He spoke very quietly. 'We'll talk more about this, Rose – if you'd like to, that is?' He gave me a look that was almost shy. 'I think I need to sleep again now.'

I fell back into my role of nurse, settling him. I stayed in the chair by his bed, thinking about what had happened after the abortive search for Mum's letter.

~

We'd gone off to our new schools. By then I'd had the first of the operations on my arm. It looked much better, Andrew told me. Marie told a series of PE teachers that I couldn't wear short-sleeved Artex shirts for games. Mostly they understood.

Dad found a job in London and bought a house. I didn't even mind too much when he and Marie married in a registry office with just Andrew and me as guests. We spent most of the school holidays abroad.

Mum's solicitor arranged for the smoke-damaged bedroom, staircase and entrance hall at Fairfleet to be quickly repaired and repainted and the woodwork replaced. Dad was impatient to see Fairfleet gone. We knew that someone well-known bought the house, but the name of Benny Gault didn't mean much to Andrew and me. All we knew was that he'd once lived in the house, one of Granny's German refugee boys.

'Forget about Fairfleet,' Dad said, after the sale had gone through and the last of the paintings and silver had been removed from the house and sold for us. 'Put it all behind you. You've both inherited a good amount from this sale, even after paying the death duties. You can probably do what you want in life without worrying about money.' We were sitting, one on each side of him, at a table in a Swiss mountain restaurant during a ski holiday. He put an arm around each of us. 'Nothing can compensate for your mother. But you must try to move forward.'

I looked at the sunlit snowy mountains, which might have represented the unmovable barrier I felt between me and any future worth having.

Andrew went on to study science at university and eventually invested most of his capital into starting his own laboratory in southern California, researching all kinds of new drugs. Sometimes I'd read an article in the science pages of the *Times* mentioning my brother's company and feel a rush of pride for him. Andrew only rarely returned to England with his family.

I had an aptitude for science, too, gaining good enough A-level results in physics, chemistry and biology to be accepted into medical school.

During my post-clinical training, I was sent to the burns unit of a London hospital to complete an elective. I thought I'd be all right in such a setting. Medical school had desensitized me, I told myself. I'd seen awful things during my time in A&E and elsewhere. I was a trained professional.

One of the patients in the unit was an Asian woman in her late thirties. Her husband had accused her of adultery and thrown a pan of hot fat over her face. I stood at her bedside with the specialist while he explained the treatment she'd need.

As he talked I tried to focus on the stand holding up the woman's drip, rather than on her bandaged face. I'd seen burns victims many times by now. I tried to rationalize. It meant nothing that this patient was a mother the age Mum had been at her death. My mind was trying to trip me up. Best to ignore it, to concentrate on the drip stand, the half-full plastic jug of water on the bedside table, the chip in the paintwork on the wall.

I smelled burnt flesh. I told myself it was simply the sickly smell of hospitals. But I kept thinking of how I'd smelled my own scorched arm that day at Fairfleet. And Mum. I'd smelled her burning body. At first I managed to keep a look of concentrated interest on my face, nodding as the consultant turned to tell me something. I even answered his questions and scribbled something in my notepad.

'Wouldn't you agree?' the consultant asked me.

I lifted my head from the pad. The ward wasn't the stationary structure it ought to have been: it was spinning slowly. And now the floor was rippling as though it was molten. I could hear a ringing sound.

'Are you all right?' The consultant glared at me.

I started explaining that I was dizzy and needed air, but by then it seemed as though all the oxygen in the room had rushed out, leaving me breathless. I slid gently onto the lino-covered floor, which continued to judder and ripple beneath me.

~

They told me it was a panic attack. They wanted me to look for triggers, have counselling.

'We know about the terrible thing that happened to your mother.' The counsellor at my initial session spoke very softly. 'Your father spoke to us. Have you ever talked to anyone about it?'

I shook my head.

'Would you like to do that with me?'

She was kind. I liked her. Perhaps it would have helped. But I couldn't afford to revisit the fire; I needed it tucked safely in my memory where it couldn't overwhelm me.

I packed my bags and wrote a letter telling them I'd changed my mind about taking my medical career any further. And went to New York for six months so that they couldn't get in touch with me. Before I left I told my father I had found the shifts as a junior doctor too exhausting and the continual studying for examinations too demanding. He'd looked at me with pain clear in his eyes.

'I should never have gone to Saudi Arabia that year,' he said. 'If I'd been in the country I could have intervened, taken you away from Fairfleet and that man.'

But that would have left Mum entirely alone with Cathal. Dad must have seen how I felt about that.

'You and Andrew felt you had to take care of your mother, didn't you, Rose?'

'Yes.' And we had failed to do this. Me, particularly.

'You could have gone far as a doctor,' Dad said sadly.

I could have gone far, perhaps, but I hadn't done so badly in my preferred career, even if my private life had been a bit of a disaster, until James had come along.

James. Shut away with Benny, I'd allowed myself to forget about James between phone calls and texts. I'd told myself it was me who was in pain, because of our recent loss. But he would have been feeling it too. I looked at my patient. Benny had nodded off in his chair. I allowed myself to further consider my life.

After my marriage failed I'd drifted from one short relationship to another. And then I'd met James. Despite, or perhaps because of, our combined sad histories – he being a recent widower – James and I had hit it off. And he'd moved in. Perhaps the moving in hadn't been such a good idea.

'There's something provisional about you, Rosamond.' He'd looked around my spacious flat. 'You've never really settled down, have you? Where are your books? Your furniture?'

'I don't like clutter.'

'You could buy up most of Heals and put it in this flat and still have room for a football pitch.'

'I like it like this.'

'Perhaps it's this way because you're always travelling.'

Something in his expression made me feel uncomfortable. 'I've enjoyed moving around the world, seeing different places.'

'Yes.' He was still staring at me. I started to feel annoyed.

'Regretting moving in with me?'

'No. I just wonder how easy you'll find it, that's all.'

'I'll enjoy it.' And I had, though it was strange to have James there every evening, to have his books, pictures, clothes and saucepans in my space. But we'd wobbled on together. Until the day I discovered, aged forty, that I was unexpectedly pregnant. Nine weeks gone, in fact.

When I broke the news, neither of us said anything for a whole minute. 'I thought it was just my age,' I said at last. 'I mean, forty!'

'Catherine's twenty.' James gulped. I knew he was wondering how on earth he'd break it to his adult daughter that she was going to have a sibling.

I went to open the fridge and retrieve the Chablis. Reminding myself I couldn't drink any more, I poured a glass for James. I sipped at a glass of tap water while I tried to process the news. 'How can I have been pregnant for two months and not known?'

'I thought you were looking a bit peaky.' James took a long drink from his glass. 'But you had that difficult job.'

I'd had a non-residential job a long drive from home. The hours had been long and the patient's house was kept very warm. I'd frequently felt nauseated.

'What are we going to do?' I looked around the apartment. 'I mean, a baby, in here?'

The nearest park was at least fifteen minutes away. I had a balcony, though. With a ten-storey drop.

He took my hand. 'We'll do just what you want us to do, Rosamond.'

I went through the next few weeks swinging from complete rejection of the prospect of becoming a mother to a kind of fierce joy. By the end of the eleventh week of my pregnancy the latter emotion was winning. James and I agreed to look for a new house. We'd sell both our homes and find something suitable for a new family of three. Something manageable, but with a garden. At the end of week eleven I was beginning to feel less nauseated. A scan showed that the baby was developing well. I rang my father and Andrew. Their delight showed just how much they'd wanted this for me. I'd been worried about how Catherine would respond to the prospect of a much younger sibling, but she seemed to take the news in her stride, hugging me when we met for lunch.

A day later I started to bleed.

'Perhaps you should think of counselling.' We sat in my empty flat the next day, James holding my hand.

Perhaps I should. I hadn't lasted long with the counsellor I'd seen after my breakdown on the ward. She'd been kind and no doubt competent but I'd backed out. But, on the bright side, I hadn't completely fallen to bits. So I'd manage this time round, too. The loss of a less than twelve-week-old embryo, something that wasn't really a person, couldn't compare to the bigger loss I'd suffered.

So I told myself. I took a month off work and then this job came up. I'd tried to resist, but Fairfleet had exerted too strong a pull.

~

Benny half-woke and seemed to be feeling discomfort. I checked the time.

'You need to take your medication. Let's get you settled.' I helped make him comfortable and he fell back asleep almost as soon as he'd swallowed the tablets. I wondered how much he'd remember of our conversation when he woke up. Perhaps he wouldn't care as much as I worried he would. If he liked the adult Rosamond Hunter, if she was doing her job well, he'd forgive the deception I'd carried out. Or, if not deception, the sin of omission I'd committed in not making it clear that Rosamond Hunter and Rose Madison were the same person.

I switched on my phone to look again at the photographs of Granny and Mum. The latter on the front steps as a young woman, smiling into the camera, still years away from the mental illness that was moving to claim her. Granny climbing out of a plane, wearing her beloved flying jacket, hair pinned back, radiant. I might have expected the photographs to make me feel sad, nostalgic, at least. But they didn't, perhaps because I'd unburdened myself to Benny. And because I'd allowed myself to think about the miscarriage. I felt as I imagined Catholics did after confessing sins to a priest: physically lighter, airy, almost.

I went downstairs to wash and refill Benny's water jug and tumblers. The snow-clearer would probably be grateful for a hot drink. I prepared a coffee for him and put on boots and coat to find him. He was sitting on a section of low wall by the back terrace, staring out towards the lake. He turned as I approached. His eyes were less red today. The deep blue was more marked.

Some of the coffee slopped out of the mug onto the snow, melting its purity and leaving a stain.

'You,' I said.

'Hello, Rosebud,' Cathal Pearse said.

28.

Cathal took the mug from my shaking hand. 'Careful, you're spilling it. Quite a coincidence, both of us showing up at Fairfleet.'

'No coincidence at all. You saw me in Oxford, on Cornmarket when I was shopping and you grabbed at me. Then you tracked me here.' I struggled to control the shake in my voice.

He took a mouthful of coffee and breathed out warm air. The vapour hung around us like a bad dream.

'So? It's a free country. I'm doing a good job.' He nodded at the path he'd cleared around the back of the house.'

'Why are you here?'

'I just wanted to see the old place. Look at what could have been mine.'

'Yours?'

'Your mother and I had plans for Fairfleet. I could still have been teaching here now. If it hadn't been for you, Rosie.'

'She was never going to let you turn it into a tutorial college.'

'She signed the papers.'

'She changed her mind.'

He shrugged. 'You and your brother couldn't have the place anyway. All those death duties. You didn't think about that when you killed your own mother.'

'Get the hell out of here!' My body was in panic mode: perspiration running down my neck, my stomach churning.

He took another lazy sip of coffee before answering. 'I'll take my orders from Sarah Smith, thanks all the same. She wants me here every day clearing snow while the bad weather lasts.' He handed me the mug. 'So the doctor can get up the drive if it looks like the old man's pegging it.'

'If she knew who you were –'

'Does she know who *you* are?' He leered. 'She doesn't, does she?'

'Tell her your arm is hurting you and go.'

'What would happen if Sarah found out you were here under false pretences?' he said. 'Would she throw you out, Rosebud?'

'I am not here under false pretences. I'm using my legal name.'

'You damaged me seriously when you hit me.' He put a hand to the side of his head.

'Even your own lawyers said you hadn't a chance of making me responsible for what happened to you. The police didn't agree with your version of events, either.'

'You were a child, Rosie, a wicked and violent child. But they didn't want to think the worst of you. Someone had to be the scapegoat for everything and they chose me. Strange, when I wasn't the one who lit the match and started the fire. And when I was trying to help your mother.'

'It didn't look like help. It looked like a drunk trying to hinder our attempts.' I started to walk away, telling myself not to break into a run, not to show him my fear.

'You drove me to drink,' he shouted. 'I'd given it up before I went to Fairfleet.'

I ignored him.

'You're probably sorry I didn't die,' he called after me. 'Pity for you they put out the fire before it could burn me to ashes, too.' And now I was running, feet sliding on the snow.

'I could still bring a claim against you, you know,' he shouted. 'For ruining my life with the injuries you inflicted on me.'

I slammed the kitchen door closed and rammed the bolts over, my shaking hands making the job hard. He couldn't get into the house through the locked front door. I was safe from him inside. But for how long? I sank into one of the kitchen chairs, hands over my face. Once again the mask had slipped and I was no longer Rosamond Hunter, forty-year-old nurse, calm, composed and professional. I was Rose Madison, not yet thirteen. With a bipolar mother who couldn't rid herself of the influence of a man with a major personality defect. A charming narcissist with violent and controlling, possibly psychopathic tendencies. These were the descriptions the adult me had come up with to describe Cathal. The child me hadn't known any of these terms.

I'd just known that Cathal was dangerous.

And the child still inside me knew that I couldn't be here at Fairfleet while he remained.

29.

Sarah came into the kitchen carrying clean drying-up cloths and dishcloths. 'I'm always amazed how many of these I get through at Christmas.' She stared at me. 'Rosamond?'

'The snow-sweeper.' I swallowed. I had a decision to make. I could tell her exactly why I feared him, who he was, why he'd come to Fairfleet. Or I could just make up some other story about him, make him sound like a nutcase who was no specific threat to me, but wasn't the sort of person you wanted round a house containing two women and a very ill elderly man.

'What about him?'

'He's . . .' I swallowed again. 'Listen, Sarah, this is going to sound mad. But he knows me and I know him.'

She put down the pile of clean cloths she was holding. 'What do you mean?'

'I used to live here, Sarah, years ago. It used to be my grandmother's house.' I watched her, expecting her to look surprised. She gave a little nod.

'I suspected you'd stayed here once. You seemed to know too much about the house, where cupboards were, where there were high beams to duck. Things nobody would know if they hadn't lived here before. But Benny was happy with you.'

'I thought you wouldn't let me take the job if you knew.'

She shrugged. 'Perhaps not. But you're here now.' Her expression turned more serious. 'But I can't let you bring old family history in to trouble Benny, you understand, Rosamond? What's all this about the snow-sweeper?'

'He wriggled his way into my mother's life when she was vulnerable.' I told Sarah about Cathal's arrival at the house, his exploitation of Mum's mental frailty, the way he'd driven out Smithy, the violence we'd seen unleashed little by little.

She listened in silence. 'Should I call the police?'

'I'd like to,' I said. 'But they couldn't find anything to charge him with all those years ago and I can't see anything has changed. He hasn't done anything wrong here.'

'Other than frighten you.'

'He'd probably deny it.'

'I'll tell him to leave,' she said. 'He can have his money and go. I just don't want trouble, Rosamond.'

'No.'

She took her purse from the kitchen table and put on boots and coat.

'Do you want me to come out with you?' I asked.

'Probably best if I do it alone.' She sounded grimly determined. 'I've had some experience of letting people go over the years. It happens. Cooks who drink, cleaners who don't clean, gardeners who sit in the shed and smoke dope. I've dealt with all the clichés, and more. Don't worry about this pathetic specimen. He'll go.'

From the window I watched her stride across the snowy lawn and address Cathal. His arms spread in that familiar open-palmed gesture I remembered from years ago. He shook his head. Sarah gave him bank notes. He took them, but threw them onto the snow. She pulled a mobile phone out of her pocket. He stooped, picked up the money, and trudged off. Sarah watched him for a while before turning back for the house.

'I actually had to threaten him with the police before he'd go,' she said, stamping on the doormat so that the snow could fall off her boots. 'He was most peculiar.' She flicked off her boots and hung up her coat, sounding unruffled but puzzled. 'He was ranting on about all kinds of nonsense. Claiming he should own the house. I almost felt sorry for him, but Benny is my main concern.'

She washed her hands under the tap and picked up her whisk, giving me a sharp look, warning me, perhaps, that Benny and his comfort would remain her priority.

'I'm sorry I didn't tell you that I'd lived here before.'

'No particular reason why you should.' But she still looked watchful.

'I didn't think I should take the job. But I did.'

'Why?'

'I'm still not sure. I liked the sound of Benny. The agency thought we'd get along. It seemed like a good time to return here, with a patient to look after.'

And distract me, if things became too intense.

She was still watching me.

'I didn't expect to feel so at home here,' I went on. 'Even though this once was my home. I thought I'd feel like an outsider. But I didn't. And that's because of you. And Benny.'

She nodded. 'Whatever's bothering him, see if you can help him with it.'

Her expression told me that this was the reason she was happy to have me in the house. She needed me to release Benny from the burden of whatever he was brooding over. I was his nurse and his welfare mattered more than anything to me.

30.

I sat by Benny all night, dozing occasionally, but awake for most of the time. He slept better than he had in previous nights. I topped up his medication in the early hours and helped him drink some water. At five Sarah relieved me for a few hours. Benny was awake when I went back to him at seven to give him more drugs and help him wash. 'I heard voices on the lawn yesterday,' he said. 'I thought I'd dreamed it, but I don't think I did. Who was it?'

I told him who the snow-sweeper had been. His eyes widened. 'Cathal came here?'

'Sarah saw him off.'

He gave a wry smile. 'She's quite fierce when she needs to be.'

'Now you know all about me, about it all . . .' I made an expansive gesture with my hand to express what it was he knew.

'Yes. And I'm glad I do. I promised your grandmother . . .'

'What did you promise Granny?'

'That I'd always keep an eye on things here. That was way back before I owned Fairfleet. I took it to mean that I'd always take care of her family, too.'

'But you were younger than her?' Surely he'd just been a teenage boy during the war? Far younger than Granny. But then

I remembered how young she'd been when she'd married her first husband, just nineteen.

'I know. Sounds strange, doesn't it? Presumptuous, almost. But things started to change between us as the war came to an end.'

And now the expression on his face was one I couldn't interpret.

'It was as though the age difference between us melted away. By the end of the war I was the last in the series of boys they'd waved off to promising futures. Perhaps it made me seem older than I was.' He considered what he'd just said. 'Perhaps both of us forgot that I wasn't really very old at all.'

~

Rainer, David, Richard, Ernst, Paul. By this summer of 1945 all were now dispersed. Lord Dorner had pulled strings as boys of Jewish German origin were still regarded with suspicion. Rainer and David had joined up. Richard had gone back to Germany, helping out with translation work in Hamburg with a British major rounding up suspected Nazis. Richard was older: nineteen. Still too young, Dr Dawes told Benny, for what he'd see and hear in Germany. But perhaps it would be useful to have one of their little group back over there, closer to the Red Cross and refugee organizations.

'Perhaps Richard can find someone who knows what happened to your father, Benny,' he said.

They were out in the walled garden this July morning, helping Lady Dorner with the gardening. Too beautiful a day to spend indoors, Dr Dawes said. And Benny had earned a break from studying.

Benny's father, Josef Goldman. Josef Goldman had driven a shiny Mercedes and had dressed very smartly. He'd possessed one of those open faces that always look as if they've just smiled or are about to smile. Very far from being a hook-nosed, close-eyed Jew like those depicted in the propaganda.

'He vanished into a camp very early on,' Benny said. 'Even before Kristallnacht.' It all seemed an eternity away now.

Dr Dawes said nothing for a moment. Benny knew he was thinking that it was unlikely, impossible, that Herr Goldman could have survived. He'd be long dead, his body flung into some pit in Poland or scattered as ashes over some desolate field. But suppose he'd been one of the few who'd lived through the horror?

Suppose he traced his son through all the confusion of the diphtheria outbreak and the Kindertransport to England and came over to claim him? Benny pictured a man in his forties, but worn down by his terrible treatment and looking older, ill and weak, coming into the house, taking off his hat, looking round at the comfortable furniture and warm, if now somewhat thread-bare, carpets. Heard him addressing Lady Dorner in stumbling English, explaining who he was.

'I have come for my only son, Benjamin.'

Lady Dorner would take Josef Goldman into the drawing room and order tea. She'd call for Dr Dawes and ask him to tell his tutee, Benjamin Goldman, known here as Benny, that he was no orphan as might have been assumed, and would be leaving this very day with his father, who'd come back from near-death to claim him. A miracle.

Benny pictured Josef Goldman's face when he saw the new, anglicized version of Benjamin Goldman and tried to find the young boy he'd loved in the seventeen-year-old's features. It was warm in this walled garden, but goose-pimples formed on Benny's arms. He swallowed hard.

'Benny, I know it's terrible for you to have all this raked up again.' Dr Dawes's hand was warm on his shoulder. He looked at

Benny, soliciting a confidence. 'If there's anything I can do to help, you only have to ask.'

'It's the uncertainty.' Benny tugged hard at a stem of couch grass in the flowerbed.

'I know that's the worst part of it. We've tried to distract you, to keep you occupied so you wouldn't think about your families too much. Everyone said that was the best thing. Perhaps it wasn't.' Dr Dawes's eyes were sorrowful. 'Perhaps we should have spoken more openly of the terrible losses you have all suffered.'

He'd really cared for the six of them, Benny thought. They hadn't just been a wartime distraction from more interesting academic pursuits. For more than six years he'd taught and guided them. They'd been boys when they'd arrived at Fairfleet, but now they were young men. Dr Dawes had been strict, but had never once raised his hand to them. The worst any of them had had in punishment was an afternoon's detention, or exclusion from a trip to the cinema.

At the time they'd taken his solicitude for granted, but now Benny wondered what it had cost him. Guiding six young men from an enemy culture, making Englishmen of them. Or trying to. Some of the older boys had proved too difficult to mould and would always be recognizably German, for all their conscription into the army and their educating in Britishness. They'd all go on to universities. Lord Dorner and Dr Dawes had made certain of this. But even then, the foreignness would stick to them, showing itself in the way they pronounced an 'r' or a 'w', or used their cutlery.

'We've made good progress.'

Benny blinked. He'd forgotten Lady Dorner, standing in front of them, looking at him now, clasping a small garden trug containing garden tools. Probably wondering why he was staring into space.

'Sorry,' he said. 'I was dreaming.'

'You're wise to take a break. It's hot out here.' She stooped to pick up clippings from the gravel path. 'What are you planning for the summer, Benny? You have three months before you do your service, don't you?'

He shrugged. 'A cycling tour. The Cotswolds, perhaps. David says he'll have a few days at home at some point. We could go together.'

'Sounds fun.' She started to pull out bindweed. Her fingers were long and strong, the nails manicured but unvarnished. He joined her. Bindweed pulling was more satisfying than tugging at couch grass. You thought you had just a small frond of the weed, but then you tugged it and saw you had a yard or more of the stuff in your hand.

'Careful to get it out by the roots,' she said. 'Otherwise it just grows back again.'

'I'll leave you to carry on helping Lady Dorner, Benny.' Dr Dawes sounded weary.

'Thank you,' she said. 'If you could pick up the weeds and throw them into the wheelbarrow. I'm trying to get some of the flowers going again.' Here and there a delphinium still lingered among the vegetables. Nobody had had time for flowers for years, but the scent of those that remained, and of mown grass, took Benny back to his childhood, to the summer afternoons when his mother had still been alive and had worked in their garden.

Harriet Dorner's hands continued to move through the stalks, cutting, straightening, tying back. He could imagine those hands on the controls of a cockpit. They worked in silence for half an hour.

'When we've finished here I should do something with the poor old topiary,' she said. 'I know we've done our best during the war, but I feel sorry for the beasts. They've lost all their shape.' She laughed at herself. 'I'm being silly.'

Benny could still just remember the box animals. The elephant with his raised trunk. The pig, the chicken and the fox. 'Let's have a look at them now,' he said.

There must have been a note of urgency in his voice because she blinked. Perhaps he felt everything shifting, changing: the older boys leaving Fairfleet, himself just about to launch into adulthood. He needed to remind himself of how it had been when he'd first arrived here. But perhaps there was more. Perhaps he didn't want this afternoon to end: Harriet Dorner and him, working together in the sunshine in companionable silence. Though there were many things he might have liked to say to her.

'Come on then.' She picked up the trug and followed him.

Over the last five or six years people had tried to maintain the shapes of the box beasts. Some had clearly been more gifted at topiary than others. The elephant might have been a cow. The fox had mutated into a kind of crocodile with a ruffle on its back. The chicken might have been anything: a lizard or a half-completed statue of a swan.

Harriet rolled her eyes, handing him a pair of secateurs. 'Just do your best, Benny.'

He undid the secateurs and cut a few sprigs off the chicken's back. Back before the war, he remembered, it had had outstretched wings. Hard to see how you could make a hen shape from the tangle of stems and small leaves. He cut a few more pieces away. That was better: the shape was smoother now. The aroma of clipped box tree was fresh and crisp.

Harriet was working on the elephant with hedging shears. 'I can see his trunk again now.' She sounded happy, absorbed in the task.

Benny cut more of the overgrown box tree and looked again at his work. He'd taken too much off around the chicken's head, which had now lost its neck and shrunk into its body. The beak was overgrown and looked more like a propeller. He tried taking more off the sides of the body, but made matters worse: it looked too cylindrical now, not like a bird at all.

He looked at the shape in despair. Perhaps if he trimmed the growths on each side, the wings, the chicken's head would look more in proportion. But when he'd finished the wings it didn't resemble any kind of avian. It looked more look like an aeroplane. An idea came to him. He cut a few more sprigs, more quickly. Stood in front of the box bush and studied the shape he'd cut. It might be possible. The overgrown beak could in fact be a propeller. In his mind it was 1943 again. A plane was carving the pale blue sky, sun glinting on its wings.

Wings. Tail. Benny cut away. He was barely aware of Harriet now, until she came to stand beside him.

'You've got it,' she said, softly. 'My beautiful Spitfire. Commemorated in a piece of box hedge.'

He closed the secateurs. She was circling the box shrub now, examining it from every side. 'Just a little bit more off this side, I think, if you're to get this port engine perfect.'

He reopened the secateurs and trimmed off more sprigs. He heard an intake of breath and stilled his hand, turning to look at her.

'It's nothing.' She gave a shaky smile. 'Just for a moment there I thought you were taking off too much.' The golden tones in her complexion had turned milky white. 'I couldn't bear to see it spoiled.' Still he was looking at her, not understanding.

'A bad memory, that's all.' She stood straighter. He didn't know what to say, wished he was older, wiser, more at ease talking to people like Harriet Dorner. She must have known bad things – male pilot friends who had lost their lives flying missions, or even just accidents, engines failing, misjudgements.

'It's perfect.' She touched his hand. 'A wonderful testament to a wonderful plane. Sometimes I . . .' She dismissed the thought with a shake of her head. 'Thank you, Benny.'

All the things he wanted to say lumbered towards his mouth and tripped over one another and couldn't be spoken.

'I must go in now.' She sounded clipped like Lord Dorner's wife again. 'I've got a friend coming to play tennis.' She gave a little smile as she left. 'Sounds almost like old times, doesn't it? Don't stay out here long.'

He raked the off-cuts on the grass together and fetched the wheelbarrow. The sun was hot as he wheeled the load to the compost heap. His head was pounding as he replaced the gardening tools in the shed and walked back to the house, skirting the topiary walk so that he wouldn't have to see the Spitfire. Was Harriet Dorner laughing about it, about him, now with her friend? *You'll never guess what that funny boy has done now.* He kicked out at the roots of an old monkey puzzle tree.

There were sandwiches for lunch, served in the kitchen to save work as there was no longer a full-time cook. Harriet didn't appear. Probably eating hers in her room while she dressed for her tennis. Benny ate his meal quickly and drank several glasses of water in succession to kill the headache.

He went up to his books. He'd moved back to the bedroom on the first floor he'd moved to during the diphtheria. There was more room for his desk and books.

'There's not much more I can teach you at this stage,' Dr Dawes had told him when he'd received his Higher School Certificate results. 'You've done very well, Benny. We'll concentrate on broadening you out for the Oxford scholarship papers. Writing essays is the thing, Benny. And reading, reading, reading.'

So this afternoon he was writing on free will. His own will seemed to be completely enslaved, pulling him away from the lined paper to the sounds coming from outside the house.

Plop, thwat, plop. A hoot of laughter. He looked out of the window. Harriet and a woman friend were out on the tennis court beside the walled garden, which had been levelled off, re-sown with grass seed and rollered. Lord Dorner must have seen his wife casting longing looks at it when she came back from flying planes.

Some of her female friends were flying for the commercial air companies, she'd told them. Some of them had even made plans to fly in South Africa or Argentina – imagine that. But the wife of Lord Dorner couldn't be in paid employment during peacetime, even though she was supposed to be one of the best pilots in the country, male or female.

'But now she'll have to get back to organizing charity balls and sitting on hospital boards,' Rainer had said in a rare visit home.

Benny himself mightn't have much opportunity to see how she adapted. He wasn't sure what he was supposed to do with himself during leave from national service and university vacations. Perhaps you weren't really supposed to return to Fairfleet once you'd left. Perhaps it somehow exceeded the terms of Lord and Lady Dorner's generosity. Benny wanted to ask Dr Dawes about it but didn't want to appear too needy. He turned back to watch Harriet Dorner on the tennis court.

She and the friend, Betty someone-or-other, a woman Benny recognized from dinner parties years ago, were laughing at missed shots and bungled serves. *Such* a long time, they told one another, their words rising crisply through the still air to Benny's window. Harriet's tennis-shoe soles had perished. Mice, little devils, had nibbled at the wood on her friend's racquet. The whites they'd last worn in 1939 had yellowed and moths had chewed holes in them.

'I'll never be able to serve again,' Betty called. But within twenty minutes they'd found a rhythm, Harriet moving across the court in light dancer's steps, making it look the easiest thing in the world, hitting forehands that sent up little clouds of dust when they landed and volleying balls back at Betty with precision. Perhaps she'd teach him to play. But why should she? Why should Harriet Dorner do any more for the refugee boy?

He watched the women playing tennis a few minutes longer until he felt guilty about the unfinished essay and forced his head down towards the exercise book. *Put simply, free will means the power to determine one's own actions . . .*

The power to stop himself being distracted by Harriet's strong yet shapely legs in her tennis skirt. This was completely the wrong essay question to attempt. He'd start again. Choose a different topic: this one on guilt. He put the lid on the fountain pen to stop the nib drying out along with his thoughts, and doodled on a scrap of blotting paper with his pencil. Easier to start this essay off; almost too easy. Keep it objective, he reminded himself. It's not about you.

Their footsteps on the bare landing floor made him look up. He heard Betty making for the guest bathroom. Lady Dorner's footsteps passed his open bedroom door.

'How was tennis?' he called, casual, friendly. A young man passing the time of day with his guardian's wife.

'Wonderful.' She came inside the room, stretching her neck out as though she wanted to see what he was doing. 'May I, Benny?'

'Please do.'

She walked up to the desk and looked over his shoulder. '*Does guilt serve any true purpose?* That's a big subject.'

He thought so too.

'Guilt is always a correct response; if one feels guilt it is probably the case that one deserves to feel it,' she read. 'Somewhat severe, Benny.'

'It's what I think.' He sounded defensive. 'I know I haven't written it very elegantly, though. Guilt is a mechanism that alerts us to areas in which we have failed, is what I meant.'

She was straightening pencils on the desk top, arranging them into a straight line.

'But you wouldn't know about that,' he added. 'You wouldn't have failed in your conduct.'

She gave a low laugh. 'You don't believe that, do you? Everyone fails sometimes.'

'You're a war heroine. You made sure the RAF had the planes at the right places.'

She flicked at the pencils and one of them shot off the desk onto the floor. She stooped to pick it up, holding it and looking at it. 'When a plane hits a hillside it looks like this.' She snapped the pencil in two. 'Not quite as neat, of course. There are bits of metal and fabric and body parts splattered around. It's seeing the personal effects that is the worst: cigarette cases, scarves, lipstick.'

'Whose body?' He realized he'd been a monumental fool, though he wasn't quite sure how.

'A pilot friend of mine. Jenny Hayes. A girl. Just twenty-two. She looked up to me, Benny, trusted me.'

Harriet dropped the two halves of the pencil onto the desk. 'I should have said we'd done enough for the day. That the cloud was too bad. They told us not to chance it. But I was impatient. I'd been promised another Spitfire, you see. I just wanted to deliver the Oxfords, old dependable buses of planes, they were. And get back in time for the Spit. If we called it a day, waited till morning, I'd have missed the opportunity. So when she asked whether we should wait, I said no. Let's do it. We'd be all right. We'd flown those Oxfords in similar conditions across that part of the country before. I saw the cloud before we hit it. I caught sight of Jenny's face just before everything went invisible.'

She took a breath. 'She was rigid, paralyzed. I knew then she couldn't do it, but it was too late. The cloud swallowed us. I heard an explosion a few minutes later and I knew. I just knew. When I touched down I made them send out an ambulance. Someone drove me to where I thought she'd gone down, near Devizes it was. I made them take me with them, Benny. I saw the plane. I saw . . . Jenny. She was . . . Her body . . . it . . .' She put a hand to her mouth. 'The fuel had caught light, there'd been a fire.'

He could see it as though he were Harriet: the young woman's blackened body, the smouldering, snapped plane.

'It wasn't your fault.'

'It was. I wanted to fly the Spitfire waiting for me more than anything else. It made me feel more fully alive than anything else.'

He didn't say anything. The confidence hung between them, thick as the cloud that had brought down her fellow aviatrix.

'So that's my guilty secret.' She gave a little laugh. 'What's yours, Benny? Do share.' From her skirt pocket she pulled out a slender cigarette box and extracted a cigarette, hand shaking. He'd started smoking occasionally and took a matchbox out of the desk, lighting the cigarette for her, pushing the ashtray towards her.

'It doesn't matter.' He was still seeing the smashed plane, the broken body of the pilot.

'I think it does matter, Benny.' She transferred the cigarette to her left hand and laid her right hand on his shoulder. He felt its warmth through his Airtex shirt. 'I've been away from Fairfleet for too long. I should have spent more time here with you boys. There, you see? Another thing to feel guilty about. I was off having fun with my planes while you were all growing up here.' She inhaled on the Player's. 'I just left you to Dr Dawes.'

He'd never thought about it like that. It had always seemed entirely appropriate that this golden creature should be up in the sky, in the air, where she belonged. He hadn't been used to having women around, in any case. Sometimes one of the other boys would talk about a mother or sister they missed, but not often. He couldn't think of a way to express this without making it sound as though he wouldn't have enjoyed her constant presence in the house. Which would have been a lie. He'd thought so many times about how she'd drawn that pink cross on the oak for him.

'Tell me what's wrong, Benny?'

'You've been so good to me. Both of you. So kind, taking me in though you didn't know me.' He forced himself to look at her.

She made a little moue. 'We had space enough. None of you were any trouble.'

'It was more than just giving us bed and board.' The words sounded harsh. He tried to soften them with a smile. 'You gave us a home.' Her hand stayed on his arm.

'Of course we did! You were all hard-working boys. Conscientious. Dr Dawes used to write and tell me you'd be a credit to this country.'

He hadn't known this. Why would a creature like Harriet Dorner have been interested in a group of adolescent boys when she had the irresistible planes to fly?

'Look at all you've achieved. Sitting a scholarship for Oxford!'

'But we were Jewish. That's why you did it?'

Now she moved the hand. 'What do you mean? That we didn't really come to be fond of you? It was all just charity?'

Someone came out of the guest bathroom onto the landing. 'Shall I go downstairs and wait for you, Harriet?'

'On my way,' she called back to her friend.

He pulled himself together. 'No, I didn't mean that you were just doing it to be charitable. But it doesn't matter.'

'It does.' She slid off the desk, the tennis skirt brushing a half-inch up her thighs as she moved. An encouraging smile curled her lips. *Poor boy*, she'd be thinking. *Working too hard, the stress has been too much. That cycling tour can't come a day too soon.*

'Perhaps I just need a break from the books.' He stood, too. He'd take a walk round the lake.

She was still studying him intently. 'Do you feel guilty, Benny?'

He gave a start.

'Guilty because you survived and all those others didn't?'

He said nothing.

'Who do you think your guilt will benefit? If you feel that badly, do something to help. Find a refugee organization and work for them during the summer before you go off to the army. Or help out at a scout troop in a bomb-damaged city centre.'

He was watching her intently now.

'Don't just moulder away. Be the best you can. That's all any of us can do.' She stubbed out her cigarette in the ashtray on his desk and came a little closer. The cells in his body remembered Mona's body pressed against his own and pulsed greedily. Mona was back in London now, but before she'd returned, there'd been a few more encounters in the dappled shade underneath the trees. Benny knew more about women now.

He knew he must be flushing. Harriet could only be in her early thirties, far younger than her husband. She'd looked after herself, even during the war years. Her lips were very close to his now, just as Mona's had been.

He moved his mouth a half-inch nearer to Harriet's. He must be making a huge mistake. She'd be appalled, tell her husband one of the boys they'd taken in had assaulted her, abused their generosity.

Still she didn't move.

They'd throw him out; his university plans would be wrecked. *The refugee who took advantage.*

He found himself moving nearer, nearer. And then their mouths were almost touching; he could still feel air between them. She pressed more firmly, just for a second, before releasing her lips.

'I've been wondering what it would feel like,' she said. 'I'm sorry, Benny.'

'I'm not.'

As he said it her eyes seemed to darken. Her tongue flickered out from between her pink lips and touched his own, just for a second. Someone was pouring molten treacle down his pelvis. He closed his eyes. Then there was only coolness. Air where her body had been just a second ago. He opened his eyes, letting the feeling engulf him, feeling the guilt melt away. She was picking up the tennis racquet from the floor.

'Forget what just happened, Benny.' Her smile was a silver stab under his ribs.

'I'm not sure I can.'

The pupils of her eyes became small black full stops. 'It was wrong of me.'

'Then . . . why?'

She plucked a string on the racquet as though it were a guitar. 'I don't know. Perhaps life is just a little too sensible these days. All my life I've been told to do the right thing, think of Fairfleet. Every now and then I just feel the need to take a risk.' She strummed her painted fingernails over the racquet face. 'I took advantage of you, Benny. It will never happen again and I can only apologize.'

'I didn't mind.' Understatement of the century.

She almost smiled. 'Sidney wants to go to America. Perhaps we should go sooner than we planned.'

Was he, Benny, the refugee youth, really that dangerous?

'Markets are opening up again,' she said, flushing a little. 'He needs to be over there. Shopping in New York – just think. No rationing over there. I might even persuade him to take me out somewhere I can do some more flying. And you, you'll be off to Oxford, won't you, as soon as you've done your bit for king and country?'

Benny looked at the uncompleted essay.

'You will get that scholarship, Benny, I know you will.'

Then she was gone, leaving the scent of her perfume in his room.

31.

'You kissed my grandmother?' Even now, in the depths of winter, I thought I could smell some of the past: the flowers in the garden, the rubber of Granny's tennis shoes, the pencil shavings on Benny's desk. The kiss they'd exchanged seemed part of the sweetness I could imagine. She hadn't been married to my grandfather, Peter, at that time. She'd been married to Lord Dorner. But a single kiss? Was that really what was on Benny's mind? I couldn't believe that was all there was to it. I wanted to smile, thinking of it. The half-century and more that had passed had surely robbed it of any iniquity.

He gave his head the slightest of shakes. 'I was a precocious boy.'

I could imagine it. In this wrinkled, gaunt old man there still lingered something of the youth he'd been.

'And then shortly afterwards you went off to university?' My grandmother had gone to America with Lord Dorner, who never returned because he'd died out there. I was wondering how much more time Benny and Granny had spent under the same roof. But Benny was asleep.

I spent a quiet day, catching up on some sleep and emailing James and Andrew. At lunchtime I helped Sarah cook us bowls of pasta. 'Better to eat now,' she said. 'While we can.'

I rang the cancer charity who were going to help with nursing care at nights to warn them that we were approaching that stage.

When I went up to see Benny I read to him again. More *Great Expectations.* Pip was enjoying his wealth in London now. Over-enjoying it. Estella was well and truly breaking his heart.

But Benny was distracted and looking for something. 'Where's Max? He hasn't been up to see me all day.'

I couldn't remember seeing the dog for hours, either. 'I'll go downstairs and bring him up,' I said.

Sarah was sitting with a cookery book in the kitchen. 'Every Christmas I swear I'll cook less and save myself the problem of leftovers.' A shadow passed over her face. 'Of course, next year . . .'

Next year Benny wouldn't be needing her to cook Christmas lunch at Fairfleet.

'I came to find Max for Benny,' I said softly.

She rose. 'I let him out. Normally he'd be barking to come back in again by now. He doesn't much like the cold.'

I opened the kitchen door and whistled for the dog.

'That's strange.' Sarah came to join me. 'Come on, Max, it's freezing with the back door open, and your master wants you.'

Still there was no sound of the terrier. I picked up the torch. 'May I borrow your boots, Sarah?'

'Go ahead. Take my coat, too.'

I whistled and called for the dog as I walked to the lake. Years ago Granny had told me how a dog of hers had chased a bird out onto the ice. The ice had cracked and the dog would have drowned but for my grandfather's speed in running along the end of the jetty and reaching out for its collar.

But the ice was already melting on the lake. Max wouldn't have run out here.

I walked back to the kitchen, rehearsing how I was going to tell Benny that his dog had disappeared.

Sarah met me in the kitchen. One look at my face told her of my lack of success. 'I'll try out the front,' she said. 'Perhaps he's wandered out that way. He's not usually as interested in that side of the house, though.'

'I'll come too.'

As we walked through the hall she stopped. 'Can you hear that?'

I stood still as well and heard scratching on the basement door.

'I'll go and get the key,' she said.

When she unlocked the door Max rushed out.

'Did you go down to the old pantry?' I asked Sarah. 'Perhaps he followed you down?'

She shook her head. 'Not today.' She bent down to pat the dog. 'How did you get down there, Maxie boy?'

Some old memory, some piece of trivia, was trying to nudge its way to the front of my mind. I must have been frowning as I stood there with the dog.

'What is it?'

'There was a door down there in the basement. They used it for deliveries.'

'I don't think I've ever noticed a door.'

'It's kept locked. Or used to be. My grandmother was worried about burglars.'

'But you think someone opened the door and Max got in that way?'

We looked at one another. 'Let's go down together,' she said. 'With the dog.'

We switched on the basement light and went down the steps. Max's wet footprints were the only thing I could see that were out of the ordinary. The old door with its faded green paint was locked.

'Where's the key?' I asked.

'I've no idea.'

'I'll ask Benny when I take the dog up to him.' And we climbed back up the steps.

But Benny was sleeping again when I opened his door. Max lay down on the rug beside his master's bed and fell into a similar state. I sat watching them, wondering whether the dog sensed that his master was very close to the end of his life. Tonight I could see signs that Benny had advanced a further stage. Death is strange in its moves, sometimes jumping several phases in just hours.

I pulled the quilt up over his hands. The skin felt very cold to my touch and the tips of his fingers were blue now. He opened his eyes.

'My secret,' he said. 'Was going to tell Harriet. But I can't, can I?' He looked forlorn, a small boy lost.

'Tell me,' I said. 'Pretend I'm Harriet.'

He was quiet for so long I thought he was drifting off again.

'One secret leads to another,' he said, sounding very old and very tired suddenly. 'You tell one person one thing. Then something else happens that also has to be kept hidden.'

He groaned.

'Pain?' I asked.

'It feels more . . . a presence.'

'I'm going to give you your drugs now and make you comfortable for the night.' It was only half-past seven, but it felt very late. 'We'll talk when you've rested.'

Death was playing Grandmother's Footsteps with us, suddenly accelerating towards us while our backs were turned. Benny's lips were slightly blue as well now. I unhooked the oxygen mask and put it over his face. He closed his eyes. When I'd tidied the room I went downstairs.

Sarah was making soup for our supper. She saw from my face that a change had occurred and put down her knife, very slowly. 'It's coming, isn't it?'

I nodded.

'But the doctor didn't seem too worried yesterday?'

'Things can change very quickly at this stage of an illness.' And I remembered the glance the doctor and I had exchanged. We'd both known.

'When?' she asked. 'Days?'

'Possibly.' Possibly less, I thought. 'There's still more he seems to want to say. Do you have telephone numbers for anyone who ought to know that he's slipping away?'

'He spoke to them all yesterday. Made it clear, from what I gathered, that he was saying goodbye.' I wondered why he hadn't told any of these old friends what was on his mind.

I checked on Benny and saw that he was sleeping. The doctor took my call when I rang the surgery and we agreed how I would manage Benny's medication from now on. He promised to look in on us the next day.

Sarah and I ate our supper quickly and in silence. When we'd finished stacking the dishes in the dishwasher Sarah told me she'd like to join me in my vigil, too. 'I'll come up at midnight, if there's no change.'

'I'd like that. Get some sleep first, though. I'll let Max out. And make sure he comes back in safely.'

'I'll send him down to you.'

Sarah went upstairs and shortly afterwards Max pattered downstairs and I let him out into the moonlit garden. He barked once and then sniffed around in what was left of the snow. I could see the black, white and tan of his coat. He raised his head, growling.

'Come on,' I urged him. 'Let's get back upstairs to Benny.'

He growled again. Someone tall stepped into view.

'Hello again, Rosebud,' said Cathal.

32.

'You,' I said. 'It was you who unlocked that basement door.'

No balaclava tonight. Cathal wore a black jacket and a pair of respectable jeans. Only the eyes were the same: those staring pale-blue eyes. And the dent in the side of his skull.

'Where did you get the key?' My heart was pounding, but I was determined he wouldn't hear fear in my voice.

'I kept hold of it when I left, years ago. Never thought I'd need it again, mind.' He sounded amused. 'But when I came back to do the snow shovelling it was useful for me to have somewhere to sleep.'

My spine tingled. But not from the cold. 'You were sleeping here at Fairfleet?'

'Just like old times, eh? Mind you, you'll remember that conditions in the basement aren't exactly comfortable, Rosebud. Still, needs must.'

My mobile was in my pocket. I wrapped my fingers round it, hoping I could press the right keys.

'What do you want, Cathal?'

'You came back here under a false name to unduly influence a dying man into leaving his house to you.'

'I came back using my lawful married name.'

He looked put out, but only briefly. 'You'll be struck off.'

'No I won't. We've never discussed his will.'

'How can you prove it, though? All those hours sitting there alone with him.'

I shrugged. But my fear of Cathal pulsed through my body. Even if I called out, Sarah might not hear; her bedroom faced the front of the house.

'I've no idea what his financial plans are,' I said as calmly as I could. 'Now get out.' I pulled my mobile out of my pocket and pushed the keyboard.

'Oh, you can call 999 if you want. But since they shut down the police station in the village you'll have to wait for a car to come out from town. Can be a twenty-minute wait this time of year.'

I kept my features neutral.

'What about the old bloke? Perhaps I should let him know.'

'He guessed.'

'Shall I tell him you wanted to kill me?'

'He knows all about the fire. And this isn't the time to discuss it.' Upstairs Benny lay close to death. I didn't want his house contaminated by this man while Benny's soul still resided here.

'I still don't know why you felt such an irrational hatred of me, you and your brother.'

'You were after Mum's property. But worst of all, because of your drunkenness, you stopped us helping Mum in the fire.'

I could still see Andrew trying to put out the flames with a rug and Cathal pushing him away.

'I loved Clarissa. And it wasn't me who started that fire.'

'Where did you hide the letter?' I asked, bringing the fight back to Cathal. 'The one Mum wrote. You must have taken it while I was in the basement.'

'Yes. I let myself in while you were down there, using the garden door. You were asleep up on the steps.'

It was so long ago. But hadn't I dreamed, as I lay on the cold stone staircase, that some devil or monster had entered?

'I knew you'd been in the storage room, Rosebud. So I searched the drawers and found an envelope addressed to the lawyer. I knew exactly what Clarrie had been up to.'

'What did you do with it?'

He didn't say anything. I was about to repeat the question.

'Now I understand,' he muttered, his eyes looking wild now.

'What?' I asked.

'That old bitch,' he said. 'That old Sappho-worshipping dyke. I was right about her.'

I waited.

'That's what she had stuffed into her skirt.'

'What are you talking about?' Again I kept my voice calm.

'Alice Smith. And your mother's letter.'

'Smithy?'

'She came back here that next morning, muttering about the police, while you were cooling your heels in the cellar and your mother and brother were outside looking for you.'

I remembered Mum telling me that she had missed Smithy. It had seemed so poignant that only a few minutes had made the difference between help coming in time to save Mum from the fire.

'I put the letter down by the telephone. She must have picked it up.' Cathal's eyes were like pale stones now.

Smithy had seen the lawyer's address on the envelope, realized that the letter was important, needed posting. But she'd failed, for some reason, to do this before she'd died.

'I followed her in the van, to make sure she'd gone. I didn't mean . . . I just wanted to give her a bit of a fright so she wouldn't bother us again.'

Smithy had had an accident on her bike. Which had killed her eventually. I remembered Dad and Marie breaking the news to us.

Smithy's death had seemed like just another manifestation of the evil shadow hanging over us.

'You ran her over, didn't you?'

'I tapped her.'

'You *tapped* her?'

'Just her back wheel, but the idiot lost control on the ice. Seemed to throw herself all over the road. I couldn't miss her.'

And Smithy had died weeks later, never recovering consciousness.

'When I saw you were back in the area I thought you'd found out what I did.'

But I was still thinking about Mum's letter. Why hadn't someone in the hospital retrieved it and given it to Smithy's niece?

Cathal's old ability to read my thoughts hadn't abandoned him. He sniffed. 'If the envelope was where I think it was, in her skirt pocket, nobody could have read it.'

'What do you mean?'

He came closer to me. 'Have you never seen someone haemorrhaging from their chest, nurse? Surely you must have. Blood soaks their clothes. And everything else.'

For all my medical training and experience I felt nauseated.

'The hospital staff probably had to cut her out of her clothes to get the lines in. They'd have thrown her things into the incinerator. And because Alice Smith never woke up again, she couldn't blab to anyone, could she?'

I thought of Mum's letter, drenched in crimson, illegible, cast into a hospital incinerator, lost for good. And as I did, all fear of Cathal burned away.

'Do your worst,' I told him. 'But tell me, Cathal, why us? Why did you pick on Mum?'

'She needed me.' His face lost its aggression. 'I knew she was a lost soul and I could help her. I'm good at being a shoulder to lean on. I helped my mother when my father died and left us homeless and penniless.' He gave a scoffing laugh and the aggression returned to his features. 'Or I would have helped the daft cow if she hadn't got the wrong end of the stick about me. My sisters poisoned her against me.'

I bet they had.

'I went from having everything – the house, the schooling, the position – to having nothing.'

And when he discovered that Mum had inherited Fairfleet, that she was single, mentally unwell and lonely, he'd found a way of clawing back his privileges.

'But people are always so suspicious, Rosebud. So inclined to judge harshly.'

He lurched towards me.

'Get out now.' Again I checked the mobile.

He stepped towards me. 'What are you doing with that phone?'

'Leave us alone.'

Sarah stood in the kitchen door. 'I heard your threats. I've already called the police and they're on the way.'

He looked from each of us to the other.

'Off you go.'

He spat at me. I stood back so that the globule landed on the slush at my feet. I watched until I was sure his dark shape had left the garden. I switched off the recorder on my mobile. 'I don't know if this will be admissible after all these years.'

'What will?'

'His confession to deliberately running over a woman in 1981.'

She let out a gasp.

'Let's go in,' I said. 'I want to check on Benny.'

I ran upstairs, not even bothering to take off my boots, Sarah following me. He slept on. I washed my hands in his bathroom and found gauze swabs, which I dipped in water.

'What's that for?' Sarah asked, from the doorway.

'Moistening his mouth.' I removed Benny's oxygen mask. 'He'll be finding swallowing hard now.'

The doorbell rang.

'That'll be the police,' Sarah said. 'They said they'd be quick, as we're two women alone with a very sick old man. They must have had a car in the area.'

'I don't want them to come into the house and disturb . . .' I blinked.

She squeezed my arm. 'Go out and have a quick chat with them. I'll take over here.'

I looked at Benny. 'He probably needs the mask back on. But . . .'

'I know,' she said. Our gazes met. 'He told me very clearly he didn't want to be kept on oxygen when it was completely hopeless.'

She stood there with the mask in her hand. 'Let me think about it.'

I sat with the police in their car. 'I can't stay long,' I told them. 'I'm nursing a patient who is going to die very shortly. He needs me.'

'Tell us about this intruder.' The female officer's voice was very gentle. 'You said you know him?'

I told her about Cathal and Mum and the fire. 'I don't know how far back your records go. You might have notes about what happened here thirty years ago. I hit him on the head when I was a child, by the way. He'll tell you that. I had to. He seemed to want my mother to burn to death. My father dug up some stuff about him after her death as well, suggesting he'd been exploiting vulnerable people.' I sensed uncertainty in her kind face. 'I know it sounds paranoid. You need to hear this.' I dug out my phone and played the recording I'd made on my phone.

They sat, looking restless for the first minute. Until they heard Cathal's sneering voice calling Smithy an old Sappho-worshipping dyke, admitting that he'd deliberately knocked into her bicycle and run over her. The atoms in the police car became charged with something more purposeful.

'I'm going in now,' I told them. 'To my patient. Thank you for coming out.'

'We'll go and see if we can pick this Cathal up,' the woman officer told me.

'We'll need a witness statement from you,' her male colleague added. 'Lock your doors and wait to hear from us. I'll make sure someone drives past the house again in half an hour and regularly through the night.'

I went into the house and upstairs to Benny. Sarah sat beside him, holding his hand. He looked wide awake now, the oxygen mask still off. Relief flooded his features when he saw me.

'Glad you're here. Stronger . . . Might not be again.'

Sarah stood up. 'You sit here, Rosamond.'

'Need you . . . read something,' he whispered. 'My past.'

'You don't have to tell me anything,' I said. 'Nobody wants you to return to events that are distressing.'

'Needs telling.' His breaths were coming in gasps now. 'Most myself when I'm writing.' He struggled for air. I reached for the oxygen mask.

'Don't speak any more for now. Rest.'

'No.' He turned his face away so that I couldn't fit the mask. 'Laptop.'

It was there beside him on the bed. I switched it on.

'Files . . . "Rudi Lange".' He gasped in a breath.

'First you're going to put this on.'

This time he let me attach the mask. I waited until his breathing settled before searching the few files loaded onto it. The first three seemed to cover Benny's financial and legal arrangements and his funeral wishes. Three other files were entitled 'Rudi Lange 1', 'Rudi Lange 2' and 'Georg Lange'.

'I'm opening the first Rudi Lange file,' I told Benny.

33.

If you're reading this it's because I'm almost dead, in my last hours, probably. Cancer wouldn't have been my preferred way to die. But what would? Dying of a quick heart attack, perhaps. At the same time as the death of my beloved wife, Lisa. But fate didn't intend that for me.

Writing this account of my last days in Germany in the form of a third-person narrative is a coward's way out, but it's the only way I can return to the events of January 1939. Kristallnacht was only seven weeks past. Those friendships between Jews and non-Jews still existing were severely tested. But some remained strong.

The story starts with an Aryan boy, Rudi Lange, offering to assist his Jewish friend Benny, who wanted to travel on a Kindertransport to Britain. Benny was already sick with what turned out to be diphtheria, so Rudi took his place at a medical examination, essential for permission to emigrate to Britain. The boys had feared that a full examination of Rudi would expose the fact that he hadn't been circumcised and had concocted an explanation. In any event, the doctor, a kindly man, didn't seem interested in anything below Rudi's waist and had stamped the form with no more than a searching look at him.

The boys' plan was for Benny to collect the completed medical form and go on to the railway station the following evening. Both of them had probably assumed that Benny, who'd hitherto been fit and healthy, would throw off his sickness.

But Benny's condition grew worse. He didn't reappear at the Langes'. So next morning Rudi played truant from school and took the tram to a part of town he hadn't visited before, to find his friend.

The buildings looked different with their crumbling plaster and unwashed steps. The people on the streets wore old clothes like Benny's, with the exception of a few women in smart coats and hats who might have belonged in the smarter cafes in the town centre.

At school they'd be reading the register now, before racial theory. There'd be a storm when Rudi's name was called and he didn't answer. He'd say a sudden illness had struck him on the way to school and he'd sat on a park bench, too feeble to return home until the faintness had passed.

The tram was slowing, the conductor removing his cap and rubbing his head in an anticipatory way. This must be the last stop before the tram turned back to the town centre. Rudi jumped off. Who to ask about Benny? A small group of men in faded black suits stood on a corner. He asked them. They looked at one another before one of them answered, in short sentences, not meeting Rudi's eye. Nobody had heard of Benjamin Goldman.

'He's only been here a short while,' Rudi insisted. 'Have you seen a new boy round here?'

More suspicious looks were exchanged. They knew someone like Rudi shouldn't be here. Perhaps they thought he was spying on them for the authorities. Sometimes you heard about children doing that. He walked off, feeling the men's eyes on his back. Across the road, observing him, was one of the older Jewish boys who'd once let him play football. Herschel had always been suspicious of Rudi. He didn't look that welcoming now.

'Herschel?'

The older boy was thinner than Rudi remembered. The challenge in his eyes was like a dagger. 'What do you want, Lange?'

'I want to see Benny.' Rudi put a hand into his pocket and pulled out the bread roll. 'I've got food.'

'A bit of bread? Your leftovers from breakfast?' Herschel bared his teeth into an expression that might have been either a smile or a snarl. 'Benny used to eat the best. His mother ordered their bread from that smart bakery in the marketplace. Know how I know that, Lange?'

He shook his head.

'My father used to own that bakery. What do you want with Benny, anyway, apart from giving him your leftovers?'

'I've got his signed medical form. For the train tonight. To England. He needs to go, doesn't he?'

Herschel slumped against the boarded window of the shop behind him and studied him in silence for a moment. He nodded along the street to a doorway. 'Through that courtyard. Second door on the right. Third floor, apartment six.' He shuffled against the boarding. 'But you shouldn't go up there.' He said it grudgingly. 'Benny's ill. Really ill.'

Rudi managed a shrug. Herschel's aggression seemed to shift to something less hostile.

'Good luck.'

Rudi didn't know whether this was intended for him or Benny.

He walked through into the courtyard, past the lidless dustbins, scrawny cats and lines of washing. The second door on the right led to a staircase. He climbed the stained stone steps. By the time he'd reached the third floor the smell was making him gag. Blocked drains. And something else, something sickly, like meat left out too long. He thought someone might be watching him and spun round to look down the steps. Nobody. Probably just another stray moggy running downstairs.

The apartment door opened to a push. Nobody answered his quiet greeting. Where was Benny's aunt? Trying to find work or food, Rudi guessed. He walked through a room that seemed to be bathroom, bedroom and kitchen combined. A woman's hat on a small table. Green lino on the floor, but worn away in large patches so that it looked like lace. A pair of shoes under a chair, Benny's probably, soles curved up like bananas. A further door opened at the end of the room. Rudi opened it and went through, blinking to accustom himself to the dark.

Benny lay on a couch with a brown blanket over him. On a small table next to him stood a jug of water, a glass and a photograph of himself as a toddler with his parents. Benny had never talked much about his father. They'd come for Herr Goldman a long time ago now.

Benny's face was the colour of paper. It was only by watching him intently that Rudi could see his abdomen actually rising a millimetre or so every few seconds. 'Benny.' He spoke the name in a whisper, still afraid to break the silence.

No response. Rudi moved closer and laid a hand on the other boy's arm. 'It's me, Rudi.'

Benny's eyes opened slowly, as though they were weighed down. 'Why did you come here?' The words were hard to make out. Benny was speaking as though someone had stuffed a cloth down his throat. One of his hands pulled at the sheet. Rudi stood back. Benny's neck was like a bull's: misshapen and swollen. Around his mouth the skin looked blue.

'I brought you some bread.' Rudi took out the bread roll. 'But you probably can't eat hard stuff.' He put it on the table. 'And I've got your medical form.' He patted his satchel. 'Stamped and signed.'

Something crackled underneath the blanket. Rudi could make out the edge of more papers and Benny's identity card. The effort made Benny slump back for a moment before he pulled the papers out. 'Please.'

Rudi took them from his friend's trembling hand. One was a sheet with what looked like English words on it, with a photograph of Benny stuck to it. Benny coughed, a horrible long rasping sound, and a thin yellow liquid ran from his mouth. He gasped, making no effort to wipe it away. There didn't seem to be a handkerchief. Rudi watched the yellow thread run down Benny's chin and onto the pillow.

'You must be on that train, Benny,' Rudi said. 'I don't know how we're going to get you there, though.'

Benny didn't seem to have an answer either. Rudi touched his arm.

'Wake up.' Benny was very still. Rudi watched him closely. His chest wasn't moving. Rudi put a hand on Benny's cheek and touched it. No response. He ran to the door. Herschel might still be out there in the alley; he'd know what to do, how to wake Benny. There must be a doctor somewhere round here. Or they could take him to the Jewish hospital where Benny's mother had gone. Rudi sprinted down the three flights of stairs to the courtyard. Herschel was still where Benny had left him, slouching against the boarded-up shop. He started when Rudi shook his arm.

'Benny's not moving. He needs a doctor.'

Herschel ran past him, reaching Benny's rooms with Rudi in pursuit. He sank to his knees beside the boy's couch, shaking Benny's shoulder and calling his name, putting his head to Benny's chest. His shoulders sagged. He turned very slowly to Rudi, looking both older and younger at the same time.

'He's gone.'

'Gone?'

'Dead.' Herschel pulled the blanket over Benny.

Benny couldn't be dead. Not the boy who could whack a ball into the goal from halfway across the park. Rudi shook Benny's shoulder under the blanket.

'You won't wake him.' Herschel spoke quietly. 'Go now. It won't be good for you to be found here. There are things I need to organize now.'

'What do we do with the papers?'

Herschel seemed to be daydreaming, his face losing some of its hardness. He looked at Rudi as though he'd forgotten who he was. 'Papers?'

'For England.'

Benny had wanted to take this train so badly. And now it had all come to nothing.

'It's probably too late now.' Herschel seemed to be thinking it over. He walked into the other room and searched among the few objects in it, finding a scrap of paper and stub of pencil. 'This man works for the *Reichsvertretung*, a Jewish organization. You'll find him at the orphanage.' He scribbled something on the scrap. 'Here's the address. Tell him Benny's dead and give him the papers.' Herschel returned to where Rudi stood, staring at Benny's shape under the blanket. 'There's probably not enough time to find another kid, though.'

'Couldn't you go?'

'Me?' Herschel blinked. 'I'm too old. They want little kids. The papers give Benny's age, see.' He showed Benny's form, with the birth date on it, to Rudi.

'You should try to get on the train anyway, Herschel. There's a bridge people sometimes use to jump on. By the old cattle market.' Rudi heard his own words with surprise. Vati had always complained about this breach in railway security. 'The trains move slowly there because of the points. It's not too hard to climb down from the roof and get someone to let you into a carriage. Hide in the lavatories at the border, when they check the papers.' He'd heard Vati talking about criminals who did this.

Herschel was gazing at him with curiosity now.

'You'll bring trouble on us now if you stay here, Rudi.' He spoke more softly than Rudi could ever have imagined. 'They might say we forced you to help us.'

The gentleness faded. He nodded towards the door. 'Off you go, little Aryan boy. You know what you need to do. Then go home and forget about your Jewish friend.'

~

Somehow Rudi was sitting on the tram with Benny's papers. But it was Benny himself that filled his mind. That liquid thread running out of his mouth. The sour smell. And Benny's stillness. Benny, the agile and fearless football player, motionless under the stained blanket. Rudi wished he could sponge out that last image.

They were already passing through the town centre again. Some of the shoppers he'd seen on his way to Benny's rooms were still out on the street, apparently unchanged and unmoved, even though Benny had died. He closed his eyes for a few minutes until they'd moved past the shops.

The orphanage was almost outside the town; fields stretched between the houses. Rudi and an elderly man were the only passengers now.

Rudi'd come out this way years ago. When Mutti was still alive. A special treat. The three of them had walked through fields. Picnicked at a lake. Vati had swum in the cool green water and Rudi had straddled his back, urging him to go faster.

The tram was slowing now. The old man tightened the scarf around his neck. Rudi grabbed his satchel and sprang out of the door.

His stomach growled. Lunchtime. He'd forgotten about eating, even though Olga always called him a boy with a healthy appetite and Vati said he was greedy. No signs to the orphanage. The first man he asked didn't seem to have heard the question, continuing to sweep snow off his garden path. A woman was pushing a pram. She considered him with narrowed eyes when he asked her, nodding up a rutted side-street. On the wall a few metres along was a sign: JEWISH CHILDREN'S HOME. Someone had drawn a rough Star of David over it.

Rudi walked up a long path bisecting an overgrown garden. The shutters were drawn. He rang the bell. After a long pause the door opened. A woman peered through a small opening. When she saw Rudi her eyes showed relief and surprise simultaneously.

'Yes?'

'These are for the man from the *Reichsvertretung*.' He tried to push Benny's papers towards her. 'The boy they were given to . . . died.' He swallowed. The door opened fully. A man appeared behind her, serious-faced.

'What is it?'

She pointed at Rudi. 'He has papers for tonight's Kindertransport.'

'How did you get these?' The man snatched them from Rudi's hand.

'Benny died.'

'What were you doing there with him? How did you know him?' The man sounded angry.

'We played football together. I . . .' He thought of Benny on the pitch, face shining with the fun of it. 'He was my friend.'

The man placed the papers on a table by the front door.

'I thought it would be too late for that boy.' The woman ran a hand over her eyes. 'They go downhill so quickly with diphtheria. They have no reserves.'

The man looked at his watch. 'We have no way of doing anything now.'

The woman touched his arm. 'If only we had more time.'

'There must be someone.' Rudi was starting to feel nobody apart from him had any will to sort this out.

The woman shook her head. 'They need sponsors, medical certificates, guarantees, entry papers. It takes days, weeks.'

Rudi thought of the morning he'd had, missing school, tracking down Benny, watching him die, bringing the papers out here without a tram ticket.

'You can't just give up,' he said, voice cracking. 'Someone must want to go to England.'

The man and woman were silent.

'They burned your shops and the synagogue. They hate you.'

'It's too late.' The man spoke quietly. 'Go away now and forget you ever came here.' Something white and angry shone in his eyes. Today was a day for angry people. But the anger didn't seem to be aimed at Rudi; it seemed to flow out of the front door, down the weed-snagged path and towards the town itself.

'Thank you for bringing the papers,' the woman said gently. 'Not everyone would have done that for us.' Rudi saw her eyes glistening.

The man nodded briefly. 'You've taken a risk,' he said, already pushing the door shut. 'I shouldn't have shouted at you.' Rudi made a lunge at the table, grabbed the papers and was away down the path before the man's shout reached him.

'*Sometimes you must rely on yourself alone*,' he remembered Vati saying. '*It's the only way of making sure a job gets done*.'

A tram slowed on the street ahead. He sprinted for it, reluctant to linger here in case the man pursued him. On the tram he examined the papers in his hand. There must be another Jewish boy of Benny's age wanting to go to England? Perhaps he was out on the streets this afternoon, lurking in an alleyway, trying to avoid the youths in uniform. As they approached the town centre he scrutinized the people in the street. Old men and women. Little girls. Babies in perambulators. Where were the young Jewish boys? *Come on, come on, show yourselves.* But of course, they didn't like hanging around in public any more; too risky.

He saw a dark-haired boy loitering on a corner. He might be Jewish; they were usually dark. The tram trundled past and Rudi shot round in his seat to look at him. Not a boy at all. A girl, in shorts, hair tied back, probably off to gymnastics training.

The tram reached the town centre. People bustled from shop to shop. Rudi saw several of his classmates walking along the streets. Lunchtime; school was finished for the day. Did any of them even remember Benny? If Rudi told them he'd died, they'd probably just shrug. If he asked for help finding a substitute for the Kindertransport they'd think Rudi was insane.

The tram was slowing. He needed time to think, to ease the image of Benny's swollen neck and grey skin from his mind. He needed his bedroom with its familiar objects: his building sets and books, the boots neatly laid out by the wardrobe. Olga would feed him. His father wouldn't be home yet, wouldn't know about the broken vase, about the truanting from school. Like a wild animal seeking refuge, Rudi needed somewhere quiet to gather strength. Then he'd make another attempt to find a Jewish kid for that train to England.

He opened the front door with his key.

'Olga?' he said softly as he removed his boots. No answer. She must have given up waiting for him to come to lunch and gone upstairs to clean. He crept into the dining room. Olga had left the tureen of stew on the table. He sat down, not bothering to wash his hands or remove his jacket, and helped himself. Dumplings as well. And carrots braised in honey and poppy seeds.

When he finished he rested his head on his hands on the table and let himself fall into a half-trance. It was warm in here; Olga had lit the stove. She moved between bedrooms upstairs, furniture thumping and groaning as she moved it to sweep floors.

The front door opened.

Rudi sat up. *Bump* went the briefcase on the tiles by the door. Vati. Rudi moved silently to hide behind the door. But Vati was going upstairs.

'Did you save me some lunch, Olga?' he called.

Rudi tiptoed into the hall. The well-polished black leather briefcase waited for its owner to descend from the first floor. Rudi eyed it as he would an adversary. Now Vati and Olga were standing in the doorway of one of the bedrooms. Something rattled and clinked. The broken vase in the shoebox.

'I have no idea, Herr Lange,' Olga was saying.

'You didn't notice the vase had gone from the windowsill? Really, Olga?'

Rudi pictured Olga shrugging, twisting her gnarled hands in the white apron she always wore, trying to think of the correct thing to say.

'It must have been an accident.'

'That boy.' Rage in Vati's voice now, blazing through the thickness in his throat. He must have a cold. 'That wretched son of mine. Lazy. Clumsy. And he didn't turn up at school this morning. They rang me. In the office.'

'I can mend the vase,' Olga said.

'It will never be the same.'

'Nobody will be able to tell. He is a good, kind boy. He didn't mean to break it. And he must have had a good reason for missing school.'

'That's not the point, Olga. You'd think joining the Youth would make a difference, but oh no, always an excuse for missing meetings.' The box rattled again. 'Why can't he be like other boys?'

'He's better than most of them.'

'If I hadn't come home unexpectedly with this damn cold, would I ever have known about this smashed vase?'

More silence.

'He needs the strap. There are camps for boys like him. A hard winter camp to give him discipline.' A pause. Rudi could imagine his father's brain whirring as he planned this. 'I'll be in my study, making calls. You can prepare his clothes. Bring me some stew on a tray. And a tisane.'

His father stomped across the landing. The bathroom door closed. Any second now one of them would come down the staircase. Rudi ran to the front door to grab his boots, which his father hadn't noticed.

He made for the kitchen, keeping to the rug, his stockinged feet soundless. As Vati's footsteps thumped downstairs Rudi gently closed the kitchen door, pushing himself against the wall to hide himself from view. The shadowy outline of his father appeared in front of the frosted-glass door. Rudi stood still. Vati walked on, towards his study with its railway maps and timetables. A second outline appeared: smaller, softer. Olga.

The kitchen door opened to the garden. Rudi closed it softly behind him. The football sat on the white-covered grass like a single full stop on a sheet of paper. Rudi scooped it up. He tossed satchel and ball over the wall and climbed over, springing down into the lane behind the garden.

He walked briskly until he reached the busier streets. People were walking slowly towards the station: shabbily dressed grown-ups holding children's hands, smiles on their faces as brittle and broken as the smashed vase at home. At the station entrance an official stood with a clipboard. A couple of policemen looked on.

Benny's papers still seared Rudi's coat pocket. He could feel them through the wool fabric. He scanned the crowd. Where was the boy he could save?

34.

I put down the laptop. 'You were very young,' I whispered to my patient. 'Your father was going to punish you severely, send you to some horrific youth camp. But even then, you were trying to find someone else to go in Benny's place. You were just a child, just eleven.'

He pulled off the mask. 'Scared. Like you, Rose.'

The effort of speaking was too much. He tried to put the mask back over his face. I took it from him and placed it on him. 'Don't say anything else,' I told him. 'I know you're trying to make me feel better about causing Mum's death. You're trying to show me I shouldn't judge myself, shouldn't blame myself.'

He nodded.

'Thank you.' I squeezed his pale, cold hand. 'I'll read on.' I picked up the laptop and resumed my reading.

~

Some of the parents were weeping. Rudi blinked. He couldn't imagine Vati weeping over him, distraught at an imminent separation. Vati would pat his son's shoulder, possibly extend the affection to a quick ruffle of his hair if he was feeling particularly emotional.

There were other parents who didn't weep either, who clung speechlessly to their boys and girls, knuckles white, as though they might collapse if they let go.

'Say *auf Wiedersehen* to your children now.' The loudspeaker cut across the weeping and the excited shouts from the kids. 'You will not be permitted to accompany them any further. Hurry along, please.' Arms locked themselves around smaller bodies. A collective wail rose.

Rudi stood alone. The emotion from the parents buffeted him like the sea against an isolated rock. He clutched Benny's papers in one hand, the football under his other arm, staring at the small family groups, at all this sorrow. Half of him wanted to run back to the street away from them all, to throw the papers into the gutter and escape somewhere quiet. The lake, perhaps, where he'd once gone on that summer picnic. He could walk around its icy perimeter and cool his mind.

'All children proceed to platform two now. Parents, you must remain behind. Do not accompany your children any further.'

Again the low wail rose. Rudi could almost smell the salt of the tears. A guard walked towards him.

'Hurry, boy.'

Rudi opened his mouth to explain that he wasn't actually going on the transport, that it was all a mistake, but the guard pointed towards the platform.

'Can't you hear me?' His eyes were narrowed in anger.

'I'm not going on the transport, I –'

'Don't try it on with me.' The guard's hand was raised now. 'I can see the papers you're holding. Get moving.'

Rudi shuffled towards the head of the queue, still searching for the right words to explain. The guard kept his stony gaze on him.

An inspector in railway uniform peered at him. Rudi knew who the man was from the time a few years ago when Vati had held a lowlier position at the railways and sometimes took his son to watch the trains pull in and out of the station. Surely the inspector would recognize Rudi, raise the alarm, forbid him from going to the platform?

Rudi waited for him to hold up a hand and detain him, but something else was working on him now, a contrary impulse making him want to do what he was told and join the other children as though he was just like them: Jewish, unwanted in this country. Rudi mightn't be Jewish, but he wasn't wanted at home, so what was the difference? The inspector said nothing, his eyes passing over Rudi's features without expression.

'Papers?' Rudi showed them to the man, who checked the photograph against his face. The two didn't match, not really. Benny and Rudi both had light brown hair and dark-blue eyes, but Benny's face was far thinner than Rudi's now, and his nose was longer. Benny's hair had a wave to it; Rudi's hung straight. Surely the inspector would notice it wasn't Rudi in the photograph. But it was as though by becoming Jewish Rudi had become invisible.

'This all you have?' The inspector stared at the football and satchel.

He nodded.

'On you go.' The inspector nodded him through.

Rudi hesitated. Surely he wouldn't get away with this? Now was the time to speak up, pass this off as a prank. The inspector might even think it was amusing. He could plead with him not to tell Vati.

'Herr Lange, you'd never guess what that lad of yours was up to last week. *Nein, nein*, no problem at all, had us all in stitches, Herr Lange. You wouldn't believe the sour looks he got from the Jews. No sense of humour. As if a proper German boy would seriously want to skulk off to England with *them*.'

'Can't you understand German?' the inspector shouted. 'What are you, a stupid Polish Yid?' And this time the guard who'd shouted at him before pushed him towards the platform.

'Think the train's going to hang around for the likes of you?' Rudi took a step forward and then another one and now he was walking towards the platform. He looked back, expecting someone to call out, to pull him back. But nobody seemed to mind that Rudi Lange was about to get on the train to England. He walked to the steps leading to the platform.

He spotted a group of boys he recognized from school a few years ago. They might well know Benny and would not regard his presence here today as a bit of fun. They'd think he was mocking them in some way. He pulled up the collar of his jacket, dropping his face down, trying to make himself invisible. A policeman pounced on the group.

'Open that case.' He pointed at one of the group. Rudi slipped past as the others helped their friend undo the suitcase.

A party of smaller children was walking very slowly towards the steps. 'How'll they manage alone?' a young woman said to another. 'They're hardly more than babies.'

'Still a youth worker short? That's bad luck.'

'Suppose the police get rough with them at the border?'

'I'll go with them.' Rudi almost looked over his shoulder to see who'd spoken, then realized that the voice had been his own.

The young women turned.

'You?'

He supposed eleven-year-old boys didn't often volunteer to assist tots.

'I don't mind. I'm alone anyway.'

'What's your name?' The older girl was pretty, with curling blonde hair and freckles. She didn't even look particularly Jewish.

'Benny. Benjamin Goldman.' He said it softly in case anyone overheard.

'Well, Benjamin Goldman, you have earned yourself a very big thank-you from us.' Her smile was broad. 'Think you'll manage them on the train?'

He nodded, bathing in the warmth of her eyes. None of those tough Jewish boys would be seen anywhere near a carriage full of babies, so he'd be safe on the train. And when they were on the ship, he'd keep to the cabin. He shoved the papers into the satchel and grabbed the hand of one of the little girls.

'Let's go.'

She trotted along beside him, the rest of the kids following. The group of Jewish boys walked past him without a backward look.

The policemen were still pouncing on children whose suitcases looked expensive or too large. Rudi was almost grateful he had only the satchel and football. He was nobody of note. His father's name could cause every man in this railway station to stand to attention, but Rudi was receiving only quick, contemptuous glances as he opened the carriage door.

Just another unwanted kid on his way out of the Reich, lucky not to have a boot up his backside to hurry him on. Invisible.

And invisibility was a state Rudi intended to preserve for as long as possible.

35.

I lifted my head from the laptop. It took me some minutes to return to the old man in the bed. I was still with the young boy, swept up onto the transport by an irresistible current, arriving in a country he'd never expected to come to, alone, with a terrible secret. Rudi Lange, not Benjamin Goldman or Benny Gault. An imposter. In his own eyes, a man who'd lived under a stolen identity for the last half-century and more.

'You never went back to tell them what had happened? To find your father?' I asked. 'And Olga?'

His hand went to the oxygen mask.

'Don't take that off. Shall I read the next file?'

He blinked at me.

I found the file titled 'Rudi Lange 2' and opened it.

When I finally told my wife, Lisa, who I really was, she had questions. As you'd expect. The first was why I hadn't told anyone this years earlier. It was hard for me to describe the fear I felt that

I would be sent home to Germany, or to some kind of internment camp, once the war started. Richard and Ernst had been interned on the Isle of Man and it had taken Lord Dorner weeks to have them released. But they had been 'real' Jewish boys. Would the Dorners have interceded for a non-Jewish German, an enemy alien? I now know they would not have been unkind to me: they were tolerant, generous people. But as a boy I read stories of ships sunk in the Atlantic, their cargo of enemy aliens drowning. Even if I survived such a voyage, the thought of years spent as a prisoner in Canada or Australia terrified me. But it was the potential disgust of the Dorners, of the kindly Dr Dawes, of the other boys at Fairfleet, that terrified me even more. As I grew up I began to see my sin in a more tolerant light, but my teenage self judged himself harshly. I'd really become Benny, not Rudi, as soon as I stepped off the boat at Harwich and Benny was who I intended to be for the rest of my life.

Lisa's second question concerned my 'real' German family. She wanted to know what had happened to my father, Georg Lange. This is what I told her.

In 1951 I contacted David, who worked with Jewish Displaced Persons. I asked David if he could find out anything about Georg Lange and his housekeeper, Olga, telling him that Georg Lange had been a loyal Aryan friend of my family. David found a German researcher who searched the town records for me.

The researcher discovered that both my father and Olga had been killed in a freak air raid in 1944. An Allied bomber had emptied its bomb hold by mistake.

I'd always feared Georg Lange would track me down to England and insist on my returning to Germany. I now experienced mixed and shameful emotions, mourning the father I remembered from my early childhood: affectionate and funny. And I had loved Olga. Now they were both dead. But I felt a relief that nobody could expose me now. Benny's father, Herr Goldman, was also dead. Dr Dawes had eventually managed to obtain confirmation of his murder at a Polish camp in 1943. Frau Goldman had died in hospital the same day as the real Benny had died in the cramped apartment with just me as company.

So they were all gone. My real parents, Benny's parents, Olga and Benny himself.

I am now dying, with good and kind companions beside me. When I feel fear of what is to come I think of the real Benny, of how scared he must have been as he gasped for his last breath. I was so young, I didn't know how to reassure a dying child. I can only hope I was of some comfort to him.

I was working on a local newspaper at the time I found out about my father, and rang in, claiming to have flu. For five days I drank myself stupid and stayed in my lodgings.

Then I returned to the newspaper office. I worked hard, very hard. I took on every assignment I was given and pursued it with a terrier intensity, whether it was a story about meat shortages or the opening of a new municipal swimming pool.

Occasionally English people I worked with would ask me if I had ever gone 'home', meaning Germany. They were probably taken aback by the vehemence with which I told them that Germany was not my home and had not been since January 1939. Eventually I became Benny Gault. I dropped the Goldman surname to sound more British. By then I had barely a hint of a German accent. I'd been ruthless with myself, listening to English people, copying their pronunciation. Nobody would have known me as the person I'd been in 1939. Alice Smith seemed at one stage to hint she knew something wasn't right about me, but she wouldn't have been able to prove anything.

I suspect I have only a few days left to write down what else I discovered about my father. I am weary now and will return to this task.

࿐

I finished reading. Benny was still awake, watching me.

Something was nudging at my memory. Something to do with the storage room. I'd opened a drawer down there and touched something, something old and brown and leather. A deflated football. The football that the real Benny had given Rudi. Of course: the three gold letters, 'O D N', had been all that remained from 'GOLDMAN', Benny's surname. Benny had given his ball away to Rudi, therefore the ball could only have come to England with Rudi.

Benny's mouth was etched with blue again. His eyes were shut now. Max, lying on the rug beside the bed, lifted his head and wagged his tail, as though offering reassurance to Benny.

36.

Benny let himself drift. He could still hear Rose's voice in the distance, telling him to rest, feel her hands pull the cover over him. She had gentle hands and a gentle voice, just like Harriet, just like her grandmother. Rose wanted to know, she wanted to know everything.

He wasn't going to tell her the rest of it. He'd promised Harriet. Back then, his word had been the only thing he could give Harriet. Rose knew enough.

This disease was breaking him up, splitting him into all the versions of himself he'd ever been. Part of him was an old man in a bed he'd never leave again. Part of him was Rudi, aged eleven, finding himself pushed onto the train, smelling the mixture of anguish and relief at the railway station. And part of him was a young man. With a guilty secret. An interloper who'd fallen for his benefactor's wife.

The three parts of Benny pulled him one way and another. Finally he let himself float towards the young man. People had called Benny handsome, but he'd never really seen it himself. He'd been tall, wide-shouldered, with a good head of hair. Was that what Harriet had seen in him? But surely a woman like her could have found handsome men anywhere? *What was it about me?* he longed to ask her.

Even if he'd put the question years ago when it had first started between them, she probably wouldn't have answered with more than that mocking laugh of hers. He was back with her now; it was summer, early August. The day had been hot and he'd been studying hard.

~

The afternoon's heat had mellowed to a warm softness. Benny hadn't seen Harriet for a month. She was back at Fairfleet now; he'd overheard her talking to Smithy downstairs, discussing which dress Harriet was to wear when they dined out tonight.

Harriet said, 'It'll have to be the short-sleeved silk, Smithy. Anything else will suffocate me.' She sounded very light-hearted, not the contemplative woman who'd told him about her friend crashing the plane.

It was quiet tonight. Dr Dawes was visiting his sister on the south coast this week, so Benny had eaten the rissoles Alice Smith served up for him in the kitchen, sitting alone at the scrubbed pine table.

'You'll have to make do with these. There's barely enough meat on the ration to feed a mouse,' she said. 'So the cook tells me. When she deigns to turn up.'

'I don't mind rissoles.'

She banged a saucepan as though suggesting that it didn't really matter whether he minded or not. When the meal was finished he wandered down to the lake and lay down on the jetty. A thin haze obscured the stars tonight, but it was already dissolving. As he watched, the stars seemed to sharpen. Nobody knew Benny was down here. He felt his isolation like a stab in the ribs: he might be the last person left on the planet. In just months he'd be away from Fairfleet and there'd be many moments of isolation like this when nobody would know what he was doing or even care, not even Dr Dawes, who'd be returning at last to his beloved university libraries.

The lake suddenly felt unbearable, as if it were thousands of miles away from the rest of humanity. He stood up and went inside. Even if the only other person in the house was Alice Smith, it was better than being out here alone on the jetty.

Too hot to go to bed yet. He stood at the open bedroom window. The tobacco plants that Harriet had sewn along the beds by the house emitted a sweetness that again took Benny back to a time before the war, before his mother had died. Had she grown tobacco plants in her garden too?

Two white lights appeared at the end of the drive, telling him the Dorners were on their way home. He sat on the bed, listening to the sound of the car coming closer, then its doors closing, the front door opening. Lord Dorner's deep voice asking his wife if she'd like a nightcap, her turning down the offer, Harriet exclaiming at Alice Smith still being up, and no, they didn't need anything to eat or drink, thank you. All was quiet again. The flowers seemed to emit even more scent and Benny could see himself back in the garden on a summer night with his mother, when he'd been Rudi, not Benny.

Rudi. A name he hadn't dared speak, even to himself. Letting himself be Rudi was risky; it dragged too many secrets into the present. If he hadn't gone to the railway station, if he'd stayed in Germany as Rudi Lange, where would he be now? A corpse buried in the ground somewhere between Berlin and Moscow, like all those boys his age who'd only been seventeen in the last months but had stood between the Soviets and the capital? Failing that, he'd be in a prisoner-of-war camp somewhere on the Steppe. No smelling the flowers at midnight for Rudi Lange.

Too dangerous to muse on this. He turned to see Harriet standing in his doorway in her evening dress. Something of Rudi must have still lingered on his features. She blinked at him.

'Benny? Are you all right? You look . . . different, somehow.'

He tried to return to Benny, to the cool, contained persona of Benny, Benny who'd mastered English so completely and was planning to shine at university.

'I was just remembering things.'

'So much to remember.' She closed the door and came to stand beside him at the window. He felt the danger. Was she going to ask him something about his childhood? 'I wonder how we're all going to know which bits of the past to remember and which bits to let go.'

'What do you mean?' He sounded sharp to his own ears. Had she read his mind, seen the projections of Rudi pass across it?

'There are some parts of the last six years I want to store in my mind for ever. There are other parts I never want to think about again.' She looked at him. 'You know about that crash. I don't think about it any more. What's the point, I ask myself?'

He, too, emphatically wanted to forget his last ever scene as Rudi: in that railway station in 1939 with the weeping parents.

Harriet was still standing close to him. The scent she wore was different from what she'd worn earlier today: earthier and more sophisticated, both at the same time. The hairs on his arms stood up.

'Benny, there's something I need to ask you –'

No. He couldn't let her ask questions. She'd have it all out of him. He'd be exposed. In a panic he pulled her to himself.

'Benny!' Her eyes were wide. He'd ruined everything, she wasn't interested, what had happened earlier in the summer was just a moment of passing kindness. Her muscles felt tense under his arms. He started to apologize, to let her go.

But she clung to him, a tiny bead of perspiration running down to her collarbone, nestling in the hollow. He wanted to bend down and taste that part of her. She'd be salty, he conjectured, but sweet, too. How could he be thinking these things about his benefactor's wife? Lord Dorner was a kind man, a decent man, who'd taken in a boy he didn't know and trusted him to behave himself. He didn't deserve this kind of reward. Benny pushed Harriet away.

'Sorry,' he muttered. 'I'm not thinking.'

'No, Benny, listen to me.' She was still clinging to his hand. 'It's all right.' She was rearranging the strap on her dress now. 'Let's sit down. We'll talk.'

He looked at the chair in front of his desk. But she sat on the bed. He knew he should sit on the chair, away from temptation, but he sat on the other side of the bed. Just to be sure, he placed a pillow between them. She eyed it with a smile. Probably thinking that a six-foot concrete wall down the middle of the bed wouldn't have made any difference. He told himself not to think about the way her chest rose and fell beneath her silk bodice. Not to look at the hollows under her collarbone. They were just sitting and talking. Like friends. Like benefactress and beneficiary.

'Benny, what were you thinking about when I came in?' Her eyes were full of concern.

'Nothing. Just musing about time passing, things changing.'

'Our little group here at Fairfleet is all dissolving, isn't it?' She sounded sad. 'I know the boys keep in touch, and some of them visit when they can, but it's not the same. But you know this will always be your home, don't you?'

Did he?

'We'll always want to know what you're up to and we'll always be here to help.' Her hand stroked the pillowcase. He watched the manicured fingers slide over the ivory linen. 'Can't you tell me what's on your mind?'

Which bit? Still her fingers maintained their rhythmic, slow, sliding movement. He put his own hand on the pillowcase. Her hand stopped. Then it started moving again, brushing his fingers, progressing to the top of his hand. She turned it over so the palm was upright and carried on stroking, very slowly. Perhaps she thought it was soothing, like comforting a child who'd taken a fall. It wasn't; it was like throwing a lighted match onto a bonfire.

All it needed was petrol. He reclaimed his hand and placed it between her breasts. He could feel her heart beating beneath the fabric. He couldn't remember feeling someone else's heart before. Harriet Dorner was flesh and blood, too. Her heart pumped blood around her body. His fingers splayed out, not wanting to rush, wanting to take time. She moved closer to him and sighed.

'I didn't mean this to happen, Benny.'

But the hand that had been stroking his palm was now touching his face, the index finger running over his lips. He pulled away the pillow between them. She lay down. He looked at her on the eiderdown of his single bed, until now just an ordinary bed with a plain wooden headboard, a marker of his youthful, novice status, but now transformed into something extraordinary. Harriet Dorner was reclining on his bed, with the bodice of her silk evening dress pulled down from her breasts so that he could see lace underwear underneath. Half of him wanted just to sit there, feasting his eyes. But the other half was impatient.

He lowered himself down beside her. His lips remembered the first kiss and almost ached to do it again. She rolled over so that her body was pressed against his; he could feel every curve of her under the light silk, even the little stud-like pressure of the buttons on her thighs that must be some kind of underwear fastener. For her stockings, perhaps. He knew so little about what women wore, what they wanted. Fairfleet had been a male cauldron, most of the time.

Perhaps she guessed that he was clueless. She took his hand and guided it over her breasts. More of the lace undergarment was exposed. It didn't seem to be covering as much of her as it was supposed to. He could see the darker colour of her –

'Goodnight, Benny.' Lord Dorner, standing outside the closed door, seeing the light on, probably thinking his protégé was doing some late-night reading.

Benny sat up. Harriet sat, too. A door opened along the landing.

'I'll go through to him.' She rearranged her underwear and dress. 'He'll think I'm in the bathroom.' The Dorners' bedroom didn't have an en-suite bathroom, something that Ernst, whose father had once run a prestigious hotel, had commented on with surprise. 'What were we thinking of? I'm sorry.' She pushed a blonde lock off her face. 'But I know there's something bothering you, Benny. Not just . . . what's happened between us. Sometimes I wonder if . . . But it's for you to tell me.'

What had he got to lose now? She must already think he was a sex-crazed lunatic. Identifying himself as a non-Jewish sex-crazed, German lunatic imposter was only one more step deeper into trouble. If she woke up in the morning and decided that Benny had to go, what did it matter?

'Harriet?' Lord Dorner again.

She got up and checked her reflection in the mirror above the chest of drawers, fiddling with her hair.

'We need to be up early for the Cheltenham trip,' her husband called.

'Listen, Benny.' She spoke quietly, urgently. 'Forget about this. It's not going to happen again.'

'Never?'

She was silent.

'You can't say that, can you, Harriet? You can't promise yourself that you don't want it to happen again.'

She adjusted her pearls. 'I'm married. And you are very young.'

'I won't always be so young. Just tell me when and I'll come to you; wherever I am, I'll come.' When Lord Dorner was no longer around, he meant. The man was old, late forties, perhaps older.

She walked past him on the way to the door.

'Just tell me,' he repeated. 'Send for me. I'll come. Will you promise, Harriet?'

'Yes.' She said it very quietly, but he heard the word all the same.

Send for me, he told her, decades, aeons, later, as he lay dying. Benny was dissolving into a collection of molecules belonging to all the parts he'd played, but for the moment it was the young man who'd loved Harriet who held the strongest outline. Harriet was standing over him, fiddling with something on his mouth, some kind of mask. She looked older than she had that August night, but still beautiful, even though her hair was brown now, not fair.

He'd last seen Harriet alone one last time, years after the encounter in his bedroom. She'd called him and he'd come, just as he'd promised. Must have been 1950.

Fairfleet had been neglected. Benny jumped over a rain-filled pothole the size of a bath in the drive and wondered if he'd been rash to risk his new flannel trousers. Not to mention the almost-new black overcoat from a market in Kingston.

Clearing out bookshelves, etc., Harriet had telegrammed. *Please return and say what we should store.* He'd held the telegram and blinked. The first words from her since Lord Dorner had died in 1948 and she'd written to tell him. She'd been in America, but now she was back. Nothing stood between them anymore.

Dr Dawes had long since returned to Cambridge. Benny himself was coming back to this house having completed basic training, three years at university and the first months of his first job on the *Surrey Comet*, based in Kingston upon Thames. Holidays had been spent with the tutor, or overseas, if Benny had money and companions. He hadn't found himself back at Fairfleet. What was the point, if she wasn't there? The place had been boarded up, in any case, left to Alice Smith to look after.

A November afternoon would challenge any building to look its best. Fairfleet seemed to glower at the end of its drive like a slouching, sulky, dirty-grey beast. Chunks of plaster had fallen off the walls. Weeds grew up through the gravel. The wings on the fountain statue had come off. He caught a glimpse of the topiary hedges, now shapeless lumps of box tree. The whole scene dared Benny to make comparisons with the way it had once been.

What must Harriet think of this battered old country after those years in America? Did she miss Lord Dorner very much? He'd taken care over the writing of his telegram in response to hers, tossing several drafts into the wastepaper bin.

Finally he'd written: *Convenient next Saturday?*

She'd sent back a single *Yes Sat.* in reply. She wouldn't be able to say much in a telegram, but they both knew what these telegrams meant.

How would it be when he saw her? He certainly wasn't the naive boy he'd been when he left Fairfleet. The one who'd been so shocked and thrilled when they'd been together on his bed. He'd had his adventures during the years away from Fairfleet.

He couldn't help excitement rippling through him. When he'd checked his reflection in the small mirror by the front door just before leaving, he'd glimpsed Vati in the glass: Vati as he'd been when Benny – Rudi back then – was tiny, before the Party had stuck its nose into Vati's precious rolling-stock, railway lines and points systems. In those days Vati left for work in the morning, eyes twinkling, tall, broad-shouldered.

'Have a good day, gorgeous,' his mother would call after Vati. The words rang through Benny's memory and, as always, he tried to blank them out. This time he couldn't.

But as he approached the house it became impossible to keep thoughts of Vati in his head anyway. On the late-autumn dun-coloured grass lay a single peacock feather. Must be one of the last. Usually the peacocks had moulted completely by now. They'd died out slowly over the war. The boys had suspected that at least one of the birds had found its final destiny in a stew pot. He picked up the feather and its eye stared at him.

When he'd lived at Fairfleet he'd always walked straight in. It took a conscious effort for him to press the bell like a visitor. He'd never rung it before and wasn't sure that it worked. No sound came from inside the house. He was about to push it again when the door opened. He hadn't expected her to open the door herself and was taken by surprise. For a moment he couldn't think of anything to say. At first he thought she was unchanged. Then he noticed small lines around her eyes, very faint. But all the same, the age gap between them had shrunk, he noted with triumph.

'You're here.' She kissed his cheek and stood back to look at him. He found himself opening and closing his mouth like a fool as he looked at her. 'Come in, Benny.'

The hall was the same, though in need of a coat of paint.

'I spend most of my time in here these days.' She took him to a room at the back that she'd turned into a kitchen. 'With just me and Smithy, there's no point having the kitchen down in the basement. And I eat in here, too.' There was a wooden table and a small sofa in the corner on which a tortoiseshell cat slept.

Smithy? He must have looked blank. She laughed.

'Alice Smith. She became known as Smithy in the munitions factory.'

'She's still here?'

'I couldn't manage without her. She does pretty well everything in the house, with a daily coming in twice a week.' She went to the stove, which looked new, and placed the kettle on the hob. 'She's out this afternoon. It's been very cosy, just the two of us here together.' She gave a laugh. Benny wasn't sure he liked the idea of Harriet being here alone with Alice Smith, with her sandy eyelashes and those all-seeing green eyes.

'Things might change, though.'

'Oh?' he said.

'I have to think hard about my future.'

Selling the house, perhaps.

'You want to stay here?' he ventured, putting the peacock feather on the kitchen table.

'I wouldn't be anywhere else.' There was a flash of real passion in her eyes. It took him by surprise. 'The taxes are becoming crippling. And they'll probably get worse, everyone says. But I couldn't bear to sell Fairfleet. It's been in my family for over a hundred years, Benny.'

Her family, not Lord Dorner's? He'd just assumed the house had been her husband's. But Fairfleet was Harriet's.

She'd waved him into a chair by the stove. On the kitchen table sat the book she was reading, something about racehorses, and her writing case. A Player's cigarette was stubbed out in an ashtray. She noticed the feather for the first time. 'How lovely. It'll remind us of past glories. Poor Vulcan is our last peacock and I don't think he'll be around for much longer.'

'What are your plans now?' They might have been distant cousins, making small-talk.

'I'm hoping to get a bit of riding in. There's a trainer in the next village. It's nearly as good as flying.'

'You must miss the planes.' She seemed slightly diminished, as though being out of her element – pure, bright light – had deprived her of energy.

'I had a wonderful time in America. I managed nearly two years out in Arizona. Perfect flying conditions there. Then there were bits and pieces out on the West Coast. Until Sidney died.'

She filled the pot, her hand shaking.

'People thought he married me because I had the house. And I was supposed to be a looker.'

She still was. He didn't say this, because she must surely know.

'In fact, it was the other way round. I set my cap at him.' She gave an amused smile at the surprise on his face. 'I knew it would be hard for me to keep Fairfleet by myself. My parents didn't leave me much capital. And Sidney always loved the place. He was a generous man.'

But then he'd died just as the post-war financial squeeze had worsened.

'Anything to keep the house.' She nodded over her tea cup. 'I know it doesn't sound very admirable, Benny. But you can love a man out of pure gratitude that he's enabled you to keep your house.'

His face must have shown what he thought about that.

'Would it be more moral to love someone just because he was young and handsome and clever?' She looked directly at him. He blushed. 'Fairfleet has been in my family for generations.'

'I know.' And he did, now. She'd never love him. He'd never be rich enough to keep Fairfleet going for her. He felt the atoms in the air between them glue themselves into an invisible barrier.

She put down the tea cup. 'Never can remember where we keep the biscuits. Smithy keeps tidying them away.'

Harriet opened a drawer and found what she was looking for. 'She can't get used to these reduced circumstances.' She opened a biscuit tin and took out a packet of digestives.

'Did Alice . . . Smithy . . . go to America with you and Lord Dorner?'

'She stayed in the house, to look after things here. It's been tough on her, having very little help. She cleans and dusts and polishes all day long. But she's always been dotty about the place.'

And about you, he thought. Harriet, Smithy and Fairfleet were a perfect little triad.

They sat silently. The cat stretched and yawned. The afternoon grew greyer. Benny felt his hopes fade. Perhaps she did, too. Her fingers reached towards his over the pile of books and paper on the table. 'I've been rattling away about myself all this time. Very rude. Tell me about the newspaper. And the rest. University. National Service. I've got them all in the wrong order.'

He didn't want to talk about the months polishing boots and trying to keep himself to himself while mastering drills. What possible connection was there between that world of unpleasant food, unpleasant smells and tedious activity and the woman sitting here with him? She belonged to light and air, not to puddle-covered parade grounds and grim barracks where you could never be alone.

He talked instead of college life: tutorials, High Table with candles and Latin grace, balls he'd been to; of rising very early some mornings to go and look at the college gardens while the dew still covered the grass and flowers. 'But the topiary doesn't compare with . . . here,' he said. He'd been about to say *with ours*, but stopped himself in time. Fairfleet wasn't his home.

'And you saw a bit of Frederick Dawes?' she asked.

'Tea on Sundays and sometimes dinner during the week. And of course the vacations.' Summer holidays spent with Dr Dawes and his sister, walking on the beach in Sussex, chatting about detective novels and nuclear weapons and what had happened to India at partition. And now the newspaper: finding lodgings in Kingston, near the river: visiting Hampton Court maze and Richmond Park, taking the train up to Waterloo and walking across the Thames to the West End to see a show or play.

'Work-wise I don't do anything very exciting at the moment.' His throat felt dry. 'Stories about lost dogs. In New Malden. Reports from council meetings.'

'It's just the start.' She broke a biscuit in two and ate a half.

'Sometimes it's fun. We sit in the pub in Kingston marketplace and pick up some good stories over a pint.'

He didn't want her to start feeling sorry for him.

'Tell me, Benny, do you feel better now about things? You once said you were feeling bad about having survived when so many Jews hadn't.'

'I still feel bad.' A useless way of trying to describe his emotions.

'But if you'd stayed in Germany and terrible things had happened to you it wouldn't have saved anyone else, would it?'

'Yes.'

She frowned. 'You mean another child would have come on the transport in your place?'

'Yes.'

'But why should they have been more deserving than you?'

He could tell her now. He could tell her he was a fraud, a deceiver. Watch the gentle expression on her face turn to disgust and anger. This afternoon was all going wrong; he hadn't meant to think about all this. He should have taken command of the situation.

He couldn't do it. He gave a half-shrug. It must have looked desperate.

'Oh, Benny.' Her hand reached for his. The fingers were firm; you could imagine them controlling a Spitfire or a thoroughbred.

'Stop judging yourself so harshly. I know you're going to do well. I was so pleased when you said you were coming here today.'

He must have made a kind of gasp because the stroking fingers became more intense in their movement. He put his other hand on top of hers so that he held it in a kind of sandwich. 'Why?' he asked.

She was smiling at him now, but her smile was uncertain. 'Oh, I'm not really sure. I liked all the others; they were good boys. But you – you were different. You had an intensity about you, a look in your eyes as though you wanted to gobble up every experience and make it part of you.'

'It sounds unappealing.'

'Rather the opposite, in fact.'

Now he had nothing to lose. 'I didn't feel so much younger than you that last time.'

She looked down at their entwined hands. 'Oh God, I think we were mad. At least I was.'

He held her hand tighter.

'If we've finished tea, why don't you sit there?' She nodded at the small sofa. 'I'll bring down your books for you to decide whether you want me to store them for you.'

'I'll get them. I don't want you fetching and carrying for me.'

'It's no trouble.'

She probably wanted to be away from him. She was embarrassed.

He didn't want to let go of her hand, but she twisted her fingers free. As he approached the sofa the cat jumped down.

Harriet laughed. 'She's not used to male company. God knows how she's going to cope when . . .' She blushed again. 'We've scared her off, anyway.'

We haven't done anything yet, he wanted to say. The afternoon was slipping away and so was Harriet. He could sense it. He must have misread the meaning of the telegram. It had just been about books after all. Desperation made him brave.

'I could walk out of this room right now,' he said. 'You could telephone for a taxi for me. And you and I can write Christmas cards to one another every year. Perhaps sometimes you could invite me down for Sunday lunch. Just as you would any of the others. And when I get married you can buy my fiancée and me a silver tea pot.'

'That's the way it should be, Benny.'

'But you remember how it was last time. That night.'

'August 1945. I remember. Just before the Japanese surrendered.' Her legs opened slightly so that one of them touched his. She wore a wool skirt. He put his fingers on it lightly. It was soft to the touch. She must have bought it in America. Nobody had wool like that over here.

'Oh God,' she said softly. 'I've been so sensible all my adult life apart from those two occasions with you.'

'You weren't that sensible when you chose to be thousands of feet up, dodging the Luftwaffe.'

'Perhaps not then.' She laughed. 'But elsewhere. I've always done what was best for this place. Until now.'

He didn't dare look at her or say anything in reply, concentrating on his hand as it moved very slowly up and down the skirt. There was a small bump. Must be the suspender. He moved the hand to her abdomen, more rounded than he remembered, more womanly, and up to her breasts, which also seemed more generous than they had last time when she'd lain down on his bed. American food had filled her out. He'd touched her like this in his wildest, most guilty dreams.

When she still said nothing he let himself look up. Her face was very still, eyes half-closed. He moved his mouth towards hers. When he'd done this with other girls there'd been a giggle, a whispered encouragement or protest. Her silence was exciting. He put a hand on her shoulder, onto her soft silky jumper. Still she didn't say anything. From its new location by the stove the cat began to purr like a small engine. The shoulder under Benny's hand rose and fell in silent mirth.

'I think she's saying she approves.' She lay back on the sofa, shook off her shoes and swivelled her legs up. 'That's better.'

Nervousness fled. Her eyes widened as he kissed her more hungrily. He reminded himself to take his time. He'd waited for this for all these years: no point in rushing. It felt better than he had ever imagined. Years of anticipation and longing had only hinted at what it would be like with Harriet.

He kicked off his own shoes. One of them must have hit the side of the stove. There was a clatter. The cat gave a squawk of indignation. 'Oh dear,' Harriet broke off to laugh. 'Poor puss.' She pulled Benny back to her. For a minute there was nothing that needed saying. She tasted and felt just as he'd dreamed she would. No, better. He unbuttoned her shirt, felt her hands moving underneath his own, stroking and brushing his skin, moving downward, unbuttoning him. The cat gave another more muted squawk, obviously still put out.

Someone was opening the door. 'If that ginger from the village's got in here again to bother my Priscilla, I'll wring its neck,' a voice said.

Alice Smith. The years had added lines around her eyes. She stared at them. They hadn't reached the stage where items of clothing had been completely removed. But there could be no doubt as to what had been happening on the sofa. Still Alice Smith stared at them, face blank.

'I didn't like the film much. Left before it finished.' She blinked, noticing the peacock feather. 'This shouldn't be inside!' She picked it up, cheeks pale. Harriet made an impatient sound.

'I'll make a start on that upstairs bathroom, then.' Smithy nodded at Harriet, turned and left, closing the door behind her very quietly.

'Oh God.' Harriet pushed him away and reached for her shoes. 'I'd better go after her.'

'Leave her.' He held onto her. 'She's just embarrassed. But you're an adult, a free woman.'

'No.'

'She can't dictate how you behave.' Still he clung to her. 'Harriet, we're always interrupted, every time. Don't let it happen now.'

'You don't understand.' Harriet rose, tucking her shirt into the wool skirt, brushing a hair from her face. 'It's complicated.'

'How?'

She stood at the table, back to him. 'There's Peter to consider.'

'Peter?'

'My . . . Well, the man I might be getting engaged to.'

'You're marrying again?' He was conscious of his mouth opening and closing. Of course. It had to be that. It had to be too good to be happening to him.

'We met in America, but he's actually English.'

'But . . .' But they'd agreed that she would summon Benny when the time was right for them to be together. She'd sent that telegram. Why?

An older, wiser, more sceptical part of him answered his own question. She'd just sent a telegram about books. That was all. The rest had existed only in his mind.

'When will you marry?'

'I haven't actually said yes yet. But I probably will.' She turned now. Her face was stony. 'It's the house, Benny. It's the only way I can keep Fairfleet.'

'He's rich?' Naturally he would be.

'Made a mint in America during the war. Peter's lived over there since he was a child. His firm built bits and pieces for American tanks. He's going to bring his business over here, open a factory in the Midlands.' She was talking very fast now. 'Metal bands used in locomotive construction. They can be used in prefabs, those temporary little houses. Peter says we still need prefabs.' She came to a halt.

'You don't love him.' He said it as a statement.

'He's very generous, very kind. He knows I love this house and he wants me to live here and restore it. How could I not love someone like that?' Her voice sounded pleading. 'Try to understand.'

'So this,' he pointed to the sofa, 'was just a kind of pleasurable diversion for you?'

She shook her head.

'A bit of fun while you waited for your fiancé to come over?'

'I kept wondering what you'd done with your life, Benny. I had to see you again.' She looked at him, seeming to see the doubt on his face. Her expression hardened. 'And I really did need to sort out the books. Smithy has been going on about them.' She couldn't keep up the disapproving tone. 'I kept imagining how our lives would have been in different circumstances. If I hadn't been older than you, if I hadn't been married.'

If, if, if.

'And when I saw you again I remembered what happened years ago,' she went on, her voice soft now. 'I just wanted you.' She gave a wry smile. 'God, listen to me. I sound like a sex maniac. That's how you make me feel, Benny.'

He strode towards her, sending the cat, still glowering at him, diving for cover under the sofa. 'Don't marry this Peter, Harriet. You know it's not right.'

'I have to, Benny.'

'Keeping your bricks and mortar is more important to you than marrying the wrong man?'

'Peter's not the wrong man.' She laid a hand on her abdomen.

'His money is the only right thing about him, I'm guessing.'

'Guess away. You know nothing.'

'This isn't Jane Austen. Women don't marry for material reasons these days. This,' he tossed his head towards the entrance hall, 'is just an old house.'

'It's my home!'

'Millions have lost their homes, Harriet.'

'Exactly.' Her back stiffened. 'Are you naive enough to believe that women in London and Berlin and Warsaw don't marry just for bricks and mortar, for new homes?'

'There must be another way of keeping Fairfleet. Rent it out to a school for a few years. Start a nursing home. A convalescent home for injured airmen, anything.'

'I have to marry Peter. It's too late.' She pinched a fold of her skirt and looked at it. 'I've been such a fool. I was lonely. For Sidney and England. And for this house and for . . .' She swallowed and looked at him. 'I have to do what's best for everyone concerned. And he's a good person. I know he'll look after both of us.'

'Both of you?' He looked at her, at the position of her hand underneath the belt of her skirt. Still didn't understand. Looked again at her and saw the truth in her eyes. She was going to have a child. 'Peter and you?' He couldn't spell it out, didn't know why it made him feel so bitter. He had never felt like this about her sleeping with her first husband, but this unknown man in America . . . Why?

'I told you, I was lonely.' Her cheeks were pink. 'And a long way from home.'

If she'd returned to England Benny would have come running any time she'd called. Just one word, *come*, and he'd have been at her side.

'I can't afford for things to go wrong, Benny.' She was pale, he saw. 'If Smithy says something to Peter about what she's seen this afternoon . . .'

'Alice won't want to harm you.' Hadn't she always doted on her mistress? 'But, Harriet, this baby –'

She sat up straight, looking every bit the landed lady, the member of the local gentry, the aviatrix. 'Don't, Benny. Don't ask me about the child.'

'Is it the reason you and Peter are marrying?'

She reached for her cigarettes and a silver lighter. 'I don't want to talk about it.'

'I'm sorry.'

'No. I'm sorry. Actually, Benny, I feel ashamed.'

He touched her free hand. 'Don't. You and I, we were made for one another.'

'It's impossible, Benny.'

He knew it then and felt his head fall forward, resting almost on his chest. He felt very weary, very old.

She drew on the cigarette and some of the strain left her face. Perhaps she smelled defeat on him, knew he wouldn't put up further resistance. 'Smithy has very high standards. She might think I've let them both down. She's met Peter several times. They think highly of one another, you see.'

'She's just the housekeeper. You don't have to worry about her. She isn't Mrs Danvers from that Daphne du Maurier novel, you know.'

She laughed, but he could see she was still nervous.

He waited for her to say something more, but she was silent. 'I suppose I'd better get those books.' He felt exhausted. Harriet wanted me, he reminded himself. Even though she's getting married. She hadn't been pretending just now on the sofa. He knew enough about women now to be sure. If Alice hadn't come in, if they'd finally consummated the affair, Harriet wouldn't have been able to resist him. A rotten film at the local cinema had finished them off. He could almost have laughed.

'What time's your train?'

'Should be one in about an hour.' She followed him out into the hallway.

'Would you like any help with the books?'

'Don't worry.' They might have been the merest acquaintances. No sign of Smithy. He climbed the stairs. The first floor seemed unchanged – darker, shabbier, perhaps. He opened his old bedroom door. The bed was covered in a dustsheet, as was the desk. The books on the shelves were ones he'd forgotten he still owned. He'd taken most of them to Cambridge and then on to his lodgings. These were mainly schoolboys' novels: Robert Louis Stevenson. John Buchan. He wouldn't be able to carry them all. He took just half a dozen, Christmas presents from Dr Dawes. He wondered where his old football was. Down in the basement, perhaps.

He took a last look round his room. He'd left here a kid and was now a man. It didn't seem right to be leaving Fairfleet; yet what choice did he have? He wouldn't return when this Peter person was installed. And the baby was born. But he needed to know that Harriet was going to be all right in the future. Something about her in the kitchen after Alice Smith had returned had made him worry for her. She was a strong, athletic woman, at the peak of her life. There was no need to be concerned about her. He was just jealous, he told himself as he closed the bedroom door. But it didn't feel like jealousy. He felt protective of her, which was absurd, as she was so very capable of looking after herself and the new husband would cherish her.

Alice Smith came out of a room on the first floor as he descended, an armful of sheets in her arms. 'That you done, is it?'

'I couldn't take all the books,' he said.

'I'll box the rest up and put them in the cellar. You might not feel able to come back again.' She watched him calmly. 'I've already called a taxi. It'll be waiting at the end of the drive to take you to the station.'

You'd never have guessed that she'd caught them together on the sofa. But he looked more closely and caught the glint of something in her eyes. Malice, he thought, at his discomfiture. But something else, too: relief. Why did she still resent him after all these years?

'Done well for yourself, have you? No surprise, given the start you were given at Fairfleet.'

'I'll always feel gratitude towards Lady Dorner for what she and Lord Dorner did for me.' He sounded very stiff.

'More than most would have done for you.'

'True.' He carried on down the stairs.

'You were always a bit different, though, weren't you?'

He stopped. Turned and looked up at her.

'Not like the other boys.'

'What are you talking about?'

She gave a little smile.

How did you know? He forced himself to keep the question to himself. He wouldn't have put it past Smithy to have carried out her own secret racial investigation. Perhaps she'd interviewed the other boys. He'd been careful about dressing and undressing in front of them, but one of them might have noticed, have passed on comments that Smithy had overheard.

Or perhaps it had been nothing more than her possessing an instinct for him being an ornament on display with the wrong collection. Or a cup stored in the wrong cupboard.

'Don't spoil it for her.'

He must have looked perplexed.

'You always were a handsome boy, Benjamin.'

Nobody had called him that for years.

'Hang on.' She put down the sheets and reached into her deep pinafore pocket. 'You can take this with you.' She laid the peacock feather on top of the books. 'Never could stand them in the house. Probably best you keep yourself busy with your career in London. Then nobody'll have to mention any doubts, will they?'

He could have said more but carried on downstairs, feeling now as though he couldn't wait to leave the place. Smithy's cold gaze followed him as he reached the bottom of the stairs. He knocked on the kitchen door and opened it.

'I've taken some books.'

Harriet was sitting at the kitchen table with a cigarette. She rose as he came in. 'You're going so soon. I thought we'd have longer.' She stubbed out the cigarette. 'I shall miss you so much.' Her voice shook, but perhaps it was just that he wanted to hear it shake. 'Maybe it's for the best.'

'Not for me,' he said shortly. Or for her, either. She looked suddenly smaller. More fragile, despite her still athletic frame and the bloom that the pregnancy must be causing. He still couldn't help feeling that she needed him – him, Benny, refugee working hard to make a career for himself. Why would Harriet, soon to be married again to another rich man, possibly need anything from him?

She looked at the books in his arms. 'You'll drop those. Put them on the table – I'll wrap them up for you.' He did what he was told. '*Great Expectations.*' She read the title of the book on top of the pile. 'Benny, you *must* have great expectations for yourself. I know you'll go far.'

'I don't really care.'

Her eyes filled. 'Please care. For my sake? Be happy and successful.' She wiped her eyes and found a sheet of carefully folded brown paper and string in a drawer. In a few folds of paper and tight knots his past was parcelled up, books and feather closely married. She cleverly wound the string into a handle so that it wouldn't cut into his hand. He wished she'd left him the luxury of feeling physical pain. It would have been a distraction.

She came towards him, hand stretched out. 'Oh, Benny, it's a mess and I didn't mean it to be.'

'It doesn't matter.' But it did.

'I do love Peter. Even if it looks . . . He has this problem with his moods,' she said. 'Sometimes he gets terribly low. The doctors think it's a chemical imbalance. They're clever, those American doctors. They've tried electric shocks, all kinds of things.'

He couldn't find a word to say about this revelation.

'Then I came back home,' she went on. 'It reminded me, of everything. Of you and me that night in 1945. And before, out in the topiary garden.'

Still speech eluded him.

'It still haunts me, you know.'

He knew she wasn't talking about her private life now, that her mind was snagged on the friend's smashed and blackened body lying on the Wiltshire hillside. He knew how it felt to be trapped like that.

'Will you write, Benny?'

He remembered the implicit threat he'd just received on the staircase. He pictured Smithy taking in the post, spotting his handwriting on an envelope. He swung the parcel of books slightly.

'I don't think I can bear it if you just disappear. Fairfleet feels strange without you.'

She looked very young now, younger than Benny himself, even though she had dark shadows under her eyes. Or perhaps because of those shadows.

'I'll always be interested in Fairfleet and everyone who lives here,' he said. It was a stilted way of responding, but he dared not risk anything else. 'How could I not be? And I hope to be able to visit some day.'

'I'd like that,' she said. 'You keeping a distant eye on me. And on the house. The house is me, Benny.'

He kissed her then, couldn't help it, even though he knew that Alice Smith was somewhere in the background, possibly even watching them.

She clung to him for a second then gently shook herself free. He walked out then, without looking at her again.

~

Then the years flashed forward again, as though his life were an express train flying past stations. Benny was an old man, lying on his deathbed. And there she was again now, Harriet, in her flying suit, waving a fan made of peacock feathers, standing laughing at him in his bedroom, at the age she'd been when she'd first fallen in love with him.

'Told you we'd meet again,' she told Benny. 'I always knew you'd come to me if I needed you. And now I'm doing the same for you.' He tried to murmur a greeting to her, but she put a finger to her lips. 'We were always interrupted, weren't we?' She smiled. 'Every single time. Perhaps it was as well.'

'There's something I need to tell you,' he said, finding that he could talk now.

'I already know, silly. Perhaps I always did. But it doesn't matter, it never did, that you're not really Benny, that you're Rudi. Not long now and we'll be together always.' She waved her fan one last time and faded away.

This time they'd be united and nobody would separate them and it wouldn't matter that there were her two husbands and his beloved Lisa. *They neither marry, nor are given in marriage, but are as the angels of God in heaven.* Words from the Bible, words he'd heard in German, as a child, came to him.

And Harriet knew his secret. And she hadn't rejected him.

37.
ROSAMOND

Benny murmured something underneath his oxygen mask and pointed at the wall. He stared hard at the blank space between the windows on the opposite side of the room. Sarah came into the room and watched him.

Something there, perhaps in the play of light and shadows, seemed to fascinate him. He gave a smile that seemed to wash away the haggardness from his features. For a whole minute he observed whatever it was on the wall. Max turned and cocked his head, giving a single gentle whine. Then Benny closed his eyes and sighed.

Sarah looked at me.

'Don't worry,' I said. 'I've seen this happen before.'

'But what was he seeing?'

'I don't know. Some people think it's a chemical reaction in the brain as it closes down. Or another reaction to the morphine. Or the effects of an undiagnosed bladder infection, though I'm pretty sure Benny hasn't got one of those.' I hesitated, not sure how to put the other alternative. 'Others say that people are having some kind of spiritual experience.'

And others yet said that there was more to it than that, that the dying were seeing those who'd died before and gone ahead. I just didn't know.

'He looked . . .' Sarah seemed to search for the right word deep in her heart. 'Joyful. I came in to tell you that the doctor is coming.'

As we watched him Benny seemed to fall deeper and deeper into sleep. Sarah and I stayed with him. After an hour had passed Sarah said we should remove the oxygen mask. I agreed. Sarah dozed for a few hours in her armchair while I watched. This was my job: watching and waiting. Perhaps even welcoming death when it came because I'd made sure that my patient was comfortable and at peace.

I moistened his mouth. And I talked to him in a low voice. I told him that Max was still curled up on the bed at his feet. I told him what had happened with Cathal. And I told him about my lost chance at having a child.

'I didn't want to admit to James how terrible the miscarriage made me feel,' I whispered to the silent Benny. 'I didn't want him to see how sad I was. I pretended it was a relief not to have to sell my flat. I *hate* my flat. I was looking forward to moving into a little house with James and the baby. And a dog.'

I hadn't known I'd felt like this until now.

Then Sarah woke and I slept until mid-morning. I washed quickly and resumed my vigil with Benny.

The doctor arrived. Benny's eyelids flickered as the doctor examined him and made sure that we had all the drugs we might need.

'Though he seems to be drifting quite gently away. Goodbye, Benny. It's been a pleasure knowing you.' He squeezed his hand. Benny made a sound that might have been an attempt to return the farewell.

I moistened his lips again while Sarah showed the doctor out. He seemed to regain a last spark of life.

'Sarah . . . truth.'

'You want to tell Sarah about what happened between Rudi and Benny?'

He nodded.

'I'll show her what you wrote. As soon as she comes back upstairs.'

'Important,' he murmured. 'File, Georg Lange.'

'Your father, Georg. We'll read that one too.' He muttered something else and I leant over him to hear.

'Baby. Sorry.' I was puzzled. Then I realized he had heard me earlier on when I'd whispered the story of my lost pregnancy.

He fell back into deep sleep.

When Sarah reappeared I explained what Benny had asked and took out the laptop to bring up the file. 'It's about his childhood, something he needs you to know.'

She gave a little smile. 'I don't need to look at that.'

Awareness came to me suddenly. 'You knew he wasn't really a Jewish refugee?' She looked away. 'You guessed? Or perhaps you overheard something when he was dreaming?'

'It was something Lisa said, years ago. I came into the room unexpectedly and they were talking. They didn't hear me. Lisa told him that just because he wasn't Jewish didn't mean he couldn't help Jewish people and other refugees.'

'Of course, Lisa already knew this, didn't she?'

'We must have been the only two who did. It shouldn't make any difference to me,' she said.

Then I realized. 'You're Jewish, aren't you, Sarah?'

She looked at me and I saw it was the truth.

'My mother . . .' She took a breath. 'My mother was three when the Germans came to Prague. She survived because a camp guard took pity on her and threw her over a barbed wire fence. A farmer hid her. But after the war she weighed the same as a child half her age.' And Benny, Sarah's beloved employer, a boy never at risk of such persecution, had taken one of the valuable spots on the Kindertransport.

'Benny was just a child. But his father . . .' She shuddered. 'Perhaps his work ultimately made it easy for them to send my mother and grandparents to those camps.'

'Let's read the other file.'

We sat together at the dressing table. From time to time I lifted my head to see whether Sarah had finished a paragraph before I scrolled down further. Her expression was serious when I looked at her.

~

Only lately have I steeled myself to research my real father, Georg Lange. By good fortune none of the papers relevant to him were incinerated in air raids or destroyed during the Russian advance.

My early childhood recollections of Georg are of a man who loved his job and his family. But my mother died. My father came under intense pressure at work. He was irascible at mealtimes and quick to reprimand me.

I don't know how much his political bosses told Georg of their plans for using the German railway system to further their new order. By 1939, my father must surely have suspected that something sinister was subsuming his beloved railway.

Whatever the reason for his bad moods, it was partly owing to my fear of my father that I left home the afternoon of the Kindertransport. Once settled in England I assumed that my father wouldn't have missed me.

Courtesy of police records recently placed on the Internet, which a researcher has found for me, I now know this wasn't true. Georg Lange was reported to the Gestapo on several occasions between 1939 and 1943. Rumours flew around that the mysterious disappearance of his son had turned his mind, making him question his loyalty to the Fatherland. He'd been overheard muttering about the loss of a child being more painful than any loss of national pride. Several of his colleagues, questioned by the police, stated that he'd also stopped wearing his Party pin, the little badge on his lapel. He made negative comments after witnessing the deportation of elderly Jews from a Berlin station.

Georg resigned from the railway and took up a job as a hospital orderly. The Gestapo were still watching him closely, possibly waiting to arrest him. But Georg died in the bombing raid before any action was taken. I am saddened at this violent end, but relieved he was never tortured and lined up against a wall, or sent to a camp.

I am proud to claim Georg Lange as my father.

I've never been a religious man, but I hope I might see the people I've lost to death again after I die. Sometimes I already seem to see them in front of me, their voices calling to me. Perhaps I am simply the victim of changes to brain chemistry caused by cancer and approaching death or by drugs. It's really very interesting, a subject on which I might have liked to write or produce a documentary: *Deathbed visitations: hallucinatory or truly spiritual?*

I have wound up my affairs. The house will be sold and the money given to various refugee charities and other causes. I think Harriet would understand that it is time to sever the threads binding us to Fairfleet. Let a new family come here and fill the house with noise.

I have never felt more completely myself: Rudi Lange, known to some as Benny Gault.

~

I glanced at Sarah. She had finished reading, too, and was staring out of the window.

'He'd started writing so much again just before you joined us here, Rosamond. He'd stopped for some time while he was ill. I worried he was depressed. Then the laptop appeared.' Her expression grew fractionally lighter. 'A top-of-the-range model. Typical Benny – nothing but the best when it came to his writing. He seemed happier when he was tapping away. But he was agitated if I came too close.' She looked back at the still form on the bed. 'It's time, isn't it?'

'Yes.' Probably this evening or during the night. It was already dark again. I went to draw the curtains. I couldn't resist gazing out at the stars, very clear tonight against a navy sky. I was just a tiny, flawed fragment of dust floating around space. My face felt wet. I realized that tears had been pouring down it for some minutes.

But surrounded by light and possibility, a voice said inside me. Alive. No more half-furnished apartments. No more running from one overseas assignment to another. Time to see what would happen if I stayed still.

Benny woke again two hours later.

'Harriet.' His hand moved across the counterpane and clung to my hand, his grip surprisingly firm. 'I knew you'd come before . . . catch the train.' A real train? I wondered. The one he remembered catching when he came to England with the Jewish children? Or did he mean something metaphorical: a train that would take him on his longest journey?

'Careful.' He looked over my shoulder. 'Don't let them see you. Both get into trouble.' He stroked my palm.

I pressed his hand. 'Don't worry.' It didn't feel wrong to stand in for my grandmother, to comfort Benny. 'They don't mind.'

'Even Peter?'

'Even him,' I said, on behalf of my long-dead grandfather, who, wherever he was now, could surely not be worrying about an encounter that had occurred more than half a century ago.

'Lisa?'

'Lisa won't mind.'

~

Anxiety had flooded Lisa's features when he'd told her he was going back to Fairfleet.

'Harriet is dead, Benny. Why are you returning there now?'

He'd returned to the country just a day too late for her funeral. Damn that East Coast storm that had blown up from nowhere, grounding planes at JFK.

'I want to pass on my condolences to her family.'

'Will they even remember you?' She shook her head. 'Oh, hark at me, sounding like a jealous wife.'

'You have nothing to be jealous of. Harriet dying just feels like a part of my youth has gone.'

Lisa nodded. 'I'm being unreasonable. I just didn't know that you'd had . . . those feelings for her.'

Seeing Harriet's obituary had shocked him into telling his wife about what had happened, almost, between him and his benefactress.

'But she was a lot older than you.' Lisa's eyes had been wide open.

'Fourteen years. That's not so much, once you're out of childhood.'

'Did Harriet know who you really were?'

'No. The time never seemed right. You're the only one who knows, darling.'

And their eyes had met, Benny's secret almost like their child, the child they'd never had, binding the two of them together.

So he'd gone to Fairfleet. They were building new houses on one of the fields. He'd slipped onto the site so he could peer across the lake at the house. He'd seen Harriet's daughter sitting on the sunny lawn with the two children. He'd wanted to tell them he was sorry, to let them know just how special Harriet had been. But he felt suddenly shy about intruding.

He should have gone over to them. A failure of courage.

Lisa was standing beside him now.

~

The pressure on my hand softened. Benny slept. Max moved himself from his position at Benny's feet to lie with his back against his side. A look in the dog's eyes told me he had no intention of leaving his station. I'd seen dogs behave like this before with the dying, and let Max stay, hoping that some of his presence would be conveyed to my patient, that Benny would know he wasn't alone.

Benny stirred, opening his eyes and again staring hard at the wall between the windows on the opposite side of the room, before closing his eyes once more. A faint smile lit his face.

'Tired,' he muttered. 'Sleep on train.'

'I think you will too.' I gave Sarah's shoulder a gentle shake to rouse her.

He gasped for air. Sarah was standing beside me now.

His breaths became more shallow and rapid, as though his own engine was running short of fuel. 'Have a safe trip, Rudi.' I kissed his brow, moving to the window so Sarah could spend a few moments alone with him.

The pause between his breaths lengthened. I returned to him. His face relaxed. When they came, the breaths were very slight. Then there was a longer break. We waited for the next inhalation.

It didn't arrive.

~

Rudi waved a last *auf Wiedersehen*. No time for protracted farewells; the train was already pulling away from the platform. Carriage after carriage passed him, each filled with waving passengers. He flung open a door and leaped up. The shiny new football fell out of his arm and bounced on the floor. Someone caught it. Benny. Looking as though he'd just come in from an afternoon spent in the sunny park.

'How'd you get on?' he asked Rudi. Gone was the swollen neck, the grimy clothes. His friend was grinning at him, bouncing the leather ball on the floor.

'We won.' He flopped down beside Benny. 'Three–nil. I scored one.'

'Goalkeeper must have been blind.' But Benny's voice was warm.

'Tickets, please.' A man came in wearing a smart uniform Rudi didn't recognize. Vati. Rudi started to scramble to his feet. But Vati waved him back into his seat. 'Hello, my son. I hear you played excellently.' The uniform was plain. No military-looking epaulettes. No Party pins. Non-political. A railway man's uniform.

The dying, ever-so-rational part of his brain wanted to protest that Vati wasn't real, that this was all merely neurons misfiring, but the more he stared at his father the more real Vati seemed.

Vati clipped his ticket. 'We're running to time. Even with the stop to pick you up.' He sounded proud, energetic, like the man he'd once been.

'You knew . . . I'd be at the station?'

'Of course I did.' He gave a little nod and handed back their tickets. 'I've been waiting to take you home on my train for years now, my boy.' His features relaxed into the smile Rudi remembered from a day years ago when they'd gone for a picnic in fields just outside the town and swum in the lake. 'Lisa's in the next carriage, waiting for you.'

Lisa. So missed, so longed for. Here, too.

'And Harriet's somewhere on board. And your mother.'

The train must have come out of a tunnel as Vati said this because light flooded the carriage, blinding him.

38.

I'm doing all that needs doing for Benny – making calls, comforting Sarah, waiting for the doctor to arrive, ringing the cancer charity to explain that we do not now need relief during the nights. I feel, as I have felt with patients in the past, that Benny chose the timing of his death. He'd said all he needed to say, explained all that needed explaining.

The kind woman police officer rang the house the day after Benny died to tell me they'd arrested Cathal. He'd been hanging around outside the village shop in the afternoon. Drunk. Rambling. I suspect he'll claim some kind of mental incapacity if they charge him. Perhaps he really is mentally disturbed and will end up in a high-security psychiatric unit. Other people may now come forward, the police officer said, to give evidence against him. I shall ring Dad in France and ask him whether he still has the information about Cathal's activities he dug up after Mum's death.

I never found my mother's letter, written all those years ago and describing what she knew and suspected about Cathal. I can't show it to my brother as proof she loved us both and wanted to do her best for us. Somehow I think Andrew already knows this.

I don't need to worry about Cathal any more.

Benny fills my heart and mind. In a moment I shall go to my bedroom and ring James. I'll tell him that Benny is dead, that my time at Fairfleet is nearly run, that I will only hang on here to help Sarah tie up Benny's affairs. I'll ask James to start looking for houses for the two of us, and for Catherine, too, if she would like to live with us. I'd like a garden so we can have a dog. If Sarah can't take Max with her to the cottage she'll buy with Benny's legacy, I want to give the dog a home. I want to cling to this living connection with Benny, the man who loved my adored granny so much.

I'd also like to try to have another baby. But if that doesn't happen I believe I will enjoy just living with James for a while. Perhaps if we bought a house in need of renovation I could spend some time planning building work and painting walls, bringing order to a neglected garden.

I want my life to start again. I am ready to be happy now.

ACKNOWLEDGEMENTS

Special thanks go to Kristina Riggle and Nicole Hayes for their comments and suggestions on various drafts of this book, and to Will Atkins, Henry de Rougemont, Maggie Hanbury and Maggie Dana for their help and support.

BIBLIOGRAPHY

The following books were invaluable to me in writing *The One I Was.*

On the women pilots of the Air Transport Auxiliary:

Spreading My Wings by Diana Barnato Walker
Spitfire Women of World War II by Giles Whittell

On the Kindertransport children who came to Britain:

We Came as Children, edited by Karen Gershon
Other People's Houses by Lore Segal
. . . And the Policeman Smiled by Barry Turner
The Ninth of November by Hannele Zürndorfer

The Marie Curie website, www.mariecurie.org.uk, was particularly useful for information on palliative care.

ABOUT THE AUTHOR

Photo © 2011 Anna McCarthy

Eliza Graham spent her biology lessons sitting at the back of the classroom, reading Jean Plaidy novels behind her textbooks. In English and history, however, she sat right at the front, hanging on to every word. At home she read books while getting dressed and cleaning her teeth, and during school holidays she visited the public library several times a day.

At Oxford University she read English literature on a course that regarded anything written after about 1930 as too modern to be included. She retains a love of Victorian novels and the poetry of the seventeenth and nineteenth centuries.

Eliza's first novel, *Playing with the Moon*, was longlisted for Richard & Judy's Summer Read category and named one of the World Book Day 2007 'Books to Talk About.'

Find out more about Eliza on her website, www.elizagraham.co.uk, and follow her on Twitter @Eliza_Graham.